There was only on

Glamour is the sounded distant, whispery. *It can be a great blessing, when one has need of it. But take care. The lesson of glamour is that seeming becomes truth.*

Elise's palms met the mirror. Or met something cool and smooth that felt like the mirror's surface, and at the same time felt like warm skin. Human skin.

The Power crested, spilled over her in a wave of tingling sparkles. A spark snapped. Elise would have been worried—that much Power in Theo's house would have brought all of them up the stairs at a run—but the Trifero absorbed the extra Power, making sure not a ripple of it escaped.

A part of her was vaguely troubled by this. To be able to work a spell like this was impressive enough, but the kind of Power that could keep the spell silent was even more impressive. And that much Power, at her command, was downright scary.

Scary, and exhilarating too. Like a fast ride or a hot jam, like a roller coaster or a thunderstorm.

The *doppelganger* stepped out of the mirror. Elise's fingers slipped free and the Power drained from her, leaving only a shaky sense of satisfaction. Fire was the element of illusion and the burning away of illusions. Why hadn't she thought of this before? It felt so natural, so *right* she could have started to cry again if she'd had any tears left.

The *doppelganger* glided to the opposite side of the bed and sat down, the springs of the mattress creaking. Its mussed hair was an exact copy of hers, and it burned with her shifting red and gold aura. Elise was now the closest to invisible she could get. The copy of her wouldn't last more than an hour or two, especially if one of the Watchers came close to it. The venomous red Power the Watchers carried would tear the illusion to pieces.

She had to hurry.

Elise crossed to the window and looked down over the street at the front of the house. Theo, Mari and the Watchers were in the kitchen. She could hear them talking back and forth in worried tones.

Don't worry, guys. I'm going to take care of it all.

She swung the window open.

To Mom, who taught persistence.

Fire Watcher

***

Lilith Saintcrow

Fire Watcher
Published by ImaJinn Books

ISBN: 1-933417-02-1

10 9 8 7 6 5 4 3 2 1

PUBLISHER'S NOTE:
This book is a work of fiction. Names, characters, places and incidents are products of the author's imagination or are used fictitiously. Any resemblance to actual events or locales or persons, living or dead, is entirely coincidental.

Books are available at quantity discounts when used to promote products or services. For information please write to: Marketing Division, ImaJinn Books, P.O. Box 545, Canon City, CO 81212, or call toll free 1-877-625-3592.

Cover design by Patricia Lazarus

ImaJinn Books
P.O. Box 545, Canon City, CO 81212
Toll Free: 1-877-625-3592
http://www.imajinnbooks.com

One

The pain was nothing new. Remy had been dealing with agony—in different forms—all his life.

He rolled over and pushed himself to his feet. Blood caked his shoulder and the side of his face, and he was limping until the Dark symbiote living inside him forced the broken edges of the bones in his lower leg together, knitting them into wholeness. The pain decreased, but he was still drawing in huge gasping breaths and spitting out blood when the call came.

Only it wasn't a call. It was more like a buzzing inside the very center of his head, a tugging toward...what? More trouble, certainly. He didn't need more trouble. What he needed was to find whatever it was the Brotherhood was scurrying around to find, and take it to Circle Lightfall. He'd already retrieved several artifacts and made himself a name as a quick and deadly opponent.

Except I'm just a glorified garbage man, he thought bitterly. *A baby-sitter for old hunks of Power-soaked junk instead of a true Watcher.*

"Maybe I shouldn't have killed him," he said out loud, the chill night wind rising and pouring through the broken windows, stripping his hair back from his face. He wiped the blood away and winced as his shoulder twitched, the flesh closing over quickly. It was a pale attempt at a joke. He'd been sloppy. The Brotherhood operative could have killed him, and *that* would put a distinct wrinkle in a Watcher's day.

He picked up the black rune-chased knives. They marked him as a Watcher just as the Darkness in him did. Then he looked back at the scorched, still-smoking patch of floor. The Brotherhood had sent some of its worst out here to the middle of nowhere, and for what? An empty iron casket buried underneath a hunk of marble flooring in an old abandoned church. Only the marble had been torn up and the casket exposed, left lying broken in front of the hole. Someone else had gotten here first. Someone had outdone both Remy and the Brotherhood.

Who would dig up a church floor without knowing what was underneath it? Someone might have found some mention of the Trifero and followed the same clues he had. Although how somebody else could have found it when it had taken him a full month of poring over research texts and a careful mixture of threats, coercion, and charm to even get a whisper of it, he didn't want to guess. It was too depressing.

Remy paused, looking down at the empty casket. There was a faint, tempting glitter inside its cracked darkness.

He crouched down. The Brotherhood assassin had come out of the choir loft. Embarrassingly predictable. *Let that be the end of it. I don't feel like killing anything else tonight.* It was bad enough that the Brotherhood kept a flash-spell on their operatives to destroy any evidence of their existence. Once you killed a Brotherhood operative, the body burst into blue flame. It was annoying, but he could see why they did it. Still, did they have to make it smell so awful?

The broken iron casket wasn't empty. There was a snapped silver chain caught on a twisted sliver of iron. Someone had yanked on something after breaking the casket open. An amulet or a necklace—something on a chain.

So the Trifero could be worn, but it was now loose. It would help if he had come across a description or a drawing of it, but the Church had been cautious. Very cautious. They'd stolen the Stone of Destruction from a Lightbringer—the last European fire witch to survive past childhood—and hidden it here, in a French church.

Remy blew out a dissatisfied breath. There was enough ambient Power hanging around in this little church to give him the scent. He could track the Trifero.

Maybe that was the buzzing in his head. But an artifact had never called him before.

He picked up the chain, letting out a short sharp sound as the Power bit him. The Trifero was nothing to mess with. It was awake and on the move. The Talisman of fire and destruction was rattling around in the world now, ready to cause some havoc.

Damn. Now the Brotherhood would be tracking it too. And the gods alone knew where it might end up next.

Remy scooped up the casket as well. He would take it in with the chain and the Trifero when he found it. Hopefully this time he would get an assignment that would put him in proximity with a Lightbringer or two. It hurt, true, but how could he ever find his witch if Circle Lightfall kept sending him on these Easter egg hunts?

Like you deserve a witch, you animal. The Darkness in his bones twisted a little at the thought of a Lightbringer. Even the thought hurt. It was agony to be near any of them, and Remy was just crazy enough to keep hoping even through the pain. Hope was like a drug, even to a Watcher. He hadn't even *seen* a Lightbringer for four damn years now, too busy chasing down the little bits of Power Circle Lightfall just had to have.

A nice little Lightbringer, he thought, winding the silver chain up and slipping it into one of the pockets of his long black leather coat. The Watcher uniforms hadn't changed much since the seventeenth century, long black coats and utilitarian breeches. Some Watchers wore T-shirts and others went for a sort of poet's shirt thing that made it easier to hide weapons. Remy himself liked T-shirts. The long-sleeved, blousy things that were the alternative seemed a little fruity for serious work. Maybe it was just the macho in him.

A nice, quiet little witch to ease the pain. It would be easier to watch over one little witch than to chase ancient artifacts all over hell and creation. And it would be good to be taken care of, have his clothes mended and maybe a decent meal once in a while. Most witches were good cooks and liked fussing over their Watchers.

As long as I'm dreaming, I'll take a Corvette and a house up in Hollywood too. I don't deserve a Lightbringer and I know it. Why even think about it?

He shook his head, examining the church one more time. He hated this sort of thing. The good news was the Trifero was on the move. Moving, it would cause a disturbance he could easily track. The bad news was that the Brotherhood was also hunting it, and it would cause a disturbance *they* would easily track.

"No Lightbringer for me," Remy said to the dusty, moth-eaten silence inside the church. The marble flooring was scarred—maybe the Trifero was why the place hadn't been looted for fixtures. The artifact would have made psychics seriously uncomfortable and given normal people a sense of foreboding. The wonder was that the church hadn't burned down. But then, if a Crusader under the aegis of the Church placed the Trifero here, he would have bound it to stay still and not cause any harm until it was found again.

"Just a glorified garbage man, sorting through trash and bringing home the trinkets." *And talking to myself again. Maybe it's time for that psych evaluation.* He kicked at the floor with the toe of one heavy boot, and then stood, shrugging a little to make sure his weapons-harness fell correctly. "I should never have signed up for this."

Except he hadn't had any choice. This was his last chance. It was either being a Watcher or rotting in a solitary cell for the rest of his life. They had offered him an opportunity to make his life worth something, and here he was, complaining to himself in the middle of an abandoned French church after midnight. He didn't mind traveling the world and seeing new sights, but he was getting tired of international food and missing the little things about the States.

He should *definitely* never have signed up for this.

Well, too late now. And was that the Brotherhood's backup, flitting through the shadows? Of course. They never went anywhere alone. Bad for the Brotherhood if any of its operatives started thinking on their own.

Remy sighed and half-turned, a gun appearing in his left hand, held low and ready.

Time to get back to work.

Two

Elise Nicholson set her guitar case down, sighed, and yawned, her ears popping slightly. She was drenched in sweat and bone-tired, and the heat hadn't helped any. Heat made most people crazy, and today had been a regular end-of-August scorcher. Elise actually liked summer, but gods above, she hated dealing with crazy people.

They'd played a whole set, and the bar crowd had been too busy fighting with each other to notice. Almost tore the damn place down. Even minor celebrity hadn't fully prepared Elise for the pain of being ignored by a bunch of restless drunks.

She'd been tempted to use a little bit of fire to restore order, but that wouldn't have been good, would it? It would have been childish of her to set a troublemaker's shoes afire. Or, gods forbid, lose control of her temper and set someone's *hair* on fire. She had contemplated it, though, and derived great satisfaction from the mental images. Too *much* satisfaction.

Even thinking about it now made sparks pop from her fingers. Elise grimaced and took a deep breath. *Control is your best friend,* she reminded herself. *I have a gift to help people, not to set their hair on fire. Although it really would have helped* me *feel a lot better.*

She leaned against the door and let her shoulders drop. Here inside her house, she could let her shields down a bit, let the tough front slip away a little. Let her neck stop its relentless aching and quit holding herself so tightly.

Just as she finally relaxed, the phone rang. Elise dropped her purse—an antique black-leather camera case with a long leather strap—and walked across the bare hardwood floor, down the hall into the living room. The punching bag swayed gently as she entered the room, and she spared it a single glance.

My temper must be really bad. She scooped up the sleek black cordless. "Hey, Theo. Tomorrow? Only before four, baby."

"You must be psychic." Theo's voice crackled over the phone, amused and serene. She sounded happy, at least, and Elise closed her eyes and concentrated. She could almost *see* Theo leaning against the glassed-in counter next to the cash register. Theo sounded happy more often than not these days. At least that was an unmitigated blessing. "I was going to ask if you could pull a shift for me tomorrow. Tina's getting out of the hospital, and I want her to be settled, and—"

Elise rolled her head back on her shoulders. Her neck hurt. She'd walked six blocks in the heat, carrying the guitar case. "Sure I can. I don't have to be at the Liberty to meet Vann and Trevor until four-thirty. I'm working all Sunday night at Brixo's to get some tips so I can spend Full Moon with you guys." *And tire myself out so I can sleep.* She took another long slow breath in. Static buzzed on the phone, subsided.

Theo was silent for a beat. Elise imagined Theo, her long dark hair pulled back from her pretty, serene face, frowning just a little. "Elise?" she said, quietly, and Elise shut her eyes. "Everything okay?"

How could I tell you if it wasn't, Theo? You've got enough to deal with. "I guess. It was a rough set tonight. The new drummer's a greenhorn, but he'll work out okay, I think."

Theo's silence intensified. Theo would be wearing her "listening look" now, as if Elise was one of her patients. She never could resist a stray cat, or someone who looked down on their luck. That was how the Watchers had horned their way into Theo and Mari's lives.

Sparks popped from the fingers of Elise's free hand. *I don't want to think about that. It will only make me upset. I don't need that. Let's hope I can sleep tonight.*

"Elise." A calm, firm tone, as if Elise had started to cry. "It's about Mark, isn't it?"

"I don't want to talk about that," Elise said hurriedly. "I'm just tired, that's all, and I had a bunch of barflies almost start a riot while I was onstage. It took some doing to insulate myself from that. Look, Theo, I hate to be rude, but I've got to catch some winks, okay?"

There was another silence, and Elise heard another voice. Male, a deep growling bass, saying something to Theo. That would be Dante. He would, of course, be hovering over Theo, his black eyes flicking everywhere at once, gauging the environment and watching for possible threats whenever he wasn't staring at Theo as if she was his own personal saint.

The thought of Dante and Hanson—the Watchers—made a cold shiver go up Elise's spine. *Nobody that big, carrying that much weaponry, is trustworthy.* She rubbed at her forehead, feeling the sweat-slick skin and grimacing.

Theo finally sighed. "All right," she said, her tone neutral.

"Dante just reminded me that we have another request from Circle Lightfall. We're going to discuss it at Full Moon."

Elise's shoulders sagged under this new weight. "My answer's going to be the same. I don't want anything to do with it. Haven't they done enough?" Anger started in the pit of her belly, a familiar warmth having nothing to do with the muggy air. A comforting, familiar, friendly feeling with razor spikes up and down its broad back.

Anger. Her oldest and most faithful friend.

Her *only* faithful friend.

Theo sighed again. "I know. Your vote has always been no, and we have to be unanimous for us to take any action having to do with Circle Lightfall. I understand."

"I don't know, Theo. If you understood—and if your pet chunk of hunk understood—would you keep asking me?" Her tone was sharp enough to draw blood.

The moment she said it, she regretted it. "Oh, Theo," she continued, hearing the whining, mortified note in her own voice and hating herself for it. "I'm so sorry. I didn't mean to imply—"

"Understood and forgiven," Theo said immediately. Her voice was soothing, restful, and full of the smell of rich brown earth. Theo could hypnotize a wounded animal into calmness with that voice. Elise had seen her do it. "Don't give it any more thought. I'll see you tomorrow."

"You bet. Blessed be." Elise's free hand curled into a fist.

"Blessed be," Theo replied.

Elise hit the "talk" button to disconnect and laid the phone back in its base. The punching bag swayed again. She'd mounted it into a ceiling beam, and it creaked a little as it moved.

She regarded it, dropping down onto the folded-up futon couch set along the wall so she could look out the windows at night. Night was when she had the most trouble, really. Night was when everything seemed bleakest, and her life stretched out in front of her like a dead carnival, the rides busted-out and broken-down, all the people gone and the trash drifted up in corners. Night was when she felt the most vulnerable, because the things that lived in the darkness were hungry, and her anger could keep them at bay only so long. Anger only put the pain off, it didn't take it away. And the more it hurt, the more Elise felt furious, a vicious cycle.

And yet night was when she felt most awake. The constant prodding of her anger was the only companion in the darkness. The gods knew men didn't stick around, and her friends were too busy with the Watchers to pay much attention to Elise anymore.

She unlaced her knee-high combat boots and dropped them to the side, then fished an elastic band out of the pocket of her frayed, skintight jeans. The leather bustier would chafe, but it would keep her chest reasonably under control. She reached up, scraping her hair back, and twisted it into a bun, winding the elastic around to keep it up. Maybe soon she'd get that punk pixie haircut she'd been thinking about. But she was vain about her hair, though wild horses wouldn't have pulled that admission from her. It was her one concession to femininity.

She walked over to the punching bag, her bare feet whispering over the smooth hardwood floor. There was a pair of fingerless sparring gloves lying neatly on the floor right under the black bag. She yanked them on roughly and glanced across the room to the neat wooden bookshelf that held nothing but books. There was a low black lacquered table that held a single Shasta daisy in a long, thin black *raku* vase she had fired herself. Next to the daisy was a small statue of a goddess with a lion's head seated on a throne.

Sekhmet. The destructive fire of the sun, the Eye of Ra. Four thin red tapers, pristine in plain copper holders, graced the table as well.

Elise closed her eyes, centered herself. As usual, the rage welled up inside her, looking for an outlet. Rage—and something uncomfortably like pain. It *hurt*. All the way down to her bones, it hurt.

If you do not control the Power, it will control you, Suzanne's voice said, dry and academic. *Fire is the most helpful of elements—and also the most destructive.*

Suzanne. Her teacher, the closest thing to a mother she'd ever had, the woman who had believed both in Elise's talent with music and her talent with magick. The only person Elise had ever totally trusted.

Dead and gone.

When Elise opened her eyes again, she threw the first punch. The bag shuddered.

Right hook. Jab. Jab. Kick, left hook, kick, jab, cover your face! Work it, work it, hit it!

The sweat filming her now started to bead up and roll off.

She punched the bag, worked it hard, using knees and fists and her elbows too. The crisp, clean punches began to blur, and before she realized it, she was hitting the bag with no finesse, no technique. Just pounding on it. And right on cue, the most hurtful thought of all showed up.

Mark.

She hadn't seen it coming. What was the good of being a witch if she hadn't seen it coming? She hadn't had any warning at all. Just *bam!* One fine morning, she'd been prodded out of sleep by a phone call. Vann calling, his voice stunned and calm. *Elise, I've got some bad news.*

And that bad news was Mark, dead under a drunk driver's bumper. Walking home from the bar they'd played in.

She hadn't *known.* She hadn't even *known.* No premonition of disaster at all. No inkling that anything was wrong. What was the bloody *good* of being a witch if it didn't warn you about your on-again-off-again boyfriend's impending death?

The funeral, with Vann holding her arm and Mark's parents and little brother glaring at her, had been a particular type of hell. Mark's parents were conservative fundamentalists, and the way they looked at Elise and Vann was as if some particularly foul things had crawled up out of the sewers into their solemn occasion and let out a stink bomb. Nobody had spoken to either of them. Of course, Vann had been wearing a black polyester suit direct from the disco era, and Elise, while dressed conservatively in a knee-length black dress, was still the only woman there wearing silk stockings and a nose ring. She honestly hadn't thought that she would be so out of place.

Mark's mother had hissed something highly uncomplimentary at her. Elise had been too busy trying to hold back tears, or she could have told the woman about her husband's affairs— or the case of the clap he was going to give her soon. At least Elise was witch enough to know about *that.* She hadn't said a single, solitary word.

But oh, she had been tempted. So tempted.

And she couldn't even *leave* this stinking place. She'd sworn to stay, with Mari and Theo, as a Guardian of the City. She couldn't leave now even if she tried. She'd taken a bus out to the city limits and tried to step over, but the invisible line in the air—like a smooth glass wall, nothing for her to grab onto so she could break it—had pulled her up short. She had the uncomfortable feeling that if she was driving a car she would have wrecked it, crashed into the invisible barrier at full speed.

Sometimes life really sucked. The thing was, Elise didn't want to leave. This was home. She loved Santiago City, loved the bay and the freeways and the river, loved the University District and the East Side, loved everything about the town. She was just beginning to make it as a singer, and her art was hanging in galleries. She was known here. Respected sometimes, even.

When she was too exhausted to punch anymore, she dropped the gloves back where they had been and went to lock the front door. The rage wasn't gone. It lay beneath the surface of her mind, waiting, receded only enough that she could breathe and shove the thought of Mark under some black mental blanket.

Denial isn't healthy, Elise. Suzanne's voice, calm and precise.

She whirled, her green eyes wide and wild. Searching.

Bare white walls, bare wood floor, futon, punching bag, bookshelf, table. That was all. Nothing else.

Elise's ribs flared as she panted, breathing in the still, muggy air. She hadn't turned the heat pump on to provide air-conditioning, just left the ceiling fan on and the windows open upstairs. The air was absolutely still, humidity hanging like a wet blanket over the entire city. "Suzanne?" she whispered. The sweat-soaked leather of her bustier chafed under her armpits and cut into her lower back. "Suzanne?"

She repeated it, stupidly, for a third time, but no breath of air stirred in the entire house. She lived in a duplex, but the McCarrens had moved out last month and there wasn't a tenant yet. She still had to go through a pile of applications and pick a new lucky neighbor.

Nothing. There was nothing there.

"Goddess." The word fell flat against the floor. She hugged herself, suddenly shivering, gooseflesh standing out on her wet skin. "I miss you, boss," she whispered, and looked at the low lacquered table.

The candles stood there, waiting. Elise narrowed her eyes, felt the heat rise behind her skin. It was so *easy* to call fire, to bring it out of the air. It was behind the surface of even ordinary things, and just needed the right touch to release it. She had never understood why other people couldn't do it.

The first candle puffed into life. Clear, ordinary orange flame. Then the second. The third. And the last, the sound of the fire starting a soft *puff!* There was the smell of burning wax, and the candle flames stood up straight and steady. As always, when she used her gift, it felt like some subliminal steam valve had been released, and the relief was instantaneous. Pressure diminished.

There was a dark mark on the paint of the wall behind the altar, and another darker patch on the ceiling, soot from burning candles every day for the years of her life here.

Elise scrubbed at her wet forehead with the heel of her hand. "I need a vacation," she muttered, and stalked toward the stairs. She wanted a shower and a cup of tea, and then a snuggle in bed with her stuffed flamingo. If she was quiet and still for long enough, she might be able to pretend she was asleep.

There was, after all, nobody to fool but herself.

Twenty minutes later, she wrung the water out of her hair as she stepped out of the bathtub, shrugging into her red silk robe and tying the belt around her waist. She wrapped the towel around her hair again, chafing it gently. A yawn caught her off-guard, so she was yawning and looking into the mirror, swiping aside the condensation so she could see herself, when *something* hit the very edges of the warding laid on her duplex.

Crap. Elise leapt for her bedroom and was yanking a clean pair of jeans on when it came again. A weak hit, something blundering against the edges of the blanket of protections over her house.

She shrugged into a tank top and shoved her feet into a pair of black canvas slip-ons by her bedroom door. Then it was down the stairs, moving as quietly as she could. Her hands began to throb with Power, tingling in her fingertips.

Elise? It was Mari, faraway and dim. Ever since that awful night in the back room at Tantan's, she had been able to hear Mari sometimes, especially when the anger rose and made Elise's skin burn. Mari's big blue eyes and flyaway golden curls, the sound of ocean waves that seemed to follow Mari just like the smell of burning followed Elise.

Elise?

Elise jammed a lid on that voice and shoved it away. *I love Mari, but I don't want her involved in this—whatever this is.* She balled up a fist and flung out her hand as she ran, and her front door unlocked, swinging inward.

She ran out onto her front step, stopped dead, and then jerked to her left. The laurel hedge right next to her door was absolutely still, not even a breath of wind.

That's where it's coming from. Someone in the bushes at the corner of the house? Well, they were going to be sorry when she finished with them.

There was a long howling scream, and something whooshed past her, streaking through the hot night air. Elise's hand jerked up, her hair raying out with static electricity, and a crackling whip of fire arced out from her right hand. It lashed across the thing, which let out a screech.

Slider! she thought grimly, and centered herself. She'd seen scuttling dark things before, but they had been easy to avoid until the Watchers had shown up. One of the dark things with four red eyes and insectile legs had attacked Theo's old shop, almost breaking the glass in its eagerness to get to Theo and drain her like a wineglass, to suck out Theo's wonderful calm light.

Light. That's what the Watchers called psychic women. *Lightbringers.*

The insect-thing let out another feedback squeal. Elise didn't flinch, though the sound was painful, slicing through her head without going through her ears. She snapped her hands up, the golden glow lining them clearly visible in the darkness, and Power crackled.

"Go ahead. Make my night, buggy. I'll be the last meal you *ever* attempt."

Because Elise was a Guardian of the City, a fire witch, and generally one tough cookie. She smiled, a hard delighted grin, and the Slider made an uncertain scratching sound.

Dante or Hanson would no doubt attack the thing, if they were here. But they were guys, and testosterone-laden guys at that. Hanson in particular treated Mari like some sort of child who wasn't smart enough to be let out by herself. Elise *hated* that. She'd dated men with similar brain malfunctions, and didn't know how Mari stood it. Mari just gave a shy smile and—most of the time—gave in. Sometimes she just quietly went ahead and did what she wanted anyway. It was those times that Elise was most impressed with her.

The Slider hesitated, then apparently decided that discretion was the better part of valor. It turned tail and ran, the wind of its passing smelling dry and venomous. Elise blew out a long breath between her lips.

Well, at least my hair's dry now. She flicked her fingers to shake the built-up Power away. Sparks popped. *Power's good for something. And so much simpler than going to a salon.*

She walked back to her door, feeling the thrill of exhaustion along her nerves. Once again, Elise Nicholson had proved she was the toughest girl around.

Now can I sleep?

The phone rang, shrilly. Elise kicked the door shut, locked it and paced into the living room, hooked up the receiver. "Hello," she said, trying to hide the anger sparking in her body. It was unsuccessful, but at least she tried.

"Elise?" Mari's soft, breathy voice, soothing through the receiver. "I had an awful feeling."

You and me both, sugar pop. "Just one of those insect thingies. I took care of it."

Mari gasped. "Why didn't you call me? I could have asked Hanson to—"

"I don't need him." Elise heard the sharpness in her voice, hating it. Why couldn't she be kind, like Theo? Or gentle, like Mari? Instead, she was the abrasive one. The loudmouth, tough-as-nails, brassy one. The crazy artist. "I can take care of myself. It's okay. I scared it off." She took a deep breath. The candle flames were tall—at least five inches tall—and burning motionlessly, bright blue.

Elise felt the bottom drop out of her stomach. The last time she had seen that, Dante had entered their lives, staring at Theo all the time and bringing all the Circle Lightfall trouble with him. Elise had never seen candles act that way before or since.

"Elise?" Mari sounded uncertain now, and frightened. "There's something else. I can feel it. What's wrong?"

"I'll see you tomorrow," Elise managed around the lump in her throat. "Okay? I'm pulling a shift at the shop before I go to the Liberty."

"Elise." Mari tried again. Elise heard Hanson's voice, asking a quiet question, and she closed her eyes. The dark behind her lids was comforting. But there was nothing to be gained by hiding.

"I have to go, Mari. I'm tired. I love you, good night." She laid the phone back in its charger, disconnecting the call. Then, as if hypnotized, she looked back at the hissing blue candle flames. "Goddess. Not again."

If there was a poker-faced Watcher for Theo, and an over-protective Watcher for Mari, and the candles were spitting blue again, it could only mean that Circle Lightfall was going to try to worm a Watcher into *her* life. A possible spy who would want to convince her to change her vote and get all three of them into this mysterious organization. They still knew next to nothing about this Circle, and it had already cost them Suzanne. Of course, the fact that Suzanne was haunting them—or was acting as a Guardian on the astral plane, Theo said, though Elise didn't put much stock in that—was a comfort, but it was only a pale comfort.

Of course, if Elise believed in the Craft and lighting fires with her mind, she could believe in the astral plane. It certainly explained a whole hell of a lot.

She made her way back upstairs slowly, stopping every so often because her legs were shaking and wouldn't quite hold her up. She had to lean on the wall for support. And oh boy was she glad nobody was around to see that.

It was exhausting, being tough all the time. Sometimes she wished she could just, for once, relax. Let down her guard.

She shook the thought away. There was no way Circle Lightfall was going to make her do anything she didn't want to do. Elise Nicholson was nobody's fool. She'd looked after her-self all her life, thank you very much, and now she was re-sponsible for looking after Theo and Mari too. The Watchers couldn't be trusted, and neither could Circle Lightfall. Elise would just have to take care of it.

When she fell into bed, she was mercifully exhausted enough that her eyes closed of their own accord, and she fell into a dreamless sleep. Now that she knew the worst was coming at last, she could relax.

Three

Remy flipped open the cell phone. He held it to his ear and said nothing. It had been a very long international flight, and an even longer search for a reasonably priced hotel room that wouldn't give him some sort of rash. Good to be back in the old US of A. He'd missed it.

"Where is the artifact?" It was a beautiful voice, soft and melodious. Witches had beautiful voices. The Darkness inside Remy's bones stirred, sent a spike of bloody pain through his mostly-healed leg, and went back to sleep.

He told her. There was a long pause, which was unprecedented.

"And where are you?"

He repeated the name of the city. "Santiago City. Do I have another assignment?"

"You're inside the city limits?"

"Yes, ma'am. I wasn't aware it was a red zone." It was the closest to a question he would ever ask this faceless voice. For four years this voice had told him what Circle Lightfall wanted of him. For a time he had even thought that this voice was something special, until he'd met other Watchers and found out they received their orders in the same way.

"It isn't." Now she sounded amused. "Well. Proceed, then. Report as necessary."

"Yes, ma'am." He closed the phone, turned it off and slipped it back into a pocket.

Now *that* had been one of the strangest calls he'd ever had. Usually they didn't care much where he was, as long as he had an idea of where his current quarry was. And as long as he didn't spend a whole lot of cash to get there, he was pretty much free to do as he pleased. If it wasn't a red zone, why had she asked if he was inside the city limits? Was there another Lightfall operation going on in here he shouldn't interfere with?

He leaned back on the bed, propping himself up on his elbows, looking at the thin, cheap curtains. The night was hot and motionless, but this place had air-conditioning, at least. Sirens resounded, and there was a brief flurry of gunfire. Not as much as some other large cities—there was a curious air of peace here, though the temperature was in the eighties even now, at one o'clock in the morning.

Remy lowered himself down the rest of the way, so he was lying on the bed, his boots hanging off the edge, and stared up at the ceiling. There was something about this city. The trail of the Trifero led here…and so did the numbing, buzzing, aching call that had settled into his head and the middle of his chest. If there had been another Watcher he could have asked about that call. It didn't feel normal.

Then again, Remy was a Watcher. Normal didn't really apply.

He closed his eyes. The call remained, whispering, shouting, strumming on his nerves. *Where are you?* He took a deep breath. *Why are you calling?*

There was no answer, but the sound of sirens and gunshots from outside faded. He lay across the cheap narrow bed, searching, his awareness spreading out, contracting as he became aware of his own body again, then slipping out to coast through the city. There was a curious stillness to the air, as if the entire city was under the magickal equivalent of a dome. Something incredibly powerful had closed off this place from the outside world.

Why hadn't he noticed it as soon as he crossed the city limits? That lapse in awareness could kill him. But there hadn't been any sense of a barrier. More like a welcoming feeling. As if he was *supposed* to be here. As if something had pulled him in, almost. He'd felt drawn all the way across the Atlantic and across the damn continent itself, wondering why the Trifero was moving so quickly, so far. And grateful that the Trifero and the call seemed to be coming from the same place.

Remy's body jerked, the *tanak* growing restless under the prodding call. He breathed deeply, control reasserting itself, and came back to find that he had clenched his fists so tightly his palms were bloody, though he kept his fingernails ruthlessly short. Superhuman strength had its price.

He opened his eyes again, stared at the white popcorn of the ceiling.

Something was here. Something or someone in this city was calling him.

Who?

Remy shut his eyes again. He needed a few hours of mind-resting trance before he could untangle the mystery. Whatever was calling him could wait until morning. And Circle Lightfall would no doubt be very interested in this.

Four

Elise's temper had not improved by the time she stamped into Theo's shop at precisely eight the next morning. The sun was just above the horizon, she had been unable to find her red silk tank top, and her leather pants would be too tight today, she could just feel it. One of the things about approaching thirty was that her PMS got to be more Bloat City every year.

So she'd settled on a red silk slip over a pair of skintight jeans and knee-high bright red Doc Martens. She hadn't found her favorite silver nose ring, either, so she'd settled on a small ruby stud. The star tattoos on her shoulder blades would be clearly visible, and she'd left her hair down, even though it was already eight-five degrees and promising to be a tar-melting hot kind of day.

"Hey, Lise." Mari greeted her from behind the counter. Her flyaway blond curls were held back with two tiny rhinestone clips, and she was grinning. Her big blue eyes danced with mischief over a snub nose and beautiful, high-spaced cheekbones. She had a cute little rosebud of a mouth and invariably looked cheerful and pretty.

Elise grunted and stamped toward the back of the shop. She carried her guitar-case, decked with bumper stickers proclaiming her favorite bands. Her purse bumped against her hip.

Theo's old shop, the Magick Cauldron, had burned down a year and a half ago, during a fight between Dante and something called a Bishop. The Bishop was part of the Crusade, a secret society that for some reason wanted to kill psychics. Elise didn't quite understand, and she didn't want to. Anything Dante and Hanson had to say about it she just tuned out. They were not to be trusted.

She had done a little research of her own and dug up little to nothing. She wasn't as good as Suzanne at finding things out, and the only people she had to ask would want something in return. Elise had precious little to offer. She was only good at setting things on fire. She'd rather save that kind of favor for when she *really* needed it.

Mari had done some research in her funny underground Library run by Suzanne's creepy sister, but Elise hadn't asked. Asking Mari about the Watchers would probably only get Elise a forty-five minute lecture on How To Be Polite To Creepy Men With Guns.

They had decided not to rebuild on the old site at Bell and Fourth. The new shop, Rowangrove Metaphysical Supplies, was directly on the Avenue, right in the center of a bunch of high-priced boutiques. Business was good, and Theo had made Mari and Elise her partners in the store. They had both tried to tell her not to, but she was determined. Mari, who had graduated and was now working as an assistant head of research at another library, sometimes opened the store; but it was Elise who generally worked there the most. Mari was always studying, and Theo had her patients to attend to.

Elise shoved aside the curtain hiding the small Employees Only section from the rest of the store. Hanson, Mari's Watcher, turned around, his pale blue eyes interested and cool as usual, and held out her red Peruvian coffee mug with the golden sun design.

Hanson was a little shorter and much leaner than Theo's Watcher, Dante. He had ice-blond hair and blue eyes, a sharp nose, and a nice mouth. Elise liked him a little more than she liked Dante, but the way he treated Mari—as if she couldn't take care of herself—was infuriating.

He wore a long black leather coat and a black KISS T-shirt, as usual, and a pair of well-worn jeans. A slight shimmer in the air—the glamour laid over him to hide his weapons from normal eyes—was by now so familiar Elise barely noticed it. A sword-hilt poked up over his left shoulder, and there were knives strapped at his chest and waist, as well as two silver guns—9mm, Elise had found out when she looked them up in a gun catalog. High-quality hardware.

Professional hardware.

She put her guitar case down and turned to snatch the coffee mug away from him. Hanson avoided her fingers. "Thanks," she said grudgingly, and took a sip, slurping in air at the same time to cool the scalding liquid. "To what do I owe this honor?"

"Mari told me you were attacked last night." His voice, an even tenor, was neutral. Elise heard the bell over the door jingle merrily, and the green witch's low, pleasant voice. *Theo's here. Hail, hail, the gang's all here, all gathered to give Elise merry hell. I shouldn't have even gotten out of bed this morning.*

"Just one of those Slider things." She took another scalding sip. "I scared it off all by my lonesome. Guess I don't need a big burly weirdo around." Her lips peeled back, showing her teeth in a bright sunny smile.

"You could have died," Hanson said quietly. "It must have been weakened, not to offer you any combat."

It was the reasonableness of his tone that bugged her, she decided. "Very few things *like* being set on fire. I can take care of myself. Besides, shouldn't you be bugging Mari? You don't seem to think she has a brain anyhow."

"She likes to hear me fuss." One shoulder lifted and dropped in a shrug. It was an elegant movement. It made her nervous, the way these guys moved. They were like cats, either immobile and sleepy, or moving much faster than a human being could—or *should.* And creepiest of all was the darkness that clung to them, a scary aura that made ordinary people hurry out of their way. Elise had seen Dante dive through a plate-glass window so quickly he looked blurry, but not so blurry she couldn't see the venomous red Power outlining him.

Nothing that moved that fast and fought that viciously could be safe.

Elise snorted rudely and pushed past him, out into the main body of the shop. The air-conditioning was on, so it was a good even seventy degrees—comfortable enough, even though the sweat on her back was chilling as it dried.

Theo turned from the counter, her long brown hair swinging as she tucked a strand behind her ear. Elise ran her eyes critically over the candle display and made a mental note to bring up some of the new shipment and face the bookshelves too. A lot of work.

Well, it would take her mind off things.

"Elise!" Theo sounded delighted and stern at once. Her voice was a low clear contralto, and it made the air in the shop turn thick and golden. Theo wore a green sundress, spaghetti-strapped and full-skirted, and a pair of strappy brown sandals. As always, she looked absolutely flawless. Her skin was pale and velvety, her eyes a deep green lit from within. Theo's eyes could stop a Mack truck going downhill.

Elise smiled. It was a genuine smile. Being around Theo always made her take a deep breath, an unfamiliar soothing calm spreading down her shoulders.

Mari folded her arms, tossing her blond curls back. "Well?

You have coffee, so don't put me off. What *happened?*"

"Something just smacked my wards a little." Elise took another sip of coffee. Blessed coffee. It was the only thing in the world that didn't make her sick. She was having more and more trouble keeping food down, and wondered if the persistent burning in her chest was acid reflux or an ulcer. *That* particular question had kept her up three nights in a row last week. "I went out and faced it down."

Dante turned away from the bank of plate windows that showed the Avenue outside. This early in the morning there were few customers, just people coming in to open the shops, hurrying to work, or stopping for a cup of coffee beforehand.

Dante was tall and had shoulders like a linebacker, short black punked-up hair, and absolutely *black* eyes in a face that looked as comforting and cuddly as a snarling lion's. He wore the standard long black coat and a *Cazotte Lives* T-shirt. His hands were scarred and callused, like Hanson's, and he always seemed to be scanning the area around him with a kind of high-powered radar. When he wasn't staring at Theo as if he wanted to eat her alive, that is.

"You left the safety of your wards to face a Slider?" he said. "That was foolhardy, witch."

Elise's hair snapped with static. "I. Am. Capable. Of. Taking. Care. Of. Myself. I have been doing it for years, thank you *very* much."

Theo put up a hand. "Not right now, you two." Even though her voice was gentle, Dante straightened and took half a step back, effectively disengaging from Elise. "There's news, Lise, and I want you to listen to me all the way through before you say anything. All right?"

Elise shrugged, the silk slip moving against her back. She took another sip of coffee and let her eyes drift half-shut. The fire inside her didn't dim, though. It only stopped flaring out through her skin. She took a deep breath. Theo's calm was contagious. The green witch could calm *anyone* down, given long enough.

They're my best friends, Elise reminded herself. *They don't mean to hurt me; they're just excited about the new boyfriends. Chicks do that sort of thing, temporarily lose their minds over men. It's happened before. When these guys go away, I'll still be here.*

Mari leaned on the glassed-in counter that held the ancient

cash register. They had scoured flea markets and secondhand stores to find a working one, because three witches in a single building could play havoc with complicated electronics. Elise had burned out quite a few computers in her time, mostly when she was upset.

Mari's big blue eyes met Elise's. She always seemed genuinely, deeply happy to see Elise, which made her two short steps from crazy. Then again, Theo seemed to like Elise too, but Theo had always had a thing for strays. Make puppy dog eyes at Theo Morgan for long enough and eventually she'd take you in.

That was one thing the Watcher was good for, Elise decided grudgingly. He served as a deterrent to wackos and crazies that would otherwise attach to Theo. And he seemed to genuinely care about her. Like Hanson genuinely seemed to care about Mari.

I know he loves her. There was the time Mari had disappeared after the earthquake, in the beginning of summer three months ago. Hanson had been frantic to find her, and Elise had been impressed by the depth of his devotion. He obviously thought she hung the moon.

Just like Dante thought Theo was the coolest thing since sliced bread.

Theo waited another beat or two, with impeccable politeness, to allow Elise to gather her thoughts. "Okay," Elise finally said, taking another long swallow of coffee and burning her tongue. "I'm listening."

"Circle Lightfall wants our permission for Lightbringers to live here," Theo said. "Since we're the Guardians, they feel this will be one of the safest places on earth once we get finished with it. But if the Lightbringers come here, it will also attract more things like those spider-things—the Sliders. Not to mention other things. So they want to send Watchers to patrol the city. Under our direction, of course."

Elise felt her eyebrows going up and she bit the inside of her tongue to keep from speaking. "Mmmh." She waited to see if Theo was done.

"Elise," Theo said gently, "I think they're right."

Elise's ears began to tingle with fury, and her fingers, too. She took a deep breath. Another.

Theo's green eyes were deep and earnest. "Dante and Hanson aren't all that bad. They really have our best interests at heart. And if we can provide some protection to other people like us, I'm not at all sure it's a bad thing. If we can offer sanctuary, shouldn't we? And we have so much to learn about the responsibility of being Guardians..." Theo trailed off.

Suzanne. Elise knew it. She was thinking about Suzanne. This whole thing had been Suzanne's idea, but the old woman hadn't been able to stick around long enough to teach them how to *use* what they'd done, despite Mari's careful research in the underground Library. It was like having a big shiny new car you didn't know how to drive. Too much Power, not enough direction. And all their gifts—Theo's healing, Mari's visions of the future, and Elise's own command of fire—had been magnified by the Power of being Guardians. Terribly magnified.

Suzanne had been the one to teach Elise that she wasn't crazy, the one who had taught her about the Goddess and about love and responsibility. Suzanne had been teacher, confidante, drill instructor, and friend. Elise could still remember hours of exhausting work, trying to hold a candle flame steady as she stared at it, feeling the Power trickling through her, fighting for control. Suzanne had given her the gift of true magick, and it was a gift Elise would be grateful for until she died.

Suzanne had taken in one terrified, half-sane foster child turned resentfully into a woman, and given her a second chance, shepherding her through her first forays into the art world. Suzanne had also given Elise Theo's ad in the local paper and said, *"This one. Apply here."*

And oh, but Suzanne had been right.

Suzanne had held Elise through many sleepless nights, humming softly, stroking Elise's long hair. The old woman had smelled like lemon and incense, a combined smell that was powerful and good and clean, a smell Elise now associated with comfort.

Suzanne had always been there, to guide and instruct all three of them. Being alone without her now was very frightening. Elise could admit that much to herself.

So it's all the more important that I take care of Theo and Mari. She squared her shoulders under the burden. *It's up to me now. Theo can do the teaching, and Mari can do the research, but it's up to me to do the ass-kicking.* It was up to her to be the voice of reason here.

She waited to see if Theo was finished. She obviously was. Elise looked over at Mari, who looked uncharacteristically serious. "I think they're right, too," Mari said. "I've seen...things. Things that shouldn't be here. Like when I was walking home with Hanson that night." She shuddered delicately, her blond curls brushing her creamy shoulders. Her blue tank top shifted a little. "And I remember what it was like before I moved here and met all of you. I was so frightened, all the time, of the things I saw but nobody else seemed to see. It was awful. I think if we could make this a safe place, if we could help some of the people that are like us—"

"Oh, for God's sake." Elise couldn't keep quiet any longer. "Don't you two *get* it? These guys carry around *guns!* So we start gathering together the people they want—the *Lightbringers*—and then these guys come in armed to the teeth? Oh, come *on.*"

"Theo," Dante began, but Theo held up her hand, and he subsided. He didn't just subside; he snapped his mouth shut as if Theo had pulled a string. At least he usually did what Theo told him to do, and did it swiftly.

Elise stared at the tall, black-eyed man for a few moments, daring him to open his mouth again. Both of her hands knotted around the coffee-cup, and the coffee was steaming a little more than it had been.

The silence filled with crackling static. "No," Elise said, finally. "No. Not now, not ever. I don't want anything more to do with these guys. We were getting along fine until they showed up."

"The mere fact that you three had escaped death at the hands of the Dark is sheer coincidence," Hanson said flatly. "And you've all been running and hiding most of your lives. We didn't *bring* the Dark."

Elise knew he was right, but that didn't make her feel any better. Instead, she felt like a bitch for being the voice of caution and reason.

Oh, well. I've been called a bitch before. It's never done me any permanent damage. "Fine." It was hard to keep her voice even through her clenched teeth. "But I will be *damned* before I let any more of you bastards in on my turf. If not for you guys, Suzanne would still be here."

"Elise!" Theo sounded horrified. "That's not true!"

"It is," Elise said grimly. The air-conditioning kicked on, and cool air drifted across her skin. "The gods know that it's true, Theo."

"I miss Suzanne as much as you do." Mari drew herself up behind the counter. "You're not the only one. Don't do this."

As if it matters who misses her more. The coffee mug trembled in Elise's hands. She turned away from all four of them, stalking across the store. The fire was back, rising in her bones like a crimson tide. If she didn't get out of here she might lose control and take out the whole rack of candles, or maybe the front window. And Theo's shop had already burned down once.

If I did it this time, would Theo forgive me like she's forgiven that big punk? She was immediately disgusted with herself. She shoved the curtain aside and tossed the coffee mug into the small sink, ignoring the splash of boiling liquid that slopped out. The smell of boiled coffee was thick and rank.

Elise scooped up her guitar case. She was powerfully tempted to use the back door, but that would be childish of her. Instead, she stalked back into the store. She hadn't even taken her purse off yet.

Dante had moved up next to Theo and had his arm over her shoulders. Hanson was on the customer's side of the counter, looking at Mari, who had her head down, golden curls curtaining her face.

Elise stamped across the store, each step seeming to echo in the emptiness. She'd painted the walls here herself, a lovely dark celestial blue scattered with stars. She'd even painted the roof, a joined golden sun and moon, her own design, wheeling around the light fixtures. She had worked a spell into it with her effort, a spell to protect everyone inside the store, to make it a sanctuary. The spell had soaked into the walls as the paint dried, and Elise could still see it pulsing. The effect was usually calming and soothing, but not right now. Pretty soon the paint would start to bubble, if she got mad enough. She could smell her own anger, a scent like burning paper.

"All right." Her voice sounded funny even to herself. "I get it. Theo and Mari have their new boy-toys now, and poor little Elise is still the odd girl out. Well, I've *had* it. You want to get nuclear with this Circle Geekfall? Fine. Go ahead. Do what you like. Just don't come crying to me when it all crashes down around your ears. I *swear,* you guys are acting like—" She heard herself and bit her lip savagely, stopping just in time. She had been about to say something truly horrible.

If she didn't get out of here, she was going to burn something. And since the Power had become so much more intense—so much scarier—Elise wasn't sure she could stop if she started while she was this angry.

Instead, she stamped for the door. If either of the two men moved a muscle to stop her, she was going to flambé them.

The Power shook and jittered, and a thin thread of smoke started to slide up from the hem of her jeans. Elise took a deep breath and pushed the door open. The bell jingled playfully.

"Elise—" Theo began.

Elise just shook her head and let the door close behind her. *I can't, Theo. I can't stay here. I don't want to hurt you. You're my friend, and I love you.* Elise swallowed the words, choked on the deep hurt boiling inside her chest. Then, clutching her guitar case in fingers that had gone white, she began to run.

Five

Remy surfaced in the late morning with the sense that something was very wrong. Of course, he'd been deep in the trance that passed for sleep, not waking when he wanted to for the first time since he'd become a Watcher. He had only awakened because something was pulling at him with invisible hands, a bone-deep buzzing that must have been what a compass needle felt when it was trying to find north. Something—or more likely, some*one*—was calling him. Hard.

The third thing that was very wrong was the cell phone buzzing against his chest. He fished it out, blinking, his head feeling as if someone had stuffed a whole hive of hornets in it, and flipped it open. On the way up to his ear, his eyes informed him that he'd missed three calls.

The pulling was still there, buzzing and jittering under his skin.

What the bloody blue hell?

"Remy," he said into the phone.

"Your assignment has changed." The faceless witch's tone, for the first time ever, was not perfectly calm. "You are to go to this address, where you will be given a dossier. There is a Lightbringer, and she is in terrible danger. We've received intelligence about the Brotherhood. They are seeking both the Trifero and this witch to use it. On your way to the address I am about to give you, you are to destroy this phone. Congratulations."

Remy blinked. The buzzing in his head abruptly calmed without losing any of its intensity, and a single sharp tugging began in the very center of his chest, slamming into him. The message hit him like a freight train.

Gods, they just abandoned me! How could they do that? I'm fine. I can take care of myself.

The sudden powerful communication was like a burst of static, a female voice bolting through his ears and whispering in the center of his skull. Remy's head whipped to the side, as if he had been slapped. Blood slid down from his lip. He barely heard the witch's voice giving him the address, his own voice repeating it. One part of his mind—the practical part—was taking down the address, memorizing it and making swift deductions. The other ninety percent of him was sitting absolutely still in shocked disbelief.

"Time is of the essence," the witch said. "Hurry, Watch-er."

"Understood," he said.

She hung up.

He sat there for maybe three seconds, staring at the sleek silver phone in his fist, before his fingers snapped closed around it and he heard a decisive, satisfying *crunch.*

A Lightbringer. Here. In trouble. In serious trouble.

The call hadn't gone away. If anything, it was more insistent, a terrible aching need. He had to follow it. What were the chances of two Lightbringers in this city—one of them in complete distress and sending out a signal he was tuned to, and the other powerful enough to be targeted by the Brotherhood? They had to be one and the same.

Have to be? Sure. Talk yourself into dereliction of duty. You've been given a job. Go do it.

For the phone to be destroyed meant that he was supposed to watch over a Lightbringer instead of doing garbage duty. He wished he could simply follow the call without worrying about the Trifero, knocking around loose wherever it was, and this new wrinkle in the plan.

If wishes were pigs we'd eat bacon for free. The shards of plastic and circuitry that used to be a cell phone cupped in his fist began to grind together. Smoke and the smell of burning plastic drifted up from his hand.

Duty or honor?

Both, the pitiless voice of his conscience replied. Remy stared at the hotel curtains, which were moving gently in a faint breeze. The air inside the room was dead and still, so he must be creating that little movement. Was his control slipping? That was the very *last* thing he needed.

The address. He would go and get the dossier and find out who this witch was. The insistent, nagging call inside his head and chest had subsided to a dull throbbing ache. But that voice—a woman's voice, with overtones of rage and agony, and an undertone of dark panic and aching loneliness—had spoken directly into his head. She must have been in a high emotional state to broadcast so strongly. He would be surprised if every psychic in the city wasn't clutching his or her head and moaning.

Unless it was a specific frequency and Remy was the only

one picking it up.

Remy's conscience spurred him again. *Hard.* He had a job to do.

He rocketed up off the bed, his booted feet meeting the floor with a thud. The smell of burning plastic was overwhelming. He looked around for somewhere to stash the mess that had been the cell phone and settled on a cheap metal wastebasket as the only possible choice. He dropped it in, and the slag thumped as it hit the bottom of the can. Smoke drifted through the room. The fire detector hadn't gone off, thank the gods, but Remy knew he had let his control slip. Just a little. But even a little slip could get him killed—or gods forbid, get a Lightbringer killed. That would be the worst thing he could imagine.

If they told him to destroy the phone, it meant they were sure of something. What could they be sure of?

His conscience pricked him again. He dug in his pockets, glancing at the small digital clock bolted to the plywood nightstand. The bed was hardly rumpled. He must not have moved very much in the depths of the mind-resting trance that passed for sleep among Watchers.

It was eleven o'clock.

Hold on, he thought as clearly as he could, at the distress call blazing away in the middle of the city. She would be lucky if something Dark didn't find her before he did. They would gather around her like moths crowding around a candle flame. Huge carnivorous moths that would snuff the candle, if they had a chance.

I can't let that happen. Panic started under his breastbone. The long harsh years of training bottled the panic tightly, turned it into icy resolve. His fingers dug in a pocket and fished out a pair of sunglasses. If he screwed up on this job—his first time watching over a Lightbringer—they would keep him hunting down trinkets for the rest of his days. He would never have a chance to find a witch who could ease the constant, grinding pain of the *tanak* melded to his body, a useful symbiote but one the human body was never meant to carry. It hurt to be a Watcher, a steady agony that was nevertheless better than the sharp spurs of his conscience.

If he failed this time, he would never find a way to make up for all the things he had done in his useless, violent life before Circle Lightfall had found him.

He would never see the Lightbringers gathered together again and feel the Power of the Light caroming through his nerves, never see the face of Heaven open up as they called on the Powers of Creation.

Hold on. The call wrapped itself tighter around his bones with every passing minute, and he wished he could be sure she heard him. *Hold on. I'm coming.*

Six

Elise banged open the pawnshop door and stepped inside, relishing the wash of cool air. She was panting and sweaty from running all the way from the Rowangrove. Her guitar case now felt as if it weighed two hundred pounds, and her boots felt as if they weighed fifty pounds each. Thank the gods she wasn't wearing heels. Her hair hung in her face, and she was *very* glad nobody was inside the shop but Vann, who looked up from behind the counter and gave her a wave. His smile died on his face and his hand stopped in midair. He chewed on his pierced lip while he regarded her, a sad-faced young man with short dark hair half dyed a bright Kool-Aid red. His long blunt fingers were tipped with thick calluses, and he drummed on the thick blue countertop, counting out time for a song running in his head. He was one of the best bassists she'd ever played with.

"Hi, Lise," he finally said, as she reached over the top of the swinging door that separated the pawnshop proper from the space behind the counter. She popped the catch and the half-door slid open. "You look like shit."

"Must be lack of caffeine." She set her guitar down next to his bass, which was stuffed under the counter, out of sight. "My day just freed up. I thought I'd spend some time practicing downstairs."

The pawnshop was a nice one, guitars hanging on a rack, jewelry in glassed-in counters, three racks of leather jackets, and an assortment of other stuff. Heavy late-summer sunlight fell in through the front window, cut into slices with curlicue edges by the iron grillwork outside the glass. Inside, it smelled like new carpeting and desperation. Elise's nose didn't wrinkle; she was used to the smell. The carpeting was new, but the smell of desperation clung in every bar and pawnshop she had ever been in, and she'd been in a fair number.

Vann shrugged. He wore a tattered blue business suit and a tie with a leaping fish on it. A cubic-zirconium earring winked in his left ear. "Trevor's coming by at about two. Guess we're going to get some decent practice in after all. You finished that song yet?"

"Which one?" Elise dropped down on a three-legged stool. The air-conditioning felt wonderful. Vann's battered yellow sneakers were the perfect added touch to his rumpled suit. He looked just hip enough to be working here. The money was good and the boss was his uncle, so Vann was well cared for.

"The one about the man with the plan." Vann grinned and blinked owlishly, visibly deciding not to ask her any hard questions. He knew her too well, and got along with her because he didn't pry.

I must be wearing my mad face. "No, haven't finished it yet. We can work on it. How are you doing?"

He shrugged. "It's only nine-thirty. Too soon to tell."

"You want some coffee?" She hadn't had more than two or three sips of hers before it had boiled in her hand during the Happy Little Discussion. As a result, she was in her morning pre-caffeination funk. "My treat."

"Sure thing." He blinked at her. "Must have been one hell of a morning. Hey, are we ever going to play that bar again? That was fun."

"At least *we* didn't get in on the fighting," she said darkly, and his mouth quirked up in a grin. "We're playing the Clair tonight and the Galaxie again next week. Okay, I'm coffee bound. Try not to burn the place down." *Get it, Elise? Burn the place down. That's your trick, isn't it?*

"No milk." His fingers went back to tapping at the countertop. "I'll just keep the crowd busy until you come back."

It was the tag line to an old band joke. Elise actually laughed. She let herself out through the half-door again and shook her hair back, wishing she'd thought to bring something to tie it back this morning. But she had overslept, dreaming of…what? A church with a wrinkled marble floor and an empty choir loft, and something else she couldn't remember. She had awakened with a start, the air in her room hot and still, steam evaporating from her skin, leaving little curlicues of salt behind.

She pushed the pawnshop's door open and stepped back out into the heat.

Liberty Loans was on Belmont Street, a fair distance from the Rowangrove. A red neon sign hung over the entrance and she could see the metal grille for the nightly defense of the storefront pushed neatly to the side. Belmont was a lot more active at this hour than the Ave, where Theo's shop was located, mostly because it was in a worse part of town. This far down Belmont the sidewalks were cracked, there were four pawnshops and three liquor stores, gangs of teenagers hung out on the corners, and a few hookers worked their respective turfs even in this heat. Elise strolled down to Bronson Deli and ducked in, grateful for the air-conditioning here too. The day was going to be a scorcher.

"Elise!" Mrs. Pauvels chirped from behind the counter. "So nice to see you!"

Mrs. Pauvels was short, and her yellowing dentures slipped in her mouth sometimes, but her blue eyes were sharp and missed little. Her gray hair was scraped back and pulled into a bun. Elise leaned over the counter to give her a peck on her soft old-lady cheek. She smelled like baby powder and fried food, a familiar smell from Elise's many restaurant jobs. "Hey there, Mrs. P. What's the word on the street today?"

"New pimp carving out some territory two streets down," Mrs. P said immediately. The deli's eight tables, all decked with plastic flowers, were deserted. There would soon be a steady stream of people coming in to buy coffee and bagels, as well as hangover cures. "Stay away from him, sweetie. Wears a white suit, got a good line and a crew of PR chippies."

"Oh, no." Elise clicked her tongue. "Give me two coffees, Mrs. P. That's terrible. Trouble for sure; Robbie won't like anyone moving in on him." Her back ached from running, so she leaned on the pink Formica counter, resting her chin on her hand. It would make her ass seem heart-shaped to anyone coming in through the door, but right now she didn't care. "And can I have a whole-wheat bagel?"

"You sure can." Mrs. Pauvels's wrinkled face spiit into a sweet smile, and Elise smiled back. "Now why don't you tell me what's troubling you?"

"Ahh." Elise shrugged, watching the old woman shuffle over to the coffeepot. "Why don't you get some help here, Mrs. P?"

"Ach, my boys help out. What's wrong, sweetie?"

"Oh, just a little disagreement with some friends of mine." Elise stared at the racks of bagels on display. Little marching soldiers. Mrs. Pauvels selected the biggest whole-wheat bagel and wrapped it up neatly. "They get boyfriends and all of a sudden it's like I don't exist anymore. Like I'm not important anymore because I don't have some hatchet-faced badass hanging on me."

"What about your friend?" Mrs. Pauvels poured the coffee, sniffing deeply. "The nice boy in the band? Tall, long hair? Of course these young men all look the same nowadays."

You mean the nice boy who died last month? It was a tragedy, Mrs. P, a real tragedy. Tears rose in Elise's throat, and she shoved them down with an effort of will. If she started crying now, she would never stop. "Yeah, I agree. They're all the same all over the world." Elise looked up at her. After a moment, the old woman's blue eyes sparkled. Elise hauled herself upright. The backs of her legs and her shoulders burned from carrying her guitar case. Her neck ached, a tension headache spilling up through tense muscles. Coffee would help.

The old woman laughed. "Ach, you're too young to know what I mean. Your friends will grow out of it. They're young, like you."

"There's one critical difference between my friends and me." Elise dug in her purse. She brought out a five-dollar bill and two guitar picks, as well as some Merry Mint Lip Polish. The picks and the lip gloss went back into the camera case. Mrs. Pauvels started struggling with her cash register. "I'm not stupid and boy-crazy. Hey, Mrs. P, why don't you get a different cash register? I could find you one."

"Ach, no." Mrs. Pauvels waved one liver-spotted hand. "Would be even worse. At least this hunk of junk, I know it's junk, so I'm not disappointed."

Elise laughed again to keep up appearances. Mrs. P was a dear sweet lady and didn't deserve the sharp end of Elise's tongue. She took the two cups, popped lids on them, balanced them on top of each other, and stuffed the bagel into her purse. "Thanks, Mrs. P. I owe you one for making me laugh. You really think they'll grow out of it?"

"I'm sure of it, sweetie." The old woman nodded, but her blue eyes were sharp and troubled. "Girlfriends are supposed to last. It would be a terrible world if they didn't."

"I guess," Elise said. "Thanks."

"Ach, don't mention it." Mrs. Pauvels waved her away. "Stay away from that new pimp."

No worries. I'm a tough girl, and being psychic kind of takes all the mystery out a man's pickup lines. "I will." She picked up the coffee carefully, hitching her shoulder higher to keep her purse on. She concentrated a little, so the edges of her personal warding solidified. No purse-snatching for her. And no pimp would mess with her with her shields this solid.

A man in a pair of blue overalls pushed his way into the

shop and held the door for Elise. She thanked him with a nod
and walked away, knowing he was probably watching her ass.
Watch what you can't have, kiddo. Don't we all.

The heat was already starting to shimmer off the pavement,
and it made her feel a little better. It wasn't as comforting as
Theo's voice humming as she stroked a fevered forehead, or
Mari's laughter, but a nice sunny summer's day, even one as
hot and airless as this one was turning out to be, was like being
wrapped in a warm blanket. Elise's Power fed on the heat.
Sometimes she felt like a solar panel, as if the sun made her
stretch just like a plant. It was a deep and happy feeling, the
sun in the sky and all right with the world.

Except that it wasn't right. She'd popped her lid on her
two best friends, her only two friends. She'd all but accused
them of murdering Suzanne.

I didn't accuse them. A construction worker whistled at
her, she ignored it. The streets were starting to wake up, the
city's heartbeat taking on a rhythm that sounded just like a jazz
bass line, and her ears began to pick out the music of the city
beating just under the pavement. *I accused those two gun-
toting psychos of bringing those horrible things here. The
Dark. But they'll believe the guys. They always do. Good-
bye, Elise. We found boyfriends so you're out. Just like
usual.* She took a deep breath. The heat shimmer intensified.
A hot wind blew down the street.

She carried the coffee back into Liberty Loans and saw
Vann had a customer, who pushed something across the counter
as the door closed, air-conditioning puffing coolness across
Elise's shoulders.

"Twenty," Vann said. "Come on, man, it's a piece of junk.
Look at the setting. It's brass."

"Fine." The man wore a black cowboy hat, jeans, and a
red flannel shirt.

Elise paused for a moment, her shields quivering. *Why does
he have flannel on in this weather?* A shiver traced its way
up her spine.

His voice sounded odd, too, as if something was stuck in
his mouth. "I don't care as long as I get rid of it."

Vann's gaze flicked up and met Elise's. She caught the
blast of worry and lifted her eyebrows, the question implicit.
He shook his head slightly. *No, the guy's not a problem, just
a weirdo.*

She set the coffee down on part of the counter reserved for just such occasions, a little empty space between a rack of silk ties and a Lucite case holding diamond earrings. She slid behind the counter and latched the half-door, then pressed her fingers over it. It was a small spell, and a simple one, but better than nothing. The rune *naithuz*, the closer of doors, shaped like a backwards-leaning X. The door would stay shut until Elise wanted it open.

"Sign this, then." Vann pushed a square of paper across at the man.

Elise carried the coffee around to Vann's side and examined the man, feeling her fingers and toes go cold. He was glamoured like the Watchers. If she hadn't been around them so much, she wouldn't have been looking for the shimmering around his edges. But she saw the faint glitter and looked *under* it before she could stop herself.

The thing under the glamour was skeletal, gray skin runneled with awful sores. Elise did not let out a horrified gasp only because she had no breath left, having just exhaled. She stared, and her heart gave one terrified leap.

Its filmy eyes were huge, watery, and red-rimmed, and it had no nose, just a collapsed ruin. The hand clumsily wielding the pen Vann had handed over was a twisted, oozing claw. Its mouth was lipless, and it had a set of wicked-looking teeth that clicked together when the thing glanced up at her.

"It's a relief to be rid of the damn thing. I never should have taken it." The little sound its teeth made as they met made Elise's heart give another shuddering leap. The cowboy hat bobbed, and Elise began to feel seriously sick.

Vann took the signed piece of paper, glanced at it, and then handed the thing a twenty. "There you go." He picked up his coffee cup. He took a healthy swallow and grimaced. "Pleasure doing business."

"Likewise," the gray thing said, and Elise had a horrible thought.

It's festering. It's not supposed to be out during the day. It's one of those thingies. Something Dark. Like the Grays—the ones Theo saw, the ones that smelled so horrible.

It's a predator.

She raised her coffee cup to her lips, as if in a dream. The thing stared at her hungrily, licking its oozing ragged lips with a long yellow tongue. Its eyes blinked, first one, and then the other, slowly, deliberately.

"Hey, buddy," Vann said. "You got a problem?"

The gray thing darted him one murderous look, and Elise's hand twitched. If the thing leapt up on the counter she was going to flash-fry it. Power hummed in her hand, a prickling, intense heat. *Not Vann,* she said to herself, to the gray thing. *Leave him alone, or I swear to God I'll sauté you.*

The thing backed up two quick mincing steps. "No problem," it said thickly, the glamour wearing eggshell-thin. Any moment now it might break.

The door opened and closed. The creature fled. Elise took in a harsh gasping breath. One of the TV sets on the shelves high above the floor of the pawnshop popped some sparks, and Vann looked up incuriously. Most of his attention seemed to be on the counter. "Now this is seriously weird." He took another slurp of coffee. "You have any idea what this is, oh freaky one?"

Elise dragged in a deep breath and looked down at the counter. Her hair was about to start standing straight up like a cat's fur if she wasn't careful. Wouldn't that be a sight?

The thing on the counter looked like a giant...What *was* it?

Elise, fascinated, reached out with one finger and touched it. A spark zapped off the smooth, carved surface.

It was as long as her middle finger, a round red stone that had been carved into a dragon. Or like a mad cross between the Chinese and European notions of a dragon. Rudimentary batwings clung to a long, sleek body, each scale carved with finicky precision. A long, flaring snout, wicked teeth, and small glittering eyes completed the picture. The dragon was looped, its tail curling just under its chin so that it made an almost-perfect circle. A heavy brass ring came up from the setting, which looked to be brass as well. It looked like a necklace pendant for a barbarian princess. There was another, smaller red stone set in the middle, the dragon curled around it, and this stone was almost definitely a ruby. Or something that looked like one.

It would look nice on a bit of black velvet ribbon, for a choker. Elise stroked the dragon's sinuous curve. It was a big, gaudy piece, and she liked it. "I like it." Her fingertip caressed one bat wing. The carving was exquisite. Was the stone a carnelian? The color of the outer stone was too deep to be carnelian, too light to be garnet, and too opaque to be ruby. Maybe it wasn't even something semiprecious. Maybe it was just a red rock someone had found and carved up.

"Yeah? Twenty bucks," Vann joked, slurping at his coffee. "Hey, you okay? You look pale."

Elise flipped her purse open, her eyes never leaving the medallion. It would fit into her palm nicely, she thought. She could cup it in the hollow part and look at it for a long time, meditating on each curve and line. "Sure. Just fine. Here's a twenty. Can you write me a receipt?"

"You're crazy."

"Well, you made back your money in less than five minutes," she pointed out practically. "I'd say it's a good bargain. And the guy didn't borrow, just wanted to get rid of it. Come on, Vann. Give it up." She waved the twenty, knowing without having to look that his dark eyes were following it.

"He was staring at your tits." Vann snatched the twenty out of her hand. He started scribbling a receipt.

"So were you." Elise scooped the dragon up from the counter. It fit perfectly in her hand, and she was hard-pressed to make her fingers let go and drop it into her purse. The dragon seemed to shift against her palm, as if it was glad to be touching her. "Thanks, Vann. I owe you one." *At least something's going right about this day.*

"Ah, crap, just go downstairs and practice." He tore the receipt off and handed it over. "I'll be down in a while. As you can see, it's Fun City up here."

Elise accepted the receipt. Now that the dragon was in her purse and the gray thing was gone from the store, she began to feel almost normal. "I'll come back up for lunch. We can do Thai or something."

Vann grunted at her and went back to drinking his coffee.

She carried her guitar to the Employees Only door and went through, turning immediately to her right and heading down the stairs to the basement. She would be able to see people's legs through the half-windows, passing by as she practiced. She did some of her best thinking down here, pacing back and forth or sitting on a barstool with her legs crossed, the guitar cradled against her like a big, balky child, watching the legs go back and forth. Suzanne had often come to band rehearsals and listened, giving little bits of advice or criticism. She'd had a good ear.

Elise shook away the thought of Suzanne.

Elise's guitar was a candy-apple red Stratocaster—christened Christopher at a post-gig party some time ago, when he had been new—that she'd saved for months to buy. She jacked in and kept the volume on the amp low so nobody upstairs would hear. She tuned up quickly and did some chords, her fingers shaking against the strings so the sound came out wavering and uncertain instead of with her usual brash confidence.

That thing was allergic to sunlight. She shuddered. *And it was dying of leprosy or something. Gods. If the glamour would have broken it probably would have come over the counter at us. I'm sure it would have.*

But that was crazy. The glamour hadn't broken. It had held. It had *held.*

Elise sat on the couch, with Christopher cuddled against her, and stared fixedly at the Felix the Cat clock hanging on the opposite wall. Felix's eyes and tail went back and forth with mad synchronization. *If I wasn't absolutely sure I was sane, I would be going out and getting very, very drunk right now. At least Theo and Mari can see the same things I can.*

She sat there, mulling it over, waiting for the shaking in her hands and knees to go away. She'd been within leaping distance of something with razor-sharp teeth and giant festering sores and *hadn't even known* until she'd looked. If it had been something like a Slider, would it have had her for breakfast? And maybe finished up with poor Vann too?

The trembling came in fits, peaking and dying down. It wouldn't be so bad if she could just dial up Theo, but Theo might be out with one of her patients by now. And Mari would be working in the Rowangrove instead of having her day off. Yet another thing to feel guilty about.

She was staring at the clock face, showing her eleven in the morning, when a single molten-hot tear rolled down her cheek.

God. They abandoned me, those guys came along and they just abandoned me. How could they do that? They promised...I'm fine. I can take care of myself. I can deal with this. I can deal with this.

Elise put her head down over the guitar. Her hair fell down in long coppery strands, cloaking the way her face screwed up into a grimace of terrible pain. She felt...well, lonely. She'd never had real friends to lose before, keeping herself distant and untouchable until she'd met Suzanne. The distance was the only way to be safe. Keep yourself closed-off, and nobody could touch you enough to hurt you.

She sat for a long time, fingers wandering over the strings, producing some awful squealing sounds like piglets trapped in a pen, until something brushed against her again. It felt like someone touching her cheek, fingers threading through her hair. A very personal touch.

Elise rocketed up from the couch, whirling. There was absolutely nobody in the basement with her. She was sure of it. She had checked automatically when she'd come down the stairs, and it would have been impossible for her not to notice someone else coming down.

Hold on. I'm coming.

Elise whirled again, her hair fanning out in a long bright streak. She even glanced up at the ceiling, her fingers loose with shock. If she hadn't had her black leather guitar-strap on over her shoulder, she would have dropped Christopher. The voice was male, dark and low, and tinged with a faint slow accent. *Hold on*, it repeated, and Elise did a full three-sixty, her eyes searching every nook and cranny of the dark, low basement she knew as well as her own house, from the stack of Penthouse mags in the corner to the picture of Al Pacino hung on the opposite wall to the dart board Mark had hung up three years ago.

Nobody home but Elise, and the chickens in her head. The thought had an edge of dark panicked hilarity she wasn't sure she liked.

"Hearing voices," Elise said, and her shaking left hand curled around the neck of the guitar. "I've finally cracked. Being a witch has finally cracked me. Oh, no. No. No, no no."

She found a chord, struck it, and then her fingers moved into their accustomed positions. Music began to come softly from the amplifier crouched at her feet. The drum set—Trevor's drum set, since they had taken Mark's down and given it to his younger brother—vibrated uneasily in the corner, the high hat ringing a little as her tension communicated itself to the air.

The music picked her up, shook her out of herself. She threw it up like a wall, the guitar crying and screaming and wailing, shielding her from whatever was hunting her. Whoever was *touching* her without her permission.

*—hold on—*it repeated once, faintly, but Elise, no longer caring about politeness, used her boot toe to jam the volume control up. It was an operation she'd performed many times before, and the resulting blast of sound shook all the thoughts out of her head.

Good. First thing tomorrow morning she was going to hit the library and the other occult shops and find out what she had to do to get out of this town. It was time to do the Locomotion right on out of here, to boogie on down to somewhere sane. If she got far enough away from the Watchers her life might get more normal.

Normal? I can set things on fire just by staring at them. Normal isn't going to be part of the bargain, Elise.

Shut up. She pushed away the mocking little voice inside her head. Grinning, tears slicking her cheeks and her lips pulled back from her teeth, Elise played.

Seven

The address turned out to be a little occult shop with not only two Lightbringers, but also a pair of Watchers. One of them—Dante—was famous for never having lost a witch. The other, Hanson, was equally famous, for being the coolest, calmest fighter the Crusade had ever faced. And from the way they both hovered around the Lightbringers—a green-glowing witch with long sandalwood-scented dark hair and the unmistakable gentleness of a healer, and a blond, blue-eyed doll with the sound of a waterfall resounding behind her words—Remy saw that the impossible had happened for both of them. They had met their witches and gotten the golden apple held out in front of every Watcher.

A witch to stop the pain.

The *tanak* in Remy's bones shifted, broken glass dragging over his nerves. The proximity of the two Lightbringers made the Darkness he had been infused with wake up, tearing jagged edges of agony through his muscles. Remy supposed he was lucky. So much time spent chasing down Talismans and Power objects meant that he hadn't been in the presence of many Lightbringers, and wasn't as familiar with the awful nerve-burning pain their presence induced, or the energy required to shelve the pain and focus on the job at hand.

"Honor, brother," black-eyed Dante said.

Remy straightened, his hand leaving the knife hilt. "Duty. Look, I was ordered to come here."

Hanson held up a slim manila file. "Yeah, this just came in over the fax. How did you get in past the shields? This is a Guardian city."

Remy shrugged. "Nothing stopped me at the limits, so I thought it was okay."

The two Lightbringers stared at him. The dark-haired one elbowed the blonde, who whispered something in her ear. Remy observed a safe distance from them, avoiding pain, and because a Watcher was trained to complete respect for Lightbringers. When a Lightbringer said *jump*, a Watcher jumped. You didn't even ask how high—you just jumped as high as you could and hoped like hell it was high enough.

The dark-haired witch threw up her hands and sighed dramatically. "Oh, I don't *care!*" she said, with the tone of a woman pushed past all patience. "Dante, you can't do this. This isn't right. Elise will go nuts, and I can't blame her."

"The border didn't stop him, Theo," Dante said. "Apparently he doesn't belong to Circle Lightfall anymore. At least, that's the only thing that makes any sense. Since all three of you are alive and well, the city's still yours." His tone was dry and ironic, but he had been ready to take Remy's head off before realizing he was a Watcher.

Remy had hoped he wouldn't have to fight him. Watchers were *dangerous*.

"Elise doesn't want a Watcher." The blond witch glanced toward the front of the store. The "Open" sign was still turned out, but the heavy layers of shielding on the shop sparked and fizzed with tension. Remy didn't think many people, witch or normal, would be coming in here until they calmed down. "You saw her. You *heard* her."

"Excuse me, ma'am," he said politely, and the dark-haired one elbowed the blonde again. They seemed to be evaluating him very carefully, but he didn't have time to pass any tests. "I have a lot of business to get done before dark. I'm searching for an artifact, and I have to protect this witch from some very nasty Dark. I was *called* to this city. There's a Lightbringer in terrible pain here, and I seem to have my wires crossed with hers."

"He called you *ma'am*." The blonde began to chuckle again. The dark-haired one seemed to find this incredibly funny as well, looking a little ashamed of her mirth but still laughing.

Did they not *understand* what he was telling them?

Remy cast a hopeless look at Dante, who shrugged. Hanson thrust the folder out, and Remy accepted it. He flipped it open and glanced through the file.

A glossy eight-by-ten picture shot in black and white, showing a woman with long hair that seemed to be...no, not blond. Not dark either. Something in between. She was standing, loose and hipshot, dressed in a low-cut pair of leather pants and a torn black T-shirt with a silkscreen of Rodin's *Thinker* on it. Something glittered in her patrician nose, and her eyes were closed as she leaned into a microphone, her lips just closed. A guitar hung in her left hand, raised up; she had obviously just finished singing something. There was a slight curl to her hair, especially around her face, where sweat had soaked in. She

looked a little on the tall side, and she wore a glittering choker
of some sort. Long slim nose, perfect eyebrows, a mouth that
seemed impossibly lush, wide even cheekbones.

She was beautiful. She was so bloody beautiful it hit him in
the gut like a fully unexpected sucker-punch. The curve of her
cheek and her lips relaxed in a gentle smile, she looked lost in
some private world. But she was holding the guitar up with
white-knuckled fingers, as if she had just finished shaking it.
Or as if it was heavier than it looked. Just the sight of that one
stray strand of hair falling across her face made his fingers
itch in a new and unexpected way, wanting to brush it back.

There was a heated discussion going on, which he largely
ignored. The other Watchers could look after their witches.
This was Remy's first, and he didn't intend to screw it up.

He flipped the photo aside and scanned the printed materi-
al. His memory, thoroughly trained, swallowed the information
whole. Birth date, favorite color, known Power, known associ-
ates, known addresses, bank accounts, and phobias. A fire
witch who had survived not only childhood but also her teen
years. He let out a low whistle. A Guardian of the city? How
had that happened? And why hadn't he felt it?

The nagging, crunching call inside his head intensified. He
flipped back to the photo and stared at it, almost forgetting his
surroundings. The call intensified again.

Her. It had to be her. If it wasn't her, he would eat his
boots. The shock of *rightness* slamming into his solar plexus
was too immediate. It was like winning the lottery with a ticket
he hadn't even bought. He had never even dared to dream
that he would ever be allowed close to a witch, let alone sent
to watch over *his* witch.

My witch? Absolutely. This is her. This is the one. There
was no room for doubt. It was as true as gravity.

The discussion got a little louder, the dark-haired witch
repeating that it wasn't right, the blonde saying something about
privacy, Dante saying that she had to be protected, and Hanson,
oddly enough, saying nothing and watching Remy very closely.

Remy closed the file folder with a snap. He rolled it up in
his fist and looked at the other two Watchers, who suddenly
gave him their full attention, reading the tension in his aura.
The dark-haired witch stared at him, a thin line between her
charcoal eyebrows. She looked worried.

"Where is she now?" Remy heard the command in his

voice and hoped the other Watchers wouldn't take offense. He hadn't hung around with many other Watchers. He'd been too busy hunting down trinkets for Circle Lightfall.

And now he *had* to find her, as soon as possible.

"Probably at Liberty Loan on Belmont. It's a pawnshop, and her band practices downstairs. They have a gig at the Clair tonight." The blond witch crossed her arms as if suddenly chilled. "That's a club up from the Creation on the Ave, very new, very hot. Look, you can go with us, and we'll try to smooth everything over with Elise—"

"Begging your pardon, ma'am." Remy dared to interrupt. "The Brotherhood's tracking an artifact—the Trifero. Very nasty stuff. And if your friend is both a Guardian and a fire witch, she's probably the only person on this continent that can use it without being eaten alive. So I have to find her. *Now*." He nodded smartly. "Nice to meet you, *madames*." Then he looked at the two Watchers. If there was anything else he needed to know, they would have told him by now. He took a deep breath. "Honor."

"Duty," Dante responded, looking a bit bemused. "Need backup?"

Remy shook his head.

"Duty," Hanson said. "Good luck. What did you say your name was?"

"I didn't. It's Remy." And with that, he turned on his heel and was heading for the door.

"Now wait just a—" the blond witch began.

"Dante," the dark-haired one said.

"The Hunter," Hanson said. "Wow. Look at that, Dante. We get the *Hunter*."

Remy still held the manila folder in one fist. He paced out into the heavy shimmering heat coming up of the pavement, and the thick paper began to smolder in his hand. First he had to find a quiet corner to burn the dossier to a smudge of ash, and then he needed to find this pawnshop.

A witch. My first witch and she turns out to be the one. Five years I've been hunting for garbage and now they throw this at me. If I'd been doing real Watcher duty all this time, I might possibly be a little more prepared. As it is, I'll be lucky if I don't get us both killed.

The thought of failing this beautiful witch with a guitar in one hand and her eyes closed, lost in her own private world, made a cold sweat break out all over his skin. He noticed that the file folder was nothing more than a fine smear of ash drifting down from his fist. He had a good glamour on, one that made people's eyes slide right over him. He could slip through the slow-moving crowd easily. The map of the city he'd examined was fresh in his head, and Belmont was a fair distance from here. Once he found the street, it would be easy enough to find her. As a matter of fact, he barely needed the map at all, the calling in his chest was strong enough to act as a compass.

She's in pain, in some kind of distress. Gods. Don't let me be too late.

Remy took a deep breath and began to run.

Eight

Elise had just come up the stairs with her guitar case when the phone beeped. Vann hooked it up. "Liberty Loan we deal in freedom," he said all in one breath. "This is Vann how can I help ya?"

His eyes met Elise's, and she shook her head, understanding in a moment. It was Theo calling, or Mari. Or even worse, one of their pet Watchers.

"No, she ain't here. Sorry." Vann lied with blithe unconcern. "Take a message?" Then he shrugged, forgetting that whoever it was couldn't see him. "'Kay." He hung up. "Was your friend with the freaky head shop. Sounded worried."

Elise shrugged, yawning a little. "Not worried enough to quit jacking me around for her boyfriend," she muttered darkly. "It's only two-thirty."

"Yeah, Trevor called to ask us if we wanted to come out to that warehouse again and practice early." Van scratched under his armpits. The door opened, letting in a blast of hot air, and Elise looked over to see Charlie roll his round body in.

Charlie was round and black-haired, wearing a rumpled orange polyester suit. "Hey, Red," he greeted, sticking his tongue out and waggling it. He was Vann's uncle. "Here I is, your dream man."

Well, at least Charlie's dependable. "Huh." Elise scanned him from head to foot. "Naw, I don't think so, babe. You're too short."

Charlie's mouth twisted under his red bulbous nose. "Be kind to an old man, Red." Even this early in the day, he smelled powerfully of gin.

"Aw, Charlie, you know you're my guy," Elise relented, shifting her guitar case, and Vann grabbed his own case. His was decorated with a large painting of a fifties cheesecake calendar girl Elise had finally broken down and airbrushed for him. The painting wore garters, a black Spanish-style skirt, and a wide smile. It was a nice piece of work. Vann already had his duffel across his thin body. With his case, he would look like a musical refugee.

"You're a real sweetheart." Charlie, as usual, tried to pinch Elise's ass as she went by, but she did a neat little skipping half-turn, almost driving her case into a glass counter.

"Better luck next time, Charlie," she said, and made it out onto the hot pavement.

Vann followed her. "So we're going to the warehouse?"

"Of course," Elise said. "We can really blast it out there. He's got the van?"

"Yeah. That was a good call, Lise. He can drum and he's got wheels." Van stripped off his suit jacket and shirt, revealing a silver mesh T-shirt. His tattoo—a Celtic knot on his upper left arm—twitched as he rolled the jacket and shirt up and stuffed the resultant wad in his duffel bag. He got out a box of Marlboros and tapped one up. "You want one?"

"No, thanks." Elise fell into step beside him. "Is he coming to pick us up or meeting us there?"

"He'll meet us at Bonton's so we can pound a brewski and get some Thai before we go out there. You game?" Vann gave her a quick sidelong look. "You gonna be okay, Elise? You look pale."

"I'm fine. And I always look pale. It's like an oven out here." *I'm looking for a subject change, Vann. Get it?*

Vann took the hint. "Yeah. Heat wave. I heard on the radio that the cops are surprised there ain't been a crime wave to match the heat wave. Isn't that weird?" Vann matched her stride for stride. They walked down Belmont, waited for the light at the corner, and continued on, their pace slowing as the heat dragged at them.

"Very weird," Elise agreed. The Watchers had told them that the more Lightbringers in a geographic area, the more the crime rate descended. This was especially marked in cities. A city under the protection of three Guardians should have a low crime level too, and Circle Lightfall wanted a bunch of Lightbringers and Watchers in the city to see if it could get even better. Just like damn monkeys in an experiment. "Hey Vann. What's the progression on that thing you're working on?"

"Standard blues thing." He hummed a few bars, the crowd parting in front of them. People were dressed in shorts and tank tops, and there were sunburns and red noses. Vann flipped out his John Lennon sunglasses and pushed them onto his face. "In sevens, F-B flat-F-B flat, F-G-C-B-F, repeat as necessary, just add a woman and a bottle of tequila. Or someone shooting your dog."

Elise laughed. "I might just steal that line, baby."

"Feel free. You're the brains, boss."

"I don't think that's true." She slowed down even more, sweat prickling under her arms and at the small of her back. *I like heat, but this is ridiculous. It feels like an oven.* She amused herself by people-watching. Rumpled office workers, wilting hipsters, a few kids out with their parents, fractious because of the heat.

I'm their Guardian. She shivered, a reflexive movement in the middle of the still hot air. All these ordinary people. Their lives were probably calmer and better than hers.

The band had a gig tonight, and tomorrow she could go find another bartending job for when Theo fired her at the shop. And Elise would start looking into how she could break the Guardian thing and get the hell out of here. She could find another city to start fresh in, and the next time she saw a man in a black leather trench coat she would run the other way. Posthaste.

She had a workable plan. Theo and Mari would find a nice little witch who didn't make waves, one who would get shacked up with a hatchet-faced hunk of Watcher and crochet nice little Circle Lightfall doilies.

Things were looking up. Things were definitely looking up. Vann was talking about another song he wanted to practice, and Elise made a noise of agreement.

She should be feeling free, and relieved.

Then why do I feel like I've been stabbed in the chest?

Nine

The Clair was a very trendy place. There was a line down the block to get in, and Remy had to use a deeper glamour to slide through the crowd and push past the pair of shaved gorillas passing for bouncers. The wall of sound hit him, and he grimaced a little.

Inside, there were disco balls spinning and a sort of industrial-Goth design ethic, lots of metal catwalks and artful plastic sheeting hanging from the ceiling. The dance floor was full, and there was some no-name house music playing. The bar was roughly the size of a beached whale.

In short, the place was a security nightmare.

Remy had missed the witch—*Elise,* he reminded himself, *her name is Elise*—at the pawnshop by only a few minutes, and had tracked her to a bar and then to a Thai restaurant. Missed her there too, and finally picked up the trail in an abandoned warehouse still echoing with the music she had played with two young normals. Then the trail had gone clear across town, very close to the occult shop where he had originally started. A merry little chase, just like tracking an artifact that someone kept moving to spite him.

As a result, he was in a little bit of a temper. The house music cut just as he drifted through the crowd next to the bar, checking the normals. There were a few borderline-psychics here, glittering under the confusion and chaotic lighting, people yelling and shouting over the music. She was in the building, and he had a good idea of what would happen next, so he just waited, scanning the place every few seconds.

"Ladies and gentlemen," someone boomed over a mike, and Remy almost winced before his ears compensated for two things—the sensitivity of his Dark-enhanced senses and the huge decibel count being used. "The Clair is pleased to bring you Live Music Thursday! And now, for your listening pleasure, I give you…" There was a long pause, and a breathless hum of excitement. Remy had picked up that this band was the current hot thing. His witch had a fair amount of local celebrity among clubbers and music fans.

Let's hope she's not a celebrity with the Brotherhood yet. What do you say, Remy? If wishes were bacon, we'd all eat for free.

The excitement reached a bloodthirsty pitch, and the announcer's voice boomed. *"I give you the Tragic Diamonds!"* he howled, and the crowd started to cheer.

The lights went up, blinding, and the stage, hidden in darkness behind the dance floor, became clearly visible. The dance floor was now jammed with normals crowded almost cheek-to-cheek. There was one massive chord that seemed to stop the world, and then a spotlight bloomed and revealed...

Remy's heart almost stopped, his hands falling loose to his sides.

No picture could have prepared him for this.

She was tall for a woman, and had a long fall of coppery hair that burned against her pale skin. The color of her hair was amazing, like nothing else he had ever seen, a pure red gold. Her eyes, heavily outlined in black, were a clear light green like sunlight through green amber. Witch-eyes, the light irises ringed by a line of deeper green. Something glittered on her nose—a piece of jewelry. A ruby, if his eyes didn't deceive him. Her face, with the force of her personality behind it, was incandescent. With her eyes blazing, her fingers caressing the guitar, and her lush mouth turned up in a little private half-smile, Remy was surprised that every man in the place wasn't storming the stage.

At that thought, the Dark thing inside his bones growled loud enough that a few people—the almost-psychics in the crowd—actually turned and looked around. The thought of another man touching this witch made red rage crawl under his skin.

Steady, boy. She's a witch, you're a Watcher. Don't get possessive. That's the quickest way to get decommissioned.

She wore a tight pair of battered jeans and a red silk slip coming down to mid-thigh, every curve and line of her body showing. He had never heard of a witch dressing like this—most of them seemed to like skirts, for some reason—and it wasn't entirely unexpected that the men stared or howled at her. She was literally aflame, glancing down as her fingers moved slightly on the neck of the guitar, a look of complete abstraction on her lovely face.

The chord resolved into a driving rhythm. The tattooed and long-haired stick of a drummer was beating the drums as if possessed, and the bass player, a thin dark-haired man who looked to be eighty percent nose, popped a riff that made the dancers start to jump.

Remy took a closer look. The drummer was almost-Lightbringer. His glow was very weak next to hers; he could probably pass for a normal if he tried. *Well*, Remy thought, *I'll tell the other Watchers.* Then all thought was shaken clean out of his head.

She had the guitar, melody screaming over the top of the rhythm, reaching right through the air and shaking his bones into glass shards. Her eyes came up slowly, scanning through the crowd, and sliding right past Remy.

Who had forgotten to breathe and stood as still as a dead tree in the middle of the crowd at the bar, people who had turned their backs on the liquor and were watching the stage.

Then she stepped up to the microphone. And the magick started.

"I ain't no mermaid, I ain't no siren,
I am no green-skinned jade
I am a child of steel and ore,
the best singer of the blade
I have walked these city streets
with nothing by my side,
Darkness take me, you can't make me,
I will be no bride—"

It wasn't the best Remy had ever heard, but the screaming music and her clear high voice, delivered crisply, mixed with the flaming red Power pouring out of her in waves. She was actually tapping into the crowd, feeding their excitement, deftly tying it into the mounting rhythm.

Remy stood absolutely still in the middle of a mass of screaming, writhing, jumping normals. How had anyone ever missed this? She was like a volcano. A forest fire. Something deadly and roaring and beautiful all at once.

Something else caught his eye. There on her slender white neck, a hank of black velvet ribbon. Hanging from the ribbon was a palm-sized medallion, barbaric against her fragile-looking throat.

Gods above and below. He almost lost his footing as a wave of normals slammed into him. *She's got a Major Talisman! What the hell?*

They were deep in the song now, on the third chorus, something about a green hill under a blood moon. She had the crowd in the palm of her hand, coppery hair swinging as she leaned into the microphone, singing to it as if she were whispering to a best friend, singing as if she were performing for a lover.

The song ended with another crashing chord, the drummer breaking a stick and grabbing another one from a box set at his feet without missing a beat.

The crowd surged forward, screaming.

"Are we having a good time?" she said into the microphone, her eyes scanning the crowd. Her voice was now a husky purr, amplified but still smooth, pitched low enough to raise the hairs on a man's nape. Remy's entire body went cold, then flamed.

The crowd yelled. This place was large, and even more people were jamming in. The bouncers were having a hard time keeping anyone out, the crowd was so bad.

"I said, *are we having a good time?*" Now her eyes searched the crowd, shifting back and forth. She looked cool and easy standing there, but something in the set of her shoulders made him think that she was a little tenser than she appeared.

Of course, she probably senses me here. A glamoured Watcher, something Dark.

Something inimical to the light shining out through her aura. That light could burn him down to bone in seconds flat.

Gods. She's so goddamn beautiful.

The crowd raised its hands and bayed at her. A small smile touched her lips, painted dark crimson with lipstick. Remy's lungs burned. He inhaled, his entire body breaking out in gooseflesh. He just had to remember to breathe, that was all. He'd been doing it all his life.

I don't care if it hurts. He watched her cast a glance at the bassist. The thin young man nodded, and the drummer gave a long roll. *I want to touch her. I don't care how much it hurts.*

She smiled. "The boys and I are having a good time too." She swayed back and forth gently, like a girl mesmerizing a cobra. It would probably work, Remy thought. The Darkness inside him watched her every movement, fascinated. "So let's get started, okay? That okay with you?"

The crowd gave out a high-pitched roar. She was still smiling when the drummer began, the bassist coming in low and complex, and her fingers flew on the guitar. It was a punked-up version of "Heaven Must Be Missing An Angel." Remy's jaw threatened to drop. *That* was just as surprising as the amount of Power she had. The bassist moved up to a secondary mike and was giving harmony in a surprisingly good tenor.

He closed his eyes briefly, habit making him scan the whole building. She was like a bonfire lit in the darkness behind his eyelids. And if she was this visible to the Dark in him, how much more visible was she to the crowding shapes sliding in through the doors? The Dark in his bones shifted, recognizing its distant kin.

The Brotherhood. Here. Great. Cold rage began, shaking him out of the dream of staring at her. He'd gotten here just in time, a miracle if there ever was one. Another ten minutes and he would have failed.

He couldn't guarantee the safety of any of the normals in the building, but he could guarantee hers.

You won't have her. Bloodlust escaped him in a low growl, loud enough to be heard by some of the almost-psychics. A few of them were edging for the door. *Not my witch. Not on my watch.*

The Brotherhood operatives drifted through the crowd like he did. The normals were dancing, hair flying and sweat dewing bright faces. The smell of alcohol and human sweat filled the place, which was so hot he was surprised more of them weren't collapsing from heatstroke. Remy slipped through the crowd, the entire building taking on the dimensions of a battlefield in his mind. His top priority, his *only* priority, was to protect the woman singing on the stage, dancing a little in place, the red guitar bobbing as she made it wail. The Power she radiated was enough to make Remy's own shielding thicken defensively. She could possibly make him very uncomfortable if she was spooked enough to strike at him.

She missed a beat, recovered almost instantly. He wouldn't have been able to tell if he hadn't been watching her so intently.

He made it to the foot of the stage, invisible to the normals, and turned to face the crowd. A few burly bouncers wearing blue *Clair Staff* T-shirts kept the well-mannered normals back. The heavy musk of some not-quite-legal cigarettes began to fill the air.

The song mutated into another one, and she was sweating freely now, glowing under the lights. Singing about Jimmy Jingo, that lowdown dirty beast. It had the feel of a breakup song. Remy waited.

The Brotherhood moved with the crowd. Six operatives, just enough for a high-strength extraction team.

Damn. They must want her very badly. Then again, who wouldn't?

He scanned the building again. It wasn't like the Brotherhood to be sloppy. It *was* just like them to possibly distract him with a frontal attack while someone came from backstage and snatched the witch right in front of a crowd.

And this beautiful, beautiful witch. What would she think? What would she think of *him*?

That, quite frankly, worried him more than the Brotherhood.

She's got to know Watchers exist. Dante and Hanson know her; she's part of the Guardians. He was thinking about this when the six operatives apparently decided a lone Watcher was no deterrent. They moved forward through the crowd in standard formation, two waves of three, thin shapes that looked cut out of black paper. The Brotherhood had different shielding than Watchers, mostly because the Dark they had bargained with didn't believe in cooperation. They were nothing more than dogsbodies for the Dark, if they were human.

And if they weren't, they were far worse.

The *tanak* inside Remy's bones woke fully, grinding against his nerve-endings. What did they have planned for this witch? And the Trifero. Was that the Talisman around her neck? It wouldn't be unheard of for a Major Talisman to go from hand to hand to reach the person it wanted. And as the only fire witch Remy had heard of on this continent, she was the perfect candidate for the Trifero.

Why weren't any of the extraction team backstage?

There was no time for wondering. Close quarters and a bunch of normals. That meant knife work. One in each hand, they slid easily from the sheaths, spinning around his fingers in a quick habitual movement.

They moved in, the first three with that spooky darting speed that he'd seen too many times. He met one of them with a bone-jarring impact, his black steel knives with their traceries of crimson tearing through muscle and Darkness. He couldn't afford to split his concentration, but he did, still scanning the backstage area.

He took a hit on his side, red pain flaring up and feeding the Dark crouching in his bones. They were using their wicked curved kukris, apparently not wanting to spook the witch either. Though why they cared, he couldn't guess; he was only grateful for it.

The first three dropped, and the second wave was on him. No, only two of them. The third—

Keep away from her. The cold crystalline rage of combat closed over him again. The space behind him holding the witch was a distraction, only because he wasn't so used to fighting with something to protect. It was usually just him and the nasties, no witch to worry about.

One of them grabbed his arm, letting out a whispered curse. The Dark in his bones stretched, shedding the curse like water. The *tanak* struck back reflexively, before he could stop it, and the Brotherhood operative, still cloaked in the glamour that made him only a stick-thin black shadow, went flying.

Someone screamed.

Remy felt the crowd's mood change and tip from freewheeling good time to something near a riot. The screams spread outward from the twisted body of the Brotherhood operative, who was revealed as a huge hulking kobold, gray-skinned and bald, with a pair of tusks sharpened to a razor's edge.

Oh, no. They're sending kobolds? Remy dealt the only operative left a short punch to the face, stunning it, and drew the knife across its stomach. A quick twist at the end broke the suction of muscle against the black steel blade. Power flared— the runes on the knife were more damaging to the Dark than the metal itself.

Kobolds. That changed things. Sending nonhumans instead of dogsbodies in to do a catch-and-transport was definitely *not* something the Brotherhood usually did. Nonhumans were only sent for assassinations. Did they want to kill this witch? Circle Lightfall didn't think so, and they had never been wrong before.

There's always a first time. He scanned the building one more time, and swore. Of course. The six had only been a test-team, sent to see if they could snatch the witch with little fuss. Since Remy had shown himself, they would come in with everything they had and hope to overwhelm him.

The music trailed off, and he heard the witch's amplified voice.

"What the *hell's* going on now?"

Remy turned and looked up. The raised stage was about

as high as his waist. He gathered himself and leapt, the long black coat flaring behind him. His side tore with pain, no time to heal it when he had to *move*. His boots met the stage floor with a solid sound, and he scanned both the humans. The drummer was slack-jawed, staring at him, his hands frozen in midair. The bassist had shoved the neck of his instrument down and looked caught between two impulses: start a fight or just stand in stunned amazement at the arrival of a man twice his size in a long black coat on a ninety-degree night.

She stood with one hand on the microphone, staring at him. It was one of the most exotic moments in Remy's life, and that was saying something. Her eyes were huge, luminous in the pulsing light. The crowd was running for the exits, crushed together. There was no time. The exodus wouldn't hold the Brotherhood outside for long.

The witch—Elise—looked too stunned to speak. Her mouth was open a little, and he was shaken with the completely uncharacteristic desire to find out if her lips were as soft as they looked. She had her right hand up, and there was something like static electricity crackling around it, the air popping and snarling with Power.

Remy drew in a deep breath. He still had his knife out. He made it disappear, and her eyes flicked down his body once, then returned to his face. "You're a Watcher." She sounded stunned, though her voice was still a purr. The microphone caught it and the sound boomed through the rapidly-emptying club. Something started to bray—a fire alarm. Someone had probably fled through a fire door. Would the Brotherhood break in through there too?

Move it along, Remy. But the witch's huge luminous eyes held him. She looked terrified.

The bodies he'd left on the floor started to smoke. Of course. Couldn't have a kobold showing up at the county morgue. That would severely disarrange the human world. There would be cover-ups, investigative journalism, all sorts of messiness and scrutiny that the Brotherhood most definitely didn't want. So each of the operatives, even the nonhumans, would have a flamework on them. It was an unintentional compliment to Remy's skill as a hunter.

The Hunter. What the other Watchers called him, too. *Why couldn't I have a better nickname? The bane of the Crusade? Or even, the one Watcher you don't want to mess with?*

I have to be very careful how I handle this. He hoped his face wasn't decked with blood. His side hurt, the Dark repairing broken ribs and torn muscle. He would have to hole up for an hour or two to fully heal, but at least he wasn't bleeding now. Not much. His black T-shirt stuck to his skin, and the copper tang of blood filled his nostrils.

The witch blinked, and then something like fury crossed her face. She half-turned, looking at the two young men sharing the stage with her. "Vann, get your axe in a case and get the hell out of here. Trevor, you too. *Go!* Don't worry about the goddamn set, Trev! *Get out of here!*" Her hair began to rise slightly, lifted on a random hot draft.

"But—" the bassist said, and her eyes narrowed. Remy's heart skipped another beat. She looked fierce, and absolutely beautiful. *If she ever looks at me like that...*He stopped the thought before it could finish.

"Get out of here," she said, not unkindly. "Please. I'll call tomorrow."

Remy saw the two boys were still stunned, so he decided to help. He caught the almost-psychic drummer's eyes and gave a small mental *push.*

Do as she says. Obey her.

It was technically outside the canons to push a Lightbringer, but Elise had told the kid what to do, and Remy was Elise's Watcher. It was up to him to do the enforcing.

Sometimes those with smaller psychic gifts were easier to influence than normals. The drummer shook his head and got up, still holding his sticks like a pair of pencils. Then Remy looked at the bassist, who still stared slack-jawed at the apparition that had just leapt up on the stage. "Do what she says, *mon ami,*" he growled, and the boy backed up, his bass hanging slackly from the strap over his shoulder. "Get out of here. Things are about to get interesting."

That was maybe a mistake, because her eyes swung back to him. Her mouth closed with a snap, and a hot breeze from nowhere was definitely playing with her hair. There was a smell of burning electrical wires.

The twisted bodies near the stage were smoking furiously now. There was a soft *wump!* and one of them burst into blue flame. Remy wasn't surprised, but the witch leapt as if stung and looked at it, her eyes almost too wide for her face. The blood drained out of her cheeks.

All told, it had only taken a few seconds. The crowd was still screaming and trampling for the door. He risked taking two steps closer to her, his boots soundless on the stage floor. "Please. Come with me, *cherie*. This is dangerous. They can't get in the building right now because the normals are crowding out, but they will be here very soon. I don't want to fight off more than a dozen assassins and worry about protecting you at the same time. I'm sorry, but can we go somewhere safer?" He deliberately kept his voice low, soothing.

"You're a Watcher," she whispered again, and her face was too pale to be healthy. Paper-pale. "Oh, my gods."

"They're after you, *m'selle*." He used a half-whisper, trying not to frighten her. "I'm here to help."

"You're too tall." She was so pale that dark circles stood out under her luminous eyes, and the crimson lipstick made her look even whiter. Her hair snapped and crackled with electricity, the red turning closer to gold. Pure flame.

Of all the things you could have said, witch, I think that's the most absurd. "Don't hold it against me." He held out his hand, offering it palm-up. Maybe it would hurt him to touch her, but he didn't care. If she set him on fire, he wouldn't care. "Please, come with me. Let's get you somewhere safe."

She took a deep breath, and the entire building seemed to shudder. The Brotherhood was here. Time was running out. If he couldn't convince her, he would have to force her, and he didn't want to do that.

Two crimson fever-spots appeared high up on her cheekbones. "No," she said, and took another deep endless breath. "NO!" She yelled it this time, and the rest of the kobold corpses burst into flame. "Get away from me! *Get away from me!*"

It wasn't quite the reception he'd expected. She backed up toward the edge of the stage, and Remy lost patience.

He moved, caught her wrist in his hand, and gave a sharp yank, pulling her toward him just as the first Brotherhood assassin made it into the building. She screamed, struggling, hooking the fingers of her free hand and trying to claw at his face.

He avoided it, thinking with grim amusement that it didn't hurt to touch her, but she might hurt him after all.

Her skin was softer than he could have believed, and the expected sensation—tearing pain—did not flash through him.

Instead, a spike of agonized pleasure jolted up his arm, spreading down his entire body. He let out a short, sharp breath, catching her other wrist and trapping them both in one hand. He didn't want to do this, but he *had* to.

In one quick movement, his knees bending, he had her over his shoulder. The red guitar dropped, hitting the floor with a violent squeal of feedback, still live. *Be damned to consequences, there's a building full of Brotherhood assassins that's going to be a pile of matchsticks soon.*

His free hand throbbed with Power, and he cast the scorching *down* without a second thought. Flame exploded. It was a Watcher spell, one that used the darker energies he was capable of channeling because of the Dark inside him. *Hellfire,* the flame peculiar to as well as peculiarly damaging to the Dark. There were too many of the Brotherhood for them to make a retreat once this spell took hold and fired the entire damn nightclub. He felt sorry for the damage to a public place, but there was nothing else to be done.

Not if he wanted this witch still alive to see sunrise.

She was struggling and screaming, and his coat started to smoke. She might try to fry him—she certainly had the Power—but he made it off the stage and kicked open a convenient fire door. The alarm was already whooping anyway. Sirens began to resound in the distance.

The door opened to an alley, and he pounded down it, moving more quickly than a human could, found a fire escape zigzagging up the side of another building. He leapt for it, having to move one-handed slowing him just a little, and she was still screaming when he reached the rooftop and unceremoniously dumped her onto her feet. She staggered, the scream switched off mid-breath as she gasped.

Remy turned, his sword whipping out. There was nowhere else to go. The rooftop had a sheer six-story drop behind the witch, and it would take time for a Brotherhood assassin to climb that, especially if they were kobolds. He would sense them before they reached the top. *Having the high ground is best when you have a witch to protect,* his trainer's voice echoed inside his memory.

Concrete gritted under his feet. He waited, his mind a dark still pool, for the first attack.

It came, blurring up over the fire escape's railing, streaking for him. He shot it twice between the eyes and then moved to meet it, carving its head from its shoulders. This was a Gray, done up in the Brotherhood way, a sort of loose black pajamas, weapons strapped to it. Grays weren't good fighters, but they were great scavengers and trackers.

Then more of the Brotherhood, boiling up over the edge. By their size, they had to be kobolds. It was a relief to be in a situation where the alternatives were so clear-cut. *Kill or be killed,* the familiar voice resounded inside his head again, the Watcher he had been apprenticed to. *Don't think. Move.*

The witch wasn't screaming anymore. He spared a quick glance and saw she was on her feet, her eyes huge, her hands knotted into fists. The medallion at her throat sparkled with crimson. She looked incandescent with fury.

He had to reload, so he backed up, waiting for the next wave. Six bodies lay scattered around the roof, two of them smoking. His breath came fast and hard, and his face was bruised from a cheap shot—one of the kobolds had feinted toward the witch and then clipped him hard across the face. He was dripping with sweat—the weather didn't make him perspire, but combat did. Go figure. His fingers blurred, shoving the clip into the gun.

There was a short, sharp cry behind him, and something whizzed by his head. The bolt of flame caught the Brotherhood assassin vaulting over the lip of the roof. Crimson flame tore a hole through the darkness. There was an unearthly scream and the sickening smell of roasting meat and Dark flesh.

Remy's sword flicked. The thing dropped. He looked back at the witch.

She stood with her hand clamped over her mouth. The fever-spots were brighter than ever. She looked horrified.

She shouldn't have had to do that. Dammit. Remy backed up toward her, his sword held in the first guard position. He kept the gun low and ready. "Are you all right, *m'selle?*" he asked over his shoulder.

She gave a jagged gasp. "I just fried something that looked like a two-legged elephant with pretensions." Her voice was very close to breaking, breathless and stunned. "No, I am *not* all right."

"My thanks, anyway. Just hold on." But then there were two of them, and he met them halfway with a clash of metal and gunfire.

When they both dropped, the first body burst into blue flame.

"Time to go," he said. The stink of battle—cordite, roasted meat, metal, his own sweat, the sharp unlovely smell of the Dark—rose in waves from the rooftop. "They're going to try and flank me now. Predictable." His lips skinned back from his teeth in a feral grimace, but he tried to smooth his face out before he turned to face the witch.

She shivered, hugging herself, sweat standing out on her skin and the fever-spots on her cheeks giving her the only color in her face. "You k-k-k—" she began, her teeth chattering.

"I did." He would have spared her this sight, the bloody brutal combat. She should never have to face anything this ugly, this beautiful witch with the clear light shining through her. "It's all right, *cherie*. Really. Come on, we've got to go."

She started to laugh, thin jagged laughter that wasn't right. Even he could tell she was in shock. He approached her cautiously, and when he got close enough to smell the fresh scent of her hair—she used a shampoo that smelled like oranges, or maybe it was just her—he slid his arm over her shoulder. The air around her was oven-hot, and touching her sent a shiver of pleasure up his spine, even through the leather of his coat.

Mine. My witch. Thank the gods she's safe. That was too close for comfort.

"Don't worry," he said. "We have to go. I—" An idea struck him. "I need your help."

She swallowed grimly, her throat working, but something like sanity came back into her big green eyes. She looked up at him, her hair falling into her face. His fingers ached to brush it back. "You *what?*"

"I need you to stick with me. We'll get out of this and then we'll have a nice long talk, hmm?"

"I don't want to talk to you." Her face had lost that staring look. She wasn't going to faint. At least, not yet.

"Well, then we'll cross that bridge when we come to it," he answered, and scooped her up again. This time he didn't throw her over his shoulder; he didn't relish the thought of his back catching fire. He simply swept his arm under her knees, picked her up and took the four steps that brought him to the edge of the roof. And then, gathering himself and hoping he had enough momentum, he leapt.

Ten

"Elise!" Theo yelled, a truly rare occurrence. The Watcher set Elise on her shaky feet, held her shoulders until she had her balance, and then stepped back just a little. She looked up at him as Theo hurried across the shop's wooden floor and flung her arms around Elise. The smell of her best friend— sandalwood and the sharp iron smell of worry—made Elise's shaking knees and pounding heart calm a little.

He'd brought her back to the shop. He had carried her up to the rooftop as if she weighed nothing. He'd calmly fought a small army of things that looked like two-legged elephants and then he'd...

Dante stood by the glass door, watching the street. "Were you followed?" His deep voice was harsher than Elise could ever remember it.

The Watcher shook his head. "Not unless they have Hounds to track me. I took out their seek-team." His voice was low and dark, with a trace of an accent making the words slow and even. He had dark blond hair, too light to be called brown and too dark to be called truly blond, with threads of gold highlights running through it. And his eyes were golden, not yellow, not hazel, but the exact color of warm mellow gold. He had the face of a Michelangelo angel, severe and relaxed all at once. Nice classical nose, a completely sinful mouth, and those eyes under dark lashes. There was mottled bruising going up the left side of his face, and he winced a little as he moved, his eyes on her. It looked like his ribs were hurting him.

He had just calmly killed *how many* of those things?

Elise let out a dry sound. She'd seen a lot in her life, but this...*this* took the cake. It took the whole bloody bake sale, too.

Theo shook her. "You little...Oh, I could just...Elise Nicholson, you irresponsible...How could you?" She was actually *sputtering*. This was so new and unexpected a fresh fit of trembling spread over Elise's entire body. The curry she'd eaten for dinner with the guys somersaulted in her stomach.

The Watcher stared at her, his uncanny golden eyes never leaving her face. She looked down at his boots. He wore jeans, and there was a dark bloodstain on one knee. She swallowed again, tasting bile. He watched her the same way Dante

watched Theo, intently, his eyes marking everything about her.
As if he couldn't take his eyes away.

"What happened?" Dante, still watching the street.

"The Brotherhood," the Watcher who had carried her here
responded without looking away. Elise couldn't place his faint
accent. It dipped his words in honey. "Trying to steal an artifact.
You didn't tell me she had a Talisman."

"She didn't this morning," Dante said. "Which one?"

"I think it's the Trifero." His eyes never left Elise's face.
She could *feel* him watching her. As if his gaze had an actual
physical weight. And yet he looked completely aware of
everything going on around him, as if he shared the same high-
powered radar Hanson and Dante had. As if he could watch
her with the kind of stare a lion would give a sick zebra, and
still be aware of everything in a five-mile radius.

"Elise!" Theo actually shook her. "I was worried sick about
you!" She *sounded* worried, too. Her face was drawn and
pale, and Elise felt a sharp prick of guilt.

She let out a jagged little laugh. "He *killed* them, Theo.
He just killed them."

"I know," Theo stroked Elise's hair back from her face,
tucking it behind her ears. "I have a hard time with it too. But
are you all right?" She held Elise by her shoulders and examined
her from head to toe. "Are you okay?"

"I guess so." Elise's voice seemed to come from very far
away. The Watcher had jumped off the top of a six-story building
and landed as softly as a cat hopping down from a chair. Well,
maybe not *that* softly, Elise's cheek had bounced against his
rock-hard shoulder, and he had made a breathless apology.

The Watcher stood, apparently not caring that his face
was puffing up and bruising or that blood was dripping from his
torn black T-shirt. He was too busy looking at Elise, who kept
staring at that bruise on his angelic face. He really was cute, in
a badass sort of way, she thought dreamily, and felt a faraway
twinge.

"She's fading," Theo said. "Dante?"

"I'm not surprised," the gold-eyed Watcher piped up. "She
threw enough Power to kill a kobold up on that rooftop. She's
probably in shock." He made a restless movement, and it
occurred to Elise that he wanted to touch her, but wasn't sure
if he should.

That managed to bring her back to herself a little. "Rum."

She pushed Theo away, but gently. "Theo, I'll be out of here in a minute. I just need that bottle of rum I left."

"Don't be ridiculous." Theo's eyebrows were drawn together, and she frowned. That in itself was a rare occurrence.

Elise returned to herself with a jolt. *Lucky me. I'm the only person in the world who can piss off Theo. I must be better than I thought.* She took two steps backwards on shaky feet and then whirled and bolted for the back room.

She shoved the curtain aside and ducked into the small room, going on tiptoe and throwing open the cupboard above the sink. It was still there, thank the gods, and she had it in her hands with the cap twisted off before the Watcher appeared, his shoulders filling up the doorway. He held the curtain aside with one callused, battered hand.

She had never seen anyone *move* like that, with such savagery and grace. It reminded her of seeing tigers on a nature show leaping at their prey, teeth bared, even their most spontaneous movements gracefully coordinated. The sword had been a solid arc of silver more than once, splitting the air with a faint sound she'd only heard in chop suey martial arts movies before. *I never knew swords made that sound in real life.*

He looked at her, those gold eyes above that sinfully cute mouth, and she felt the pit of her stomach drop again. The attraction was instantaneous. And unwelcome. She *never* felt this way about guys. Especially not bad-news guys like Watchers.

"Leave me alone," Elise managed, and got the bottle to her lips. She took two long swallows and lowered it, waiting for the alcohol to hit. There was a wire of warmth in her stomach now. His eyes flicked to the bottle and back to her face.

"Can I have a drink?" With his bruised face, he looked like he *needed* it. And that voice, like dark honey. She could even *smell* him, leather and blood and the clean healthy smell of a man who'd just had a hard workout.

"Who *are* you?" Her hand shook so badly the rum slopped around in the bottle.

"I'm Remy," he said, making a little movement, as if he wanted to bow and stopped himself just in time. He still stared at her, his golden eyes intent. "Some of the other Watchers call me Hunter, but I never did like that." He paused for the barest of seconds. "I'm your Watcher, *cherie*."

She swallowed, hard. *Oh, gods above. This can't be happening.*

The rum hit her middle like a bomb going off, and the sudden warmth steadied her. She took a deep gasping breath and wiped at her lips with the back of her hand. "You saved my life," she said inconsequentially. "Though if you hadn't brought those things with you, I wouldn't have needed saving."

He looked puzzled by that, his eyebrows drawing together. "I didn't bring the Brotherhood, *m'selle.* They're chasing that pretty thing around your neck. I think it's a Talisman."

That was like a pinch in a sensitive place. The vision of the pink-eyed thing covered in running sores that had put the dragon medallion down on the pawnshop counter popped up in her head again. She took another huge gulp of rum. "What do you *want?*" she screamed, and he didn't even flinch. "Leave me alone! *Why won't you all just leave me alone?*"

"Careful, *cherie,*" he said, and she placed the accent. Creole. Kind of like a Deep South French kiss. He had a nice voice. Too bad he was a Watcher. Elise could almost see dating this guy if he kept his mouth shut—and if he wasn't a Watcher. He was pretty cute. "You could hurt something in here, hmm?" He watched her for a second, as if trying to figure out the best way to deal with a screaming crazy woman. Then he held out his hand.

Elise flinched.

That seemed to stop him. He didn't touch her, just kept his hand out like it was perfectly normal to hang your hand out in space.

The look on his face was considering, now, as if she was a puzzle he was trying to figure out. "I won't try to touch you. Can I have a drink, *cherie?* I haven't had a fight like that in something like two years."

Her hands were still shaking. "I guess so," she said numbly, and handed him the bottle. She had to take a step forward to do it, and her fingers accidentally brushed his. Usually the Watchers avoided touching her. Theo had told her that it hurt them to touch a Lightbringer—until they found the Lightbringer that they *could* touch.

Lightbringer. Witch. Psychic.

In Elise's case, *freak* was the only word that applied.

He lifted the bottle to his lips and took a healthy swig, closing his eyes for a second. Elise's heart gave a single huge leap inside her chest, and she realized she was in trouble.

"Hmm. Stings a little." He looked at her, steadily. "Your friend the green witch is worried about you. You have a bruise on your cheek." He lifted his free hand, touched his own face, high up on his right cheek. It was weird, especially because the other half of his face—the left side—was mottled with purple and yellow swelling. "I think she wants to heal it. I think you should let her."

"Look at you," Elise said. "Half your face is swelling up. Have her work on *you*."

The corner of his mouth lifted a little. "I'll heal. I'm more worried about you."

Elise snatched the bottle back from him. "Leave me alone. Get out of my way."

He stepped aside, holding up the curtain as she stalked through it. Elise was beginning to feel a little bit more like herself. She shook her hair back over her shoulders.

She was *not* going to fall into this trap. She was not going to even think about this incredibly cute hunk who had just fought off a whole load of elephant things. Theo and Mari could act like ditz-brained girlies if they wanted to, but not Elise Nicholson, resident tough girl.

Yeah. Right. Get the hell out of here, Elise. Go home, lock your door, and drink. That sounds really good.

Theo was saying something to Dante, who had his hands on her shoulders. He was tall—Theo reached just under his collarbone—but he was very gentle as he stroked her shoulders with his thumbs and replied in a voice too low for Elise to hear.

It kind of hurt to see the two of them, Theo looking up into Dante's face, his mouth gentle and his eyes warm as he looked down at her. You could see they were really involved. Really nuclear.

Elise took another hit off the bottle. If she didn't slow down it would hit her all at once like a train wreck, and she would be glad when it did. She didn't want to deal with life anymore.

She shook her head and started across the wooden floor, threading between racks of ritual cloaks and robes in all different shades, racks of organic-cotton clothing and bags made out of hemp. She was heading for the front door. If she was lucky they wouldn't notice.

He fell into step right behind her. Elise turned on her heel, and he stopped, still looking down at her with a fixed expression.

A sort of bemused, wondering concentration. He winced again, as if his ribs hurt, and blood pattered on the hardwood floor. Elise felt the rage rise again, shoved it down with an almost physical effort.

"You're making a mess," Elise said. "Let Theo bandage you."

"She's busy." That trace of an accent made the words rounder, deeper. Like he was half-singing instead of talking. "What about you?"

"I'm no good at first aid," Elise found herself saying. *Wait a minute. Didn't I tell him to leave me alone? Didn't I just tell myself I wasn't going to get all ditz-brained?*

He shrugged. "I'll suffer, then." His mouth quirked up a little. "It's just a scratch, *cherie.* I'll live."

"Oh, damn it. You're getting blood all over Theo's floor. Jeez." Elise shoved the bottle into his hands and went around a rack of robes, stamping for the back room again. The first-aid kit was under the sink.

Okay. So she'd bandage him up and *then* hit the road. It was the least she could do.

She retrieved the kit, and while she was bending down under the sink the alcohol rose up and ignited inside her head. That was what she'd been waiting for—the rest of the night to take on the quality of a dream. The rum helped even more, burning in her stomach and insulating her from this madness. She stamped out into the store, and Theo and Dante separated, Theo looking troubled. Dante wore his usual cool expression. The shop door was locked, and the sign turned to "Closed." If Elise looked, she could see the glimmer of Power that would make the store seem empty and deserted to any passerby.

That was a good trick, one she had thought up herself. Theo had been delighted.

"Sit down," Elise snapped at the tall, lean man, who immediately folded himself down on the floor right where she pointed, in front of the candle racks. "No, you idiot, on the stool. It's right there."

He nodded, hauled himself up, and walked over to the three-legged stool. Theo used it to stand on when she needed to reach a high shelf.

The rum made her vision a little blurry. "Take your coat off. And that shirt, too. I can't have you going around bleeding. *Jeez.*" It was impossible to put all the aggravation in the one syllable, but she tried.

"Elise?" Theo said.

"I'm busy," Elise threw over her shoulder. "I'll get out of your hair, your store, and your life in a minute."

"I don't want you out of our shop or my life, fireball. You're being childish. Mari and Hanson are on their way. We'll need you to listen to us instead of—"

"Oh, that's nice." Elise didn't bother to sugarcoat the sarcasm. "Let's just make it a party. You guys managed to sneak in a Watcher to follow me around and scare me into doing what you want. How typical. How utterly *typical.*"

Dante opened his mouth. "If you really believe that, why are you bandaging him up?"

You did not just talk to me, you Neanderthal psychotic. "You know, I've never liked you. So shut up."

The blond Watcher dropped his coat on the floor. It made a strange clunking sound. Of course. They carried a lot of hardware in there. Weapons and other things. Elise shivered. He undid the leather harness thingy that kept his sword strapped to his back and the guns to his sides, and dropped it on the coat. Then, obediently, he peeled off the T-shirt.

Elise and Theo made identical hissing sounds. Elise glanced over at Theo, who was paper-pale. "I'm bandaging him because it's the right thing to do," Elise informed Dante haughtily. "He got this fighting off something that looked like a...I don't know what it looked like anymore, but I know enough to know that it was after me." Her voice broke, and she cursed herself for being a ninny. "And as soon as I patch him up, I'm *outta* here. You can't fire me, I *quit.* I've had enough. I am *so* sick of this." She opened up the first-aid kit, setting the rum-bottle to one side. "You guys just shove me around from place to place. *Elise, you need a Watcher. Elise, you're in danger. Elise, let Circle Lightfall walk in and finish destroying our lives. Elise, you're so mean.*" She tipped peroxide out onto a gauze pad and rose to her knees, looking at the mess of blood and torn skin on Remy's side. She unceremoniously slapped the peroxide on and began cleaning it, none too gently.

He made no sound. He simply looked at her with that heart-stopping expression, like an art student staring at a Rembrandt.

Don't think about that, Elise. "And then you sneak this guy into the city without my permission—you know I thought I had a *vote,* and I voted to keep Circle Lightfall *out* of here, and he just shows up and totally destroys my gig! The cops are going to want to talk to me, and I'll never play another gig at the Clair again. And why, do you ask?" She was in fine form. "I'll *tell* you why. Because even as we bloody well *speak* the Clair is in the process of being burned down by a bunch of guys with elephant tusks and big bald heads! This was my big break, and I'll never play there, or anywhere else maybe again, because—" Elise had to stop to take a breath, and she decided not to say any more. She didn't have the breath to waste on arguing with them. Let Mari and Theo have their big bad Watchers. Elise was going to ride off into the sunset just as soon as she finished bandaging this guy's wound.

Elise blinked.

The scraped and torn skin under her hands was healing, flesh closing at an alarming rate. She looked up at the golden-eyed Watcher, who was—well, what else?—watching her. He said nothing. His mouth was a straight line, his dark-blonde hair mussed and his golden eyes darker now. Maybe from pain. She hadn't been very gentle. Abruptly her conscience bit her. If they had just called this guy in, he probably didn't know what was going on. He was just doing what he thought of as his job.

"Doesn't this hurt?" She wondered why the hell she cared. Wondered why she'd said it so softly.

He shrugged, his beautiful sculpted mouth even and tense under those watchful golden eyes. "It doesn't matter." His voice was calm now. With the ghost of an accent, his voice was exactly the color of pure amber. Just as golden as the rest of him. His hair would probably glow in the sun. If she could get home in time, she wanted to draw his face. It was almost too beautiful to be real. "You should let the green witch heal your bruise, *cherie.*"

Yes, in the sun his hair would probably look like a furnace of gold.

Not that Elise was ever intending on seeing him in sunlight. She just wanted to get the hell out of here.

"I'm not your *cherie,*" she told him, archly. "How the hell did you sneak into the city? We told Circle Lightfall to stay out."

"I didn't sneak in. And I'd guess that I was able to cross the city limits because Circle Lightfall doesn't own me anymore."

Theo made an inarticulate noise, protesting. Elise's hand stopped cleaning the awful, messy wound. "What are you talking about? You're a Watcher, aren't you? You work for Circle Lightfall. I know the drill."

He nodded, his hair falling forward a little, across his forehead. "*Your* Watcher. I wouldn't have been able to cross the city limits otherwise, if you've banned the Circle from the city."

Elise looked back down at the first-aid kit. "You're crazy. I don't need some psychotic samurai messing up my life. I have my own problems. I'll probably have to find another band. Vann won't like this, and Trevor's drum set...gods above, I'm going to have to buy him a new one. There go my savings."

"Better to lose a drum set than his life, *m'selle,*" he said quietly.

"He wouldn't have to make that choice if I wasn't a freak. *And* if you hadn't gone all Dresden on the nightclub." She picked up some fresh gauze. "Hold still."

He nodded and seemed to freeze, immobile while she bandaged him up, tearing the adhesive with quick jerks. The rum burned in her middle, a warm steadying glow. She had a little trouble with some of the adhesive, and she glanced up at him, pushing her hair away with the back of one hand. "You *can* breathe, you know. I didn't tell you to hold your breath or anything."

"I'm sorry for your friends," he said, when she finished taping the gauze over the quickly-healing wound.

"Well, thanks." She got to her feet, leaving the open first aid kit on the floor. "I'll be sure to pass that along. Have a nice life."

With that said and done, she turned around and walked away.

Theo, who had watched this whole interchange from a safe distance, reached out and caught Elise's arm. "Elise. I'm sorry. I didn't mean to hurt your feelings. We didn't 'sneak' a Watcher in. We didn't even know he was here until this afternoon."

Elise looked down at her. Theo was barefoot, as usual, probably having kicked her sandals off behind the counter, and Elise was wearing boots so she topped her friend by two inches or so. "Maybe *you* didn't know, but maybe your pet gargoyle did. Did you ever think about that?"

"Dante can't lie to me," Theo said, softly, patiently. "You know that. And you've seen what it does to him, to protect us. Remember two months ago, that thing that went berserk in the park while we were doing a Circle? It broke his arm *and* half his ribs, you helped me heal him. Why are you being like this, Lise?" Her eyes, a deep green lit from inside like sun seen through a forest canopy, were wide and worried. Theo wouldn't hurt a fly. She was so gentle it drove Elise nuts, trying to get her to observe some precautions for her own safety.

The bell over the door jingled. Mari burst in, her golden curls flying and tears running down her cheeks. She ran across the wooden floor of the shop, her breasts bouncing under her blue silk tank top, and threw her arms around Elise.

"I was so worried," she gasped against Elise's shoulder. She smelled like the hot night outside and salt and the peculiar Mari-smell of clean ocean and spice. "Lise, Lise, are you all right? Gods, I was so *worried!* Why did you just leave like that?"

Hanson slipped in the door after her, closed and locked it with a click, then leaned against it.

Elise patted Mari's back awkwardly. "You mean you didn't know he was here?" She shook her head. The unreality of what she had just witnessed combined with the rum to wallop her, and her unsteady legs nearly gave out. Mari let go of her only to grab her upper arms and proceeded to shake. Elise's head bobbed back and forth.

"Of *course* we didn't know. How could we know he'd be able to get into the city? Are you stupid? No, you're not stupid, but I swear you're pigheaded stubborn, and if I didn't love you so much I'd—" Mari sounded half-hysterical.

I feel sick. Elise drew in a deep, shuddering breath. "Stop it. I think I'm going to pass out," she said, in a high, unsteady voice. Mari quit shaking her and hugged her so hard Elise's ribs creaked.

"I wouldn't be surprised," Dante said. "How much did you drink?"

"Not nearly enough," she informed him smartly, and swayed. "You guys…you guys, there was…I thought that spell was supposed to keep shit like that *out* of here!"

"The Brotherhood hasn't been specifically banned. And they're not here to kill you. Or at least, that's what intelligence says." Remy was up from the stool, shrugging back into his leather coat. His ruined T-shirt was left on the floor, but he had another one, plain black like the first. Had he had it in his pocket? *So useful*, Elise thought, and surprised herself with a tired giggle. "They're after the Trifero, and a fire witch with enough Power to use it. If that thing you've got on your neck is the Trifero, which is becoming very likely, then they're trying to capture, not kill."

Capture, not kill. "That's so comforting. I bet whatever they'd do to me would make me wish I was dead, right? That's the standard threat."

"With the Trifero, you're the equivalent of a magickal nuclear bomb." He rolled his shoulders back and forth as if they hurt. They probably did. He looked awful with the bruising spreading over the left half of his face. But his eyes were still beautiful, and his mouth held her attention for that entire sentence. A small rebellious part of her wondered what it would feel like to touch his lips, and she shoved that part into a deep drawer. "They would use you against Circle Lightfall, and against other people like yourself. Psychic people. Lightbringers. *Witches.*"

Her jaw dropped.

His golden eyes were still fixed on her. "They have several ways to do it," he said, softly. "I've seen it, *cherie*. The best is with a combination of drugs and alchemical magick to make you into a nice, obedient little girl. If that doesn't work, they try classic brainwashing techniques—sleep deprivation, torture, rape. And other things that aren't half as nice."

"Stop it. Just stop it." Theo clasped her hands together, but Elise could see her shaking. "Gods." She shivered so hard that her skirt made a small rustling noise.

Elise swallowed. "Well, what are you planning on doing to me? Huh? What are *you* going to use me for?"

He shrugged and made a brief sound of annoyance. It was the first such sound she'd heard from him "I'm here to *protect* you." His accent drawled through the words, turning them into something slow and literal so that even an idiot could understand. "Nothing Dark will touch you and live." His lips twisted up in a humorless smile, exposing white teeth. "Nothing but me, apparently," he amended.

"I don't date outside my species," Elise said, her teeth starting to chatter. "You're just another reason for me to mistrust these Circle Lightfall jokers."

"She's tired," Theo said. "Let's just stop this. Elise, why don't you sleep at my house tonight? There's my spare bedroom."

"No." Elise tried to push Mari away, but the small blonde wouldn't let go of her.

"You flaming idiot, stop it," Mari said sharply. "You're acting like *we're* the enemy! What is *wrong* with you?"

"She thinks that because Dante and Hanson are here, we've forgotten all about her." Theo sighed. "Oh, Elise. Really." She sounded disappointed.

You know, it's truly a bitch to have psychic friends. "Well, it's not like it hasn't happened before." Elise was suddenly exhausted. It had been a long, hot day, and she had ditched her best friends, seen a leprous *thing* trying to pawn a Talisman-thingy, played half a gig, and been attacked by two-legged elephants with razor-sharp tusks. Not to mention getting thrown off a six-story building in the arms of a total golden-eyed hunk who was even now standing here looking at her as if he was a starving man and she was a three-course meal. "And you guys are always hanging around with them. When was the last time *we* did anything? You know, girls' night out?"

There was a long silence, Theo and Mari both looked suitably chastened, and it was the first time in the entire day that Elise felt anything like satisfaction.

Finally, Theo sighed. "We have been very serious lately. And...well, it's hard not to be frightened, with what we've seen."

"Great Power, great responsibility." Mari rolled her eyes. "I know. I can't do *anything* without that man fussing at me as if I'm made of glass. You've got that to look forward to." The corner of her mouth twisted up, a lopsided smile that was pure Mari. "That is, if the way he's staring at you is any indication."

Elise felt her cheeks start to flame.

"I'm sorry," Theo said, interrupting Elise's aggravated sigh. "I've been trying so hard to get the shop off the ground and make sure all of us can get through..." She stopped, took a deep breath, tried again. "Through the emotional repercussions of Suzanne's death. I've neglected to think that you might be feeling a little left out." She reached up, stroking Elise's cheek with warm fingers. As always, the crackling rage that never seemed to go away abated under the calming weight of Theo's peace.

The calm moved into her, cool and deep. What would it be like to live that serenely? Elise couldn't even imagine it. "A little left out? You guys never even *talk* to me anymore." *I sound exactly like a whiny little baby.* The flare of self-disgust that caused almost made her angry again. "Theo...I just...It's so...I'm just so *angry*." She heard the helplessness in her voice, hated it.

Theo nodded consideringly. "I had thought that the intensifying of our Powers when we met meant an equal intensifying as we continued working together." Her hand smoothed Elise's shoulder, a comforting touch. "Suzanne and I often talked about it. And now the Guardian spell, it's magnified our Powers tenfold. With Mari, it means that her ability to see the future has become a constant drain on her emotional resources. Hanson has had to bring her back from visions several times, and just today he saved her from walking out in front of a car again, she was so distracted."

Elise felt her own eyes widen. She looked at Mari, who was now holding her hand. "Really?"

"Oh, yeah." Mari shrugged. "I just haven't said anything lately because...well, you were closer to Suzanne than either of us. You knew her for years." Her hand was warm, and she squeezed Elise's fingers, gently. "She was so cool with you. I didn't want to worry you. You're already dealing with so much."

"With me," Theo continued softly, "the effect has been slightly different. I find myself compelled to heal people. And not just people, but plants and animals. Dante's been hounding me to take better care of myself. I can slip very easily into giving away so much healing that my physical body becomes drained and ill." Her beautiful eyes were troubled now, and Elise saw—truly saw for the first time—the circles under Theo's eyes and the fine lines around her beautiful mouth. "And you, Elise. I suspect your anger is part of your Power to call fire. Fire needs fuel, and there's no better fuel than anger. But watching you struggle with your anger and your grief over Suzanne, and your sudden isolation...It's been hard."

The strength seemed to run out of Elise's legs. She swayed. Theo held her arm and leaned into her, providing support. "You know, Theo, you've got an answer for everything." Elise felt her mouth turning down at the corners. "I kind of hate that."

Theo smiled. "I hate that too. The things I wish I had

answers for, I can never find out to my satisfaction." She reached up, brushing a few strands of Elise's hair back. "You need some rest, Elise. As your mother hen, I'm prepared to cluck and peck until you get some."

Elise swayed again. *Well, all right. So I've been an idiot. Big deal. Lots of people are idiots. I'm going to have to work this one off at the punching bag tonight. If I don't just fall down and die first out of sheer sleepiness.* "I threw a firebolt tonight. It was my first one. An actual bolt, not just an arc."

"Your first?" The blond Watcher sounded shocked. "Your *first?*"

"I didn't know if it would work." She was suddenly so tired he seemed blurry. "I had a split second to decide whether I was going to let it jump you and tear your head off, or whether I was going to get a few licks of my own in." She lifted her chin, daring him to say the wrong thing.

Remy nodded, his eyes suddenly thoughtful. "Thank you, *cherie,*" he said, with a short nod. The gesture managed to convey the impression of a respectful bow.

If he had said anything else, Elise's temper might have exploded. As it was, she just nodded. Maybe he wasn't so bad.

Then again, he'd tracked her down, burned down the Clair, ruined her gig, and yanked her off the roof of a building. Not to mention throwing her over his shoulder like a complete barbarian. "So what is it you want? You said you were chasing a Talisman or something. What does that have to do with me?"

"The medallion you're wearing. May I see it?" He held out his broad callused hand.

Elise's fingers leapt up to touch the medallion. Her immediate reaction was a panicked denial, and she shook her head, her hair swinging.

His hand dropped back down to his side. "It's the Trifero," he said, flatly.

"Can't this wait?" Mari said. "She needs rest. Everything's okay now, right?"

"Doubt it." Dante said in a low tone. He seemed to slump, though his shoulders didn't relax. "There's always a catch."

Hanson didn't peel himself away from the door. "The Brotherhood will not stop trying to acquire the Trifero or Elise. I know them well enough for that. They're not like the Crusade, just a bunch of religious nuts. The Brotherhood are businessman, motivated by profit. Any one of you would be incredibly valuable on the market, but a fire witch with the Stone of Destruction? They'll throw everything but the kitchen sink."

"Doesn't it ever end with you guys? The market? What market? No." Elise shook her head hurriedly when she saw the golden-eyed Watcher take a breath to answer her. "No. I don't want to hear it. Tomorrow. I'll hear it tomorrow. Right now I just want to go home and sleep. Like for two hundred years, until the police come knocking on my door asking me if I set fire to the Clair."

"We can take care of that." Hanson's face was set and level. "Circle Lightfall—"

Mari gave him a warning look, and he shut his mouth.

"I'll walk you home," Mari said, gently. "I want to make sure you get there all right."

"No." Elise shook her head. "I left my purse at the Clair. I have to go get it."

"Dante?" Theo turned to look at the black-eyed Watcher. He'd been watching all this with a great deal of interest.

He nodded. "Don't leave the wards, Theo. I'll be back in ten minutes."

"There's no need—" Elise began, but he was already out the door. "Theo!"

"Oh, for goodness' sake, fireball, just let it go. Come on, let's get you relaxed, and then we'll call a cab for you." Theo had that look on her face. The "I'm-the-healer-and-I-know-best" look. Elise knew argument was hopeless. Even with *her* fiery temper and quick tongue, she couldn't hope to budge Theo. The worst thing was Theo was so *nice* it was hard to disagree with her about anything when she got like this. "Now, you just let me work on you a little bit. I know you haven't been sleeping very well. So just let me help you."

"Theo—"

"Oh, Elise. It's all right. You're safe now." Theo hummed the words, and the sound of her voice seemed to filter in through Elise's skin. The world seemed suddenly very slow, and Theo smiled. It was her hypno trick, the one that calmed people down and made them sleep.

Elise blinked. The world fluttered like a candle flame in front of her weary eyes. *Maybe I should just close them, just for a minute,* she thought, relieved at finally being able to relax. Theo was murmuring something about just relaxing, about everything being all right.

Everything was blurry, and she felt a half-familiar sensation—being lifted up and carried, leather against her cheek. *Oh, that witch,* she thought through a warm honey lassitude. *She's put me to sleep. I'm going to—*

That was as far as she got before the rest of Theo's spell took effect and Elise's entire body went limp. She gave in gratefully, and fell instantly, deeply asleep.

Eleven

Theo turned the key and opened the door. Remy carried the sleeping witch through a short wood-floored hallway and into a sparsely-decorated living room. There was a futon folded up in a shiny black wooden frame serving as a couch, and a black Everlast punching bag hung from the ceiling. A low lacquered table acted as an altar, holding a statue of Sekhmet, a daisy in a black vase, and four candle holders with red candle-stubs. Two bookshelves—of course, Lightbringers loved books—stood sentinel against bare white walls. The kitchen off to his right was similarly spare and clean. There was a bank of windows looking out on a small backyard full of bamboo and a square patch of raked sand and gravel under a flaming-red Japanese maple. The leaves of the tree fluttered in the uncertain breeze. Clouds had moved in, and the city waited, hushed and breathless, in the muggy heat.

It felt like a thunderstorm was coming.

Theo clucked her tongue, setting down the guitar case. The red guitar was chipped and a little scarred, but probably all right. The case had only suffered some minor scratching and scorching. Elise's purse—an antique camera case—had been retrieved too, and Dante set that down on the couch.

"Well." Theo leaned back, her hands at her lower back. The guitar case looked heavy for a witch. "We'll be going home. I suggest you sleep on the couch. I'm not too sure about Elise's temper before coffee, but I've heard it's spectacular."

Remy nodded. His witch was deeply asleep, curled against him, her dark coppery eyelashes a perfect half-circle against her pale cheeks. There was a smattering of perfect golden freckles on her nose, and the ruby was dark now instead of glittering. She was wearing silver and garnet earrings that would swing against her cheeks if she was awake and moving.

The green witch had quietly and efficiently sent her to sleep, and then called a cab. The ride had been short, and the cabbie was waiting outside for Dante and Theo. He seemed as blasé as a normal could possibly be with two Watchers and two witches—one of them unconscious—in his car. In other words, he hadn't noticed a thing, probably thinking Elise was dead drunk and her friends were taking her home. Theo had taken the front passenger seat over Dante's objections.

Remy had spent the entire ride watching Elise's sleeping face. Memorizing it.

"He looks stunned." The green witch slipped her arm through Dante's with easy grace. Remy's bones twinged, the heat of Elise's skin spilling through them like velvet lava. He wondered if the other Watcher felt this kind of agonized pleasure from Theo's touch. If Dante felt anything, his face didn't betray him.

"I can relate," Dante replied dryly. "Honor, brother. Good job."

"Duty," Remy replied, automatically. "Thank you."

"Lock the door." Theo smiled impishly. Green lights moved in her dark-green eyes, and her Power was a deep glow probably even sensed by normals.

Dante actually rolled his eyes, ushering her away. "Gods above, Theo, he's a Watcher. He knows to lock the door."

"He looks too busy contemplating to do it." But it was a gentle teasing, and the witch grinned before she disappeared.

Remy listened to the banter fade as they left, the front door closing behind them with a click. He could not imagine ever speaking to this fire-haired witch that way. She could probably take the skin off his face with words alone.

He'd never seen a Watcher with his Lightbringer before. As a matter of fact, he'd only really *seen* five or six Lightbringers in his life, including the one who had told him about Circle Lightfall while he crouched in a corner of the solitary cell, his arms wrapped around his knees, rocking back and forth, banging his head against the concrete wall.

Remy shook the memory away. It served no purpose here.

He was left standing in his unconscious witch's house, holding her in his arms and wondering what on earth he was supposed to do next. He could have stood there, frozen, and held her all night, feeling the steady burn of pleasure-soaked pain bleeding into his body from her skin. She needed a bed, though, or she would be stiff in the morning.

I'm being ridiculous. I don't want to put her down.

The Dark melded to his bones gave him strength, speed, and endurance, and his training taught him to disregard pain as well as how to deal with just about every conceivable combat situation. However, this particular chain of events seemed to have fallen through a crack or two in his training.

Well, first things first. He guessed that her bedroom was

upstairs and carried her up, careful not to knock her head or her feet against anything. The stairs were wooden, creaking reassuringly under his weight. Even as strong as he was, carrying dead weight told on him, and he was glad to finally reach the top and find a hallway painted with what looked like stone archways in the dim light. She had done something to the paint to make it look like marble columns, and a pair of high-heeled shoes were thrown carelessly against the wall at the top of the stairs. It was the first sign of any messiness, one he felt a little relieved to see.

There were two bedrooms and a bathroom upstairs. The bathroom was painted yellow and orange, with a long swath of gold chiffon hung over the mirror and a crimson shower-curtain patterned with golden suns.

One bedroom was obviously an artist's studio, but he was more interested in the other one, which lay behind a closed door. He shouldered it open and stopped, looking.

Her bed was rumpled, black sheets pulled up but a red velvet comforter rucked down at the bottom. Of course, it was too hot for a comforter, even with air-conditioning. The red velvet looked slightly worn, probably a thrift store find. The bed itself was an antique brass thing, curlicued and bed-knobbed to within an inch of its life. Elise, however, had apparently found a quantity of crystal chandelier drops and hung them all over the bedstead, as well as from a collection of wires hung over the bed, creating a mobile. It had probably taken a long time to find so many pieces of chandelier.

When the sun hits that, it probably fills the whole room with rainbows. He laid her on the bed, sweeping back the sheet. Then he straightened and looked around.

There was a paper screen painted with flying cranes in front of the closet, with a few articles of clothing tossed over it. Her nightstand was a rattan cabinet draped with a fall of crimson silk, with a statue of Brigid holding the sun-wheel placed at what he suspected was a precise angle, a tensor lamp, and a book—*It's Not Fair: The Grieving Process and How to Get Through It.* There was a small red candle in a beaded holder, and a hairbrush with strands of red-gold hair still caught in it.

The thought of her sitting in bed and brushing her hair made his entire body tense with frustrated pleasure.

There was an old red-velour chair pulled up to the window,

where she could sit and watch the light change in her garden, looking down the hill at the lights of the south end of the city. One entire wall across from the bed was taken up by a mural of fiery horses racing through a star-dotted sky. It was beautiful, but what caught his attention was the figure standing to the left in the painting, arms crossed. It was an angel, with half-furled wings burning just as the horses were. Crimson flame curled around the angel's hard-muscled body, and its face was severe and relaxed at once.

A chill touched Remy's back. The angel's face was similar enough to his that they could pass for brothers. It was like looking in a mirror. She had obviously spent a lot of time getting the angel just right.

How long ago had she painted that?

Remy looked back down at the sleeping witch. He unlaced her red boots and worked them off her feet, then pulled the sheet over her, tucking her in securely. It was far too hot for the coverlet, but he would find the air-conditioning, if she had it. She would probably be more comfortable if she took her clothes off to sleep, at least her jeans, but he didn't trust himself to pop even one button. She was just so...beautiful.

He touched her cheek, skating his callused fingers over the perfect curve. Her lipstick had worn off, and her lips were paler now, but still...perfect. It was the only damn word in the English language that applied.

His entire body tightened. The feel of her skin under his fingertips sent a spike of intense, almost-painful pleasure through him. The feeling threatened to stop his heart. The same heart the *tanak* lived behind. The same dead heart he had promised himself would never trouble him again.

I'm only supposed to watch over her. They can't send me on another assignment; I won't go. But she'll never look at someone like me. Never in a million years. I'm not her type. I'm just another annoyance to her. She doesn't want anything to do with a Watcher.

But she had bandaged his side, her fingers unconsciously gentle once she had finished cleaning the awful mess. He had been too busy looking at the fall of her glowing hair to feel the pain.

I don't need another psychotic samurai messing up my life. Her voice, slightly husky but clear as a soprano bell.

There was a low rumble of thunder. The air was sticky

and breathless, hot and motionless. He should find out if she had air-conditioning.

Yeah, I'll get right on that. First thing on my list.

He touched her hair briefly, his fingers lingering. The wound low on his side itched fiercely, healing. So did his face. Tomorrow he would be better, up to full strength.

And, hopefully, better equipped to handle one flame-haired witch.

He spent a few minutes going through the house, closing the windows, and found the thermostat for the heat-pump. As soon as he fiddled with it, it breathed into life, and cool air was soon wandering through the house. The relief was instantaneous.

He spent a good twenty minutes carefully setting Watcher shields on the entire duplex. The shields *she* had put up were strong and defensive, but they still shouted to the night that she was a Lightbringer, and therefore vulnerable. The thought of something Dark cracking the house open like an egg and chasing her through her carefully painted rooms was enough to make an almost-soundless growl work its way through his chest.

With that done, he went back upstairs and pulled the coverlet up over her. The house was beginning to cool down, and he didn't want her to catch a chill.

She was dreaming, her eyelids fluttering, and he stayed for as long as he could to watch. Then he retreated to the bathroom and washed his face gingerly. The cold water helped wake him up.

Afterward, he walked into her studio. It would help him understand her, he told himself, and tried to ignore the guilty feeling of spying on her.

The door had been taken off its hinges, and there were high-quality lights on tracks attached to the ceiling. The walls were bright white. Two paintings hung on the walls. One was a woman with her back turned to the viewer, a tattoo of black wings on her supple back. She sat on a stone bench in a garden that on closer inspection was full of carnivorous plants, Venus flytraps and the like. The painted sky was a deep thunderous blue.

The other painting was an abstract, a wheel of fire spinning through a river of stars. It almost pulsed with life.

There was an easel with yet another painting perched on it. This was an older woman with long silver hair braided and twisted up into a coronet. Her hazel eyes looked out of the painting, direct and challenging. She had a sharp, intelligent face, and she wore a yellow silk suit, a canary scarf draped around her elegant neck.

The background of the painting was unfinished, formless dabbles of blue as if Elise had tried to start a background and couldn't decide on one.

There was a rough wooden sculpture of three leaping dolphins in one corner. The smell of sawdust in the air reminded Remy of other times, other lives. Back home he had worked as a carpenter off and on, to bring in some extra money. A sculptor's hammer and a set of chisels lay neatly at the statue's foot.

There was also a small round rug with a candle in a red glass holder set in front of it. He had a flash of her sitting there, her hair spilling over her shoulders, meditating. The air in this room vibrated with Power. Here was where she did her serious magickal work. A fire witch practicing in a room full of wood, paint, and turpentine.

No wonder she needed a Watcher.

He had the uncomfortable feeling of trespassing, so he didn't examine the rack of paintings in the closet or the delicate mobile made of wire and fragments of glass hanging in the window. There was an incense holder, and if he sniffed deeply he could smell dragon's blood incense, red and spicy.

Remy paced back into her bedroom and lowered himself gingerly into the red chair, first turning it around so he could watch her sleep and glance out the window occasionally. His side ached. So did his face. He wanted nothing more than to touch her hair again and feel that spike of agonized pleasure.

He put his head back against the high back of the chair and closed his eyes. An hour or two of trance would bring him back to full strength. He would know if anything tested the shields, or if she woke up.

Remy fell into a thin, troubled meditation, listening to her deep even breathing and feeling the breathless electricity in the sticky air. A storm coming, in more ways than one. What would she do when she woke up?

Twelve

"You're being absolutely childish." Suzanne folded her arms across her chest. *"You are being given a gift, and you spit in the face of it."* She wore yellow, as always, a long canary silk dress and a necklace of pale amber. She looked younger than Elise had ever seen her, and happier too. Her long silvery hair was braided back and fell in a long rope to her waist.

"Gift?" Elise blinked and looked around. White walls, white ceiling, white floor, or was it just a blank field of static? But she felt like she was standing in a room—with Suzanne.

Suzanne.

Suzanne's funeral had been awful. She had tried not to cry, tried not to make the low keening sound of grief that swelled her throat. Theo had cried without restraint, Dante's arm over her shoulders, and Mari had sobbed on Hanson's shoulder. But Elise had merely sat woodenly in the church, and then she'd stood at the graveside with her jaw clenched and her teeth grinding together, her eyes dry and burning terribly. The grief had been locked beneath the surface, impossible for it to come free.

She had to be strong, for Mari and Theo.

Afterward, she had gone down to the docks and sat shivering in the cold, watching the sun sink like a ship of gold into dark water. The air had crackled with electricity, and if she had let go of it, the Power would have leapt free, destroying the icy dock she sat on, boiling the water and killing whatever fish managed to survive in these industry-tainted waters. A vivid vision of boiled fish floating belly-up, all the destruction she was capable of unleashing, had risen in her mind's eye as she struggled to contain herself, snow touching her hair with cold little kisses.

Elise felt the sobs rise, choked them back down. *"What gift? I'm trying to protect them. It's my job, Suzy, in case you didn't notice. You went and left us, and now it's my job to protect them both."*

"You have help," Suzanne pointed out pitilessly. *"The Watchers will help. I've been helping, too. You know I'm not gone, only changed. Why do you fight this so hard?"*

"I don't want it." Elise's fists clenched. *"The Watchers don't help with anything. We were just fine until they came along!"*

"Were we?" Suzanne asked. *"We were always frightened, remember? We could feel things gathering around us, things standing in the shadows, just waiting to devour us. We were doing protection work every day for months. And now? The Watchers at least keep the Dark at bay. And they are truly dedicated, Elise. You've seen this."*

"Dedicated." Elise felt her lip curl. *"They want us dragged into Circle Lightfall by the hair."*

"They have never forced you, Elise. Only asked." Suzanne shook her head. *"Practice some kindness, child. You are to learn to hold Power with compassion. That is your path."*

"I'd rather roast them all," Elise muttered, then clapped both hands over her mouth. A witch had to be careful what she wished for.

Her teacher's face was infinitely kind. *"Please, Elise. Be kind to him. For my sake."*

"But he's one of them!" Elise cried. *"How can I—"*

"You're being ridiculous. He saved your life." Suzanne was fading, her yellow dress leaving a burning afterimage.

"No!" Elise screamed, reaching out to touch her. *"Suzanne! Don't!"*

It was too late. Suzanne was gone, and Elise fell through whiteness, falling toward her dreaming body lying so far below, falling, falling...

Elise woke all at once, to unaccustomed coolness. She sat straight up, gasping, clutching the coverlet to her chest, and smelled coffee.

Her breathing came in harsh tearing gulps. Her cheeks were wet. She blinked, wiping them dry.

Someone had been in her room, and moved her chair. Anyone sitting in that chair could look out the window, or at Elise's bed.

Elise hugged her knees, resting her forehead on them. The air-conditioning was on, but the air had a flat, still quality to it. She didn't have to look out the window to see the black clouds massing over the city. The light had an eerie yellow-green before-the-storm cast she only saw in late summer. A shocker of an end-of-summer storm, coming this way.

Why am I not surprised? She began her deep breathing. In, out. In, out. Let the anger fade. Let the heat sink down into her body. *There's been a storm coming for a long time. I've always known it.*

There were footsteps on her stairs. Someone heavy, moving gracefully and making noise deliberately. She already knew who it was.

She still wore her slip and her jeans, and had the rumpled feeling that came from sleeping in her clothes. Someone had taken her boots off, though. They sat right next to the bed.

Well, at least he was a gentleman.

The golden-eyed Watcher appeared in her bedroom doorway. Elise looked up, opening her mouth to say something probably extremely rude, when she saw that he had a cup of something that steamed gently in the morning light and smelled like coffee.

He paused, apparently gauging her mood. "The green witch told me your mood was uncertain before coffee." His voice was soft, conciliatory, but the hard edge to it hadn't faded. He had an angel's voice, true, but it wasn't the voice of a sweet little cherub.

It was the dark honey voice of an angel with brass wings and one hell of a sword, the kind of angel that would go through Egypt just carrying out orders.

That was an unpleasant thought, and Elise shivered. "Hi." She met his eyes squarely. "Coffee. Now." That was about as polite as she could be without caffeine.

He approached her cautiously. The sight of him—a guy twice her size carrying a sword, four black knives she could see, and two shiny guns, acting as if he was afraid of one disheveled witch he could have probably snapped in half like a chicken bone—made Elise want to laugh. As it was, she just smiled and watched his shoulders relax a fraction.

He was watching her face anxiously, as if looking for clues.

She blew across the top of the coffee, measuring him in daylight. Last night she'd been too tired and scared to really *look* at him. The bruise mottling his face was gone now, just a faint blush to show where it had been. Well, Watchers were quick healers.

Her weirdness meter had gotten a lot harder to trip lately, but this guy was doing a good job of it.

He stripped his hair back with his fingers. It was slightly

damp, the gold muted, and curled a little. He had it really too short to take advantage of the curl. It was almost a military cut, but if he grew it out a little and let it fall forward over those golden eyes...Wow. Ultra wow. He wasn't as cute as she'd thought.

He was even more attractive, if that was possible.

She wanted to paint him. She wanted to see if she could get his face right, the straight severity of his expression and the slight quirk to his mouth managing to convey an impression of irreverent laughter even when he was serious. She wondered if she could get the planes of his cheeks right, and the shadows under his golden eyes, and the way his face fit together like an angel's.

Elise swallowed. She took a sip of coffee, and was surprised to discover it was pretty good. "Huh. At least you know how to make coffee."

"It was a religion, in my part of the world." He folded himself down into her red chair. The pile of books by the side of the chair had been left undisturbed, and that made a traitorous little wire of warmth uncurl inside her chest. She could just see him carefully moving the chair, making sure the books didn't fall over. "I took a shower," he said, in the silence. "I felt a little sticky."

Elise nodded. She did too. Sweat had dried to a crackle glaze on her skin, yesterday's fear and anger both making her smell like burned paper. "No problem." She took another sip of coffee, watching him over the cup's rim. He'd picked her favorite mug, the big one with the pattern of gold leaves on it. "So where are you from? You sound Creole."

He looked a little surprised and shifted in the chair. "Was born outside Baton Rouge." His eyes dropped. Elise got the idea it hadn't been a happy time. Or maybe he just didn't want to talk about himself. The Watchers were like that—only interested in the Lightbringers, not giving out any personal information. It was kind of creepy.

"Oh." The more she looked at him, the more intrigued she found herself. He sat absolutely still, watching her with a vaguely-uncomfortable intensity. "Hey, have you had breakfast?"

He shook his head a little. Elise waited for more, but that was all she got. He watched her, leaning forward in the chair, his elbows braced on his knees and his fingertips meeting. It seemed to be a habitual pose. The hilt of his sword stuck up over his right shoulder, a grim reminder glittering in the eerie storm light.

"Okay," she said. "Look, you're kind of grim. Do you think you could talk to me? Tell me what's going on? I have *no* clue."

He nodded. "I just don't have much to say, I guess. This is my first time watching over a witch. It's a little nerve-wracking"

"Your first time?' That almost made her feel charitable toward him. "You seem pretty professional."

"The training's good. I've spent a long time doing other things. Hunting down artifacts, mostly, outwitting the Brotherhood and other groups. There's a lot of stuff being activated now, since Circle Lightfall's found so many Lightbringers. The whole world's waking up again." He looked down at his scarred, battered, callused hands. Elise took another drink of coffee, watching him. Her mouth felt foul and she would have to go visit the bathroom soon and stand under some hot water for a while, but all in all she felt a lot calmer.

Something about this guy, weird as he was, seemed to help keep the anger down. And that was so new and unexpected she wasn't quite sure what to think about it yet. It helped that he was so calm. *As long as he's calm, I can probably hang loose with the situation.* Then she chided herself. It wasn't like her, to feel comforted by a member of the male species.

He made a quick movement, holding up the medallion she'd bought yesterday. It glittered in his hand, red stone glowing in the weird stormlight. Elise's hand flew to her throat. She hadn't even noticed it was gone. And that made a squirrelly little thread of panic start under her breastbone. "How did you get that?"

"The ribbon looked uncomfortable." He leaned forward, holding it out. "And it's dangerous, *m'selle*. Best to keep it on one of us until we sort this out." He held it there until Elise reached forward and took it from him. Their fingers brushed, and his eyes were half-lidded, their gold turning dark and hot for a few moments.

"I thought Watchers couldn't touch people like me." She folded her fingers over the stone medallion. The sharp edges of the brass setting cut into her palm a little, and it vibrated against her skin. It felt perfect. It felt *right*. "I thought it hurt them."

"It does, until the Watcher finds his witch. That doesn't

hurt. The Lightbringer that can touch a particular Watcher...that's the carrot, that's the bait. We get to do something with our useless lives and protect the Lightbringers, and we get to..." He paused. "It doesn't hurt."

Elise took another sip of coffee. "So what does it feel like, if it doesn't hurt? Does it just feel normal? Like someone touching you?"

"No." Was he blushing?

He was. He was actually *blushing*. He finally dropped his eyes, looking down at his hands. Even sitting there, completely still, he looked ready to leap up at any moment.

Elise swallowed dryly, and her own cheeks began to burn. "Oh. I get it." It made sense. It must be the exact opposite of pain. That made a whole lot of sense, especially with the way he was blushing and looking down, as if embarrassed. "Okay, so I'll...um, you know, this is embarrassing."

"Kind of. I know you're angry, *m'selle*, and you don't understand or believe the Watchers are here to help. But I promise you, I'm only here to make sure you don't get killed, or worse, by something Dark. Can you believe that, at least?"

Elise opened her mouth to inform him that she did all right on her own, but then the memory of the gray thing in the pawnshop struck her. The razor-sharp teeth and the running sores, and the way it had looked at her, considering and hungry. If it hadn't been so weak and sick, what might it have done? She took a hurried gulp of coffee and met his eyes again. He watched her so intently it made a funny little hitch start under her breastbone. There was something almost hungry in his face, but it wasn't the murderous hunger of the thing in the pawnshop. This was a sort of desperate hunger that she recognized from her own life.

Loneliness. And longing.

"Yesterday, when I went to the pawnshop, this thing came in," she said, slowly, watching the light play over his face. She wanted to get out paper and pencil and draw him. She couldn't do him in watercolors. She'd have to use oils—his coloring demanded she use oils.

She lifted the medallion, its gem giving a bloody gleam against her palm before she dropped her hand again. "It wanted to get rid of this. The thing had a glamour on it. If I hadn't been so used to Watchers by now, I would never have seen the glamour, but I'm looking for it all the time now, you know?"

He nodded and made a little movement with his shoulders, as if to tell her he understood, and she could go on. She took another deep breath and looked down into her coffee cup. "It was gray; I mean it had gray skin. It had big pink eyes like an albino rabbit. And teeth, razor-sharp teeth. But the worst part was, it was really weak, like it was sick. It had all these awful oozing sores all over it. And it just wanted to get rid of the...the medallion. I didn't stop to think that it might have been the medallion that made it so sick. I just thought it was being in sunlight that hurt it so badly."

There was a low rumble that wasn't thunder. Elise looked up from her coffee.

His eyes were closed, and his aura was black with fury. Elise didn't normally see auras, that was Theo's specialty, but she saw his, a kind of hungry crimson blackness spreading out from him in pulsing waves. She stared at him, her jaw dropping for the umpteenth time in twenty-four hours. The low thunderous sound was a growl, and it was coming from *him*.

Something cold and dark exhaled through her bedroom. Elise, frozen, felt her arms and legs start to tremble. "Remy?" She wondered why it should occur to her to even *think* about attracting his attention. Her voice trembled.

His eyes snapped open, found hers. They were sane but terrible, with a kind of inhuman rage that could burn a body down to ash in seconds flat.

Elise dropped the coffee cup, scrambling out of the bed on the opposite side. When she was on her feet, she whirled to face him. *If he comes over the bed, I'll have to hit him, but I don't think it'll stop him. Oh gods—*

He was on his feet, too, holding the coffee cup. He hadn't spilled a drop. "Please." His voice was rough, like honey gone grainy with age. "Please, Elise. I'm sorry. I wasn't prepared for that."

You're not the only one. Elise shook. The medallion bit into her left hand, thrumming with Power. "What was that? What did you *do?*"

He offered her the coffee cup. "The thought of you, so close to something Dark. It strains my control." He sounded as calm and matter-of-fact as if he was giving her a laundry list. "Please, drink your coffee. You're in no danger. Just the thought of what *could* have happened to you..." He shook his head, stripping his hair back from his forehead with stiff fingers.

He looked almost gaunt, his cheeks hollowed out and his eyes burning.

Elise found her hands still jittering. "What did they *do* to you? You were human once, weren't you? *Weren't you?*" Her voice hit the pitch right before "screaming in terror," and she was both glad and terrified that there was nobody in the duplex next door. If he went ballistic, she didn't want anyone else getting hurt.

I could go without him getting ballistic this morning, too.

"If you want to call it that. Did you mention breakfast?"

"I want to know." Her voice shook. "I want to know everything."

"Didn't Dante and Hanson explain it to you?" His dark eyebrows drew together. "Haven't they told you?"

"I didn't want to know. I just…It's been crazy. It's *crazy*. I've spent so long thinking I was nuts, and now I find out I'm sane and the world is nuts. And what do you *want* from me, anyway?" The medallion throbbed inside her hand, the stone hot and curiously alive. "And what is this *thing*?"

"I was sent to protect you," he said very slowly and clearly, his accent making the words thick and golden. "To watch over you. You don't know what's out there. You just don't know."

"Then tell me," Elise whispered. "I think I'd better find out before I faint."

He shrugged, a lazy catlike movement. He was still holding out the coffee cup. "I think you need breakfast, Elise."

He pronounced her name differently, like a caress. *It must be the accent.* She had to strangle the mad urge to giggle. *Why am I not afraid of him? I should be. I should be really afraid of him.*

"I should be really afraid of you, shouldn't I." Her heartbeat began to slow down, as if her pulse didn't know she was stuck in her bedroom with a man who had just gone into ultra scary-mode.

He shook his head slowly. He still stared at her, as if he was memorizing her. "No," he said, softly. Very softly. "No, you shouldn't. Never, *cherie*. Never."

Elise closed her eyes and counted to ten. Opened them. He still stood there, holding the coffee cup. To catch it, he would have had to move faster than any human could. She closed her eyes and counted to ten again.

Opened them.

Still there, watching her with that puzzled, intense look on his face. He was taller than any man had a right to be, and he was almost as big as Dante, although he was leaner, built like a dancer instead of a linebacker.

The man had no right to look at her that way. And he had no right to just stand there with his eyes glowing in the stormlight and his hair drying and raveling over his cute forehead. And his mouth turned down at the corners with worry.

"Those things," she said. "The...the elephant-things. They wanted to kidnap me."

He nodded.

"The gray thing, in the pawnshop." She watched him carefully. But his eyes just narrowed a little. "I know it would have tried to jump me, if it hadn't been so weak. So I guess I know what the alternative is."

He nodded.

"The sixty-four million dollar question is, what do you want me to do? Can I go on and live my own life and count on you not to try and jerk me around?"

He actually looked shocked. "I was trained to obey a Lightbringer," he said finally, carefully. "You say jump, I jump. I'm supposed to obey you, unless we're in a combat zone and your safety's an issue. Good enough?"

"I guess." This whole conversation was beginning to sound like a lunatic game of checkers. "Okay." She took a step forward, another, and leaned across the bed to take the coffee cup from him. It took more courage than she thought such a simple movement would require. "I've got some stuff to do today. You can tag along for the time being. But if you try to force me into *anything*..." She trailed off, deciding not to make a specific threat. Threats were best when they were vague.

He nodded. "Understood. *Je comprends, cherie.*"

"I'm not your *cherie*," she told him, sharply. "I'm going to go take a shower. Try not to burn the place down while I'm doing it, okay?"

"I'll do my best." Was it sarcasm? No, he looked too serious. But there was a glimmer in his eye when he said it, and she examined his face for a long moment before shaking her head and turning away to excavate something from her closet to wear. *I don't want to know.* She pushed aside the paper screen she had painted before she'd moved in here. Suzanne had cosigned on the loan to buy this duplex, Elise's graduation gift.

"Elise?"

"Huh?" She stood in the closet, looking at her dresser and hangers full of bright clothes. "What?" She sounded irritated, even to herself.

"I won't fail you." His voice was rough. She heard his footsteps as he crossed the room for the bedroom door. "I swear I won't."

She didn't have an answer for that. She waited behind the paper screen, sipping at her coffee and bracing the cup with both hands because otherwise she was afraid she would drop it. The medallion chattered against the ceramic of the cup. The stone was merely warm now, instead of scorching.

He must have taken the medallion off her while she slept. And Theo had put her to sleep in the store. He must have carried her. Again.

The thought made her cheeks flush—and a few other places too. The first time in months she'd been that close to a man and she'd been unconscious. Great. Par for the course. Just when she'd decided to date Mark, he'd died. What would she do to this guy?

"Gods," she whispered. "What am I thinking? I just *met* this guy!"

Yeah, the snide little voice of her conscience replied, *but how long has he been Watching you?*

Thirteen

She came stamping down the stairs as Remy was finishing daily drill. The sky was turning the bruised purple-yellow that meant thunderstorm, a color he associated more with the hot, humid city of his childhood than this more temperate climate. He had even heard more faint rumbles of thunder.

His sword blurred through the last few complex moves and ended up back in its sheath, and he turned to find his witch standing in the living room doorway watching him.

She'd braided her red-gold hair back, and it was wet and dark from the shower. Small silver hoops glittered in her ears, she had traded the ruby stud in her nose for a silver ring, and she had tied the Trifero to another bit of ribbon, this time crimson. It just served to make her neck look even more slender and fragile. The Talisman itself seemed to pulse with dangerous Power.

Her black T-shirt said *Princess* in hot-pink cursive across her breasts, and she wore another pair of frayed jeans. Both shirt and jeans were artfully torn, the shirt with its neck ripped out and its sleeves clipped off, exposing pale satiny shoulders, her jeans showing flashes of pale thigh and one smooth knee. A pair of chunky scarlet sneakers completed the vision, as well as a thick leather cuff on her right wrist. She carried the coffee cup, and her eyes were wide and clear, the light green of her irises ringed with a darker, smoky green.

Remy's heart gave a leap that threatened to strangle him.

One coppery eyebrow quirked. She looked half-amused, half-amazed. "You were waving that sword around in my living room?"

He opened his mouth to apologize. Instead, what came out was, "Practice makes perfect."

"No." She shook her head. Her braid bounced against her back. "*Perfect* practice makes perfect. That looks pretty cool. You think you could teach me some?"

His mouth went dry. "You mean, teach you sword fighting?"

"Yeah." She shrugged. "And I should start carrying a gun, don't you think?"

Nothing in Remy's training had prepared him for *this*. The lump in his throat felt suspiciously like stone. "I thought witches practiced nonviolence." He wanted to touch her so badly his hands burned.

"I don't get violent unless someone gets violent with me. That's *practical* nonviolence." Her green eyes glittered for a moment, her perfect mouth twisting slightly. "And if you're going to be doing some ass-kicking to keep these guys away from me, I should be helping as much as I can."

How could he possibly explain this to her? "You don't understand. It takes Dark to fight the Dark. I can fight them because I can be as ruthless as they are. I can fight better if I don't have to worry about you catching a stray bullet."

She considered this, chewing her lower lip. "I need more coffee," she muttered darkly. "Are you saying you won't teach me?"

"No," he said. "I'll teach you all I can. But I want you to let me do my job. Fair?"

He watched her face go through a myriad of emotions— thoughtfulness, anger, worry, and finally a kind of acceptance. At least, he hoped it was acceptance. *That's probably the key to her. Fairness. A sense of fair play.*

"Fair enough. I'd offer to shake on it, but..." She trailed off, watching his face.

He forced himself to shrug casually. The thought of her skin against his made frustrated need twist under his skin. He *wanted* it, but he didn't want to frighten her. Or disgust her, and he knew the Dark living inside him would be disgusting to her. There was no hope for it. "You don't have to. I know how much you must dislike me."

That made her frown. "I don't dislike you." She crossed her arms, the coffee mug dangling from one of her slim fingers, slipped casually through the handle. "I just don't like the thought of anyone telling me what to do."

He nodded. He wanted to touch the angle of her chin, run his fingers over her cheekbone, to see if her skin was as soft as it looked. He wanted to see her eyes gone half-lidded with pleasure and—

Her eyes flicked over the living room and came to rest on her guitar case. They widened, and she looked up at him. "You brought my guitar case home?"

He shrugged. "The green witch brought it in."

She absorbed this. "Thank you."

He could find absolutely nothing to say.

She stood there for another moment or two, thoughts he

couldn't decipher moving behind her incandescent eyes. Her skin was so fair it seemed to glow in the strange light. A slice of her pale belly peeked out between the hem of her shirt and the waistband of her jeans. He could even see her belly button. It didn't help to look at her midriff; that only made him want to kiss it. Instead, he raised his eyes to hers, but that didn't help either. That meant that he could see her mouth.

"Okay," she said, finally. "I guess I'll get some more coffee, and then we'll get started on some research."

"Research?" He had some research of his own that he'd like to do, starting with her lips and then—

He tore his mind away from that fascinating chain of thought. *What is wrong with me? My job is to keep her skin whole, not to have stray thoughts of getting close enough to do half of what I'd like to do to her. Starting with that mouth of hers.*

"Yeah." She turned away, heading for the kitchen. "I want to find out what this Trifero thing is, and I want to find out more about being a Guardian. I want to find out how I can leave the city if I want to, and I want to find out everything I can about this Circle Lightfall, and whether or not they can be trusted. And I want to find out—"

He couldn't stay quiet. "All in one day?"

She looked back over her shoulder at him. That one moment, with her half-smile and her long rope of wet hair, she was the single most beautiful thing he had ever seen. It took every ounce of discipline he had to stay still, because all he wanted to do was cross the distance between them, take her face in his hands and kiss her until he drowned.

"I've always been an overachiever." She tipped her head toward the kitchen. "Come on. Do you drink coffee?"

"Sometimes," he said, hoarsely. She seemed not to notice.

"Well, then. Let's have a cup."

What else could he do? He obeyed.

Fourteen

They finished their coffee while standing in her kitchen, and Elise was waiting for the man to say something, but he never did. Instead, he stayed carefully on one side of the kitchen and just watched her, taking occasional sips from his cup. She had found her favorite silver nose-ring and the exact T-shirt she wanted, so she was happy to caffeinate herself in silence.

Usually she had music playing while she drank her coffee and worked out. But today her head felt thin and bruised, not ready for a morning helping of pounding drums. And she had no desire to even go near the punching bag after seeing him practice, his face calm behind the blurring silver arc of his sword. He moved like oil over water, every strike perfectly controlled. She could just imagine the kind of shape he had to be in to move like that. She knew enough about fighting to know that he must have trained for years to be that fast, that coordinated.

She'd seen a lot of scary things on the city streets, but he looked scarier than all of them combined.

Elise prided herself on being tough, but Remy looked *lethal*.

She shivered a little when she remembered last night. Looking down from the stage at a golden-eyed Watcher standing in the middle of a pile of gray-skinned, razor-tusked bodies with long fringed ears and big black eyes while the people she had been entertaining less than fifteen seconds before screamed and ran for the exits, she'd only felt stunned relief that the worst had finally happened. Another Watcher had invaded her city. And when the bodies had started to burst into flame, she had wondered if she'd finally lost control of her Powers and would start to make things burn willy-nilly. But when he had leapt up on the stage and turned to face her, his golden eyes fierce and his entire body tense, she hadn't fried him. It had been a relief to find out that she could still control the flames.

I don't want to fight off more than a dozen assassins and worry about protecting you at the same time, he'd said. And then done just that. He'd thrown her over his shoulder like a barbarian and dropped her on a rooftop, then started fighting. She had watched, horrified, as he waded through his attackers, sword blurring, kicking and punching when he had to, his entire body seeming to come alive with graceful, deadly intent. And he was so calm about it, so matter-of-fact.

And those eyes, pure gold, watching her every movement...
*This is useless. I'm dithering. What's wrong with me?
He's not that cute.*

Except he *was* that cute. Elise sighed, feeling the heat rise
in her cheeks again. *I do not date Watchers. Look what
happened to Theo and Mari. They're...well, they're happy.
Even if these guys are overprotective.*

*Stop it. You've got work to do, Elise, quit mooning over
this guy. He's not in your league.* As soon as she set her cup
down, he did too, his eyes following her as she slid past him.
Thank the gods this kitchen's big enough for two. She felt
a little burst of disappointment. What would it feel like to brush
against him, smelling male and leather?

Elise shook that off. *I'm just in shock,* she told herself—
and her hormones—sternly. *I'm not dating, remember?* Her
purse sat on the counter, and she flipped it open and looked
inside. Her shades were there. They were pink heart-shaped
sunglasses with tinted-pink lenses, which meant the stormy
light coming in through the windows took on an odd orange
shade when she slipped them on.

It was weird, the way her emotions were whipsawing back
and forth. She swung her purse over her shoulder and was
heading for the door when Remy inserted himself between her
and the front hall. He did it so quickly and smoothly she barely
saw him move. He just sort of *appeared* in front of her.

"Let me." He went down the hall, pausing for a moment
before opening the front door. Elise rolled her eyes. She could
feel the Power rolling out from him. He was checking the wards
and scanning the street outside. Looking for danger.

"What exactly do you think is going to be waiting out there?"
She stamped after him. "An army?" There was another layer
of shielding on her duplex—Watcher shielding, tough and
perfectly done. Elise decided not to even say anything about it.
If she got rid of him, the shielding would fade. If she didn't, it
would be nice to have another layer of protection. She'd just
pretend not to notice.

"No. A storm. Are you sure you don't want to wait, *m'selle*?
It looks like it might rain." His accent made the words slow
and lazy, and he glanced back over his broad shoulder at her.
"At least, a coat might be a good idea."

Elise waved a hand at him. "I'll just borrow yours," she
said, sarcastically. "What is *up* with you? A little rain never

hurt anyone. Maybe we'll get a cab, although I'm not sure you'll fit, tall guy."

"I fit in a cab last night. The green witch called one. We brought you home."

"You have no sense of humor." She followed him out the door and turned to lock it, then dropped her keys back in her purse.

"I'll try to develop one. Where are we going first?"

"First to a place I know where we can get some answers. Then breakfast, and after that we're going to see if Vann showed up to work today. I owe him and Trevor a big apology, and we're going to have to come up with some story to give them." Elise hopped down off her front step, brushing past the laurel hedge right next to her door. The path led down to her street, and a dozing heat simmered up from the pavement. Cars were parked on either side of the road, and Elise automatically turned right, heading toward the Ave. He fell into step beside her, and she looked up at him. "Don't you get hot in that thing?"

He shrugged. "No. Or cold, either. Rain is a little uncomfortable, and ice, but the training makes us largely indifferent to weather conditions."

"Wow." She fussed with the strap of her purse, sliding it over her head so it lay diagonally across her body. "Theo told me once that they—Circle Lightfall—put something in you Watchers. Something that hurts."

He nodded. His boots resounded against the pavement. He moved like a cat, all supple motion and slinking grace. "It's called a *tanak*. A Dark parasite. Or symbiote might be a better term, since it needs me as much as I need it by now. It does hurt, but pain?" He shrugged. Elise's feet automatically carried her down the pavement. "Pain can be controlled. It can be ignored. I've dealt with pain all my life. At least this way I can do something good. Something useful. I spent long enough being a useless waste of flesh."

Now that's an interesting way to put it. "How? I mean, what did you do?"

He looked ahead at the street, his eyes flicking over pavement and parked cars. The light was yellow-green now, giving the entire world an unreal tinge. There was a low, sliding roll of thunder in the distance. Elise was glad. The heat was a sticky blanket.

"Are you sure you want to know, Elise? I'm not a nice

guy."

No guy worth dating is, sugar. She bit back the comment, it was too sarcastic. The way he said her name was almost like being touched, his fingers brushing up her back. She took a deep breath, trying to squash the way her heart was hammering. "I should know, don't you think? If you're going to be hanging around me for any length of time, I want to know. I have to know."

"Certainly, then." But his head came up and he scanned the street. Thunder muttered again, much closer now. Elise looked up, saw a spear of light go from cloud to cloud. She counted habitually, and when she got to six, another low rumble of thunder vibrated through the air.

"Come on, let's hurry." Elise actually took hold of his arm, forgetting that she didn't want to touch him. "If we hurry, we might be able to make Abra's before the rain starts. I wanted to stop at the Whistle Bar for breakfast, too. I don't suppose you have a car?"

"No. Although I could requisition one, if you needed it."

"Requisition?" She couldn't keep the disbelief out of her voice. "You mean, *steal?*" *A car thief as a Watcher? Why didn't Mari mention these guys were so damn interesting?*

"No, I mean notify Circle Lightfall that I need one, and go into a dealership to pick one up," he said absently, as if his attention was somewhere else. But he glanced down at her and slowed, shortening his long strides so that she didn't have to trot to keep up with him. That was nice, but she still had her hand on his leather-clad arm. She could feel muscle under the leather, and remembered seeing how *fast* he could move. It was kind of scary, how quick he was.

Scary and exciting at the same time, like a fast car or a loud beat. Like getting up on the stage for the first time, or like the first time she ever lit a candle with will alone. Heart-hammering and ecstatic, all at once.

"Why am I not scared of you?" She didn't mean to ask him out loud.

"I'm your Watcher." As if that explained everything. His eyes were fantastic. Would she be able to catch that mellow gold color if she painted him?

"What if Circle Lightfall ordered you to make me let them into the city?" Lightning flashed again between the bruised clouds.

"They can't. I'm *your* Watcher."

"What about Dante and Hanson?" She heard the challenge in her voice, hated it. But she couldn't afford *not* to ask him the hard questions. She was responsible for looking after Mari and Theo now.

Although I've done a bang-up job of being rude and mean to all of them. Her heart actually fell. *Why can't I be nice once in a while?*

She knew why. Nice hadn't let her survive in foster care. Nice hadn't let her fight her way through her adolescence, and nice certainly hadn't saved her during the spell that cost Suzanne her life.

Remy didn't sigh, but she got the idea he wanted to. "They're not my problem. They're Watchers, responsible for their own witches. I'm only supposed to watch over you."

"Great," she said. "My very own pet psycho." She waited for him to take offense.

Amazingly, he didn't. "I'm not psychotic. We undergo severe testing. It takes some coping to maintain sanity in the face of what we have to deal with to become Watchers." He still scanned the street, his eyebrows drawn together. "Like the first time you face a zombie Crusader. Or a *s'lin.*"

"What's a slin?" Elise had the sinking feeling that she didn't want to know. The light made him look even more otherworldly.

"*S'lin.* A kind of Dark thing. Looks like a manta ray. With lots of teeth." He said this with a slight smile, just a hint of good cheer around his mouth and eyes. "A good fight."

Her hand was still on his arm. It was awkward, so she slid her arm through his, just like a prom couple. *Only I never went to the prom. I was too busy trying to survive.*

"Do you actually *like* fighting?" she asked. These were the straightest answers she'd gotten from any of the Watchers. Granted, she hadn't listened to anything Dante or Hanson had to say. But this man seemed to carefully consider each question, and he was so *calm*. No obfuscation and none of the irritating condescension the other two used, as if she had to be shielded from knowing.

And the sharp bite of irritation and anger hadn't surfaced yet. Something about his unruffled expression made *her* feel calmer too.

He shrugged. "It seems unlikely that I'll never have to do it again. Might as well just accept it." More thunder. They reached the corner of Fourth Street and Elise paused. Theo's new shop was only three blocks away. But Elise turned right instead of left. They weren't going to the Rowangrove.

I don't think I could handle seeing Theo and Mari right now. Not if I'm actually considering letting this guy hang around. They'll probably start laughing their heads off to see me with him. I think I'm about to break some of my own rules about dating hunks with shiny hardware.

Especially if I might be able to control the fire. That's worth keeping him around for, isn't it?

He turned with her smoothly, his boots ghosting over the pavement, eerily silent next to Elise's own footsteps. People scurried past them, heading for cover before the storm broke. A kid on a skateboard with a *Bloovers* T-shirt rolled past, lazy and hipshot, his eyes hidden behind green sunglasses. Elise wondered if he guessed the guy she was hanging on was carrying enough hardware to start a street war.

"I asked if you actually liked it." Something else occurred to her before he could reply. "Remy. You have a last name?"

"I used to have a last name." He moved slightly, bringing his shoulder up as the thought made him flinch. "But Watchers only have one name. The person I was before I became a Watcher is dead."

He said it so matter-of-factly that Elise stopped to look up at him. The pink lenses turned his golden eyes a strange color. But his face was still an angel's face, and he stopped and waited, his eyes slipping over the street in smooth arcs.

Watching.

"What are you waiting for?" Her skin roughened into gooseflesh. Of course, the fact that the wind had finally started moving over the city might have had something to do with it. It caressed her bare shoulder, and she shivered. She didn't want to get in his way when he looked at the street with his eyes narrowed and his entire body seeming to listen, ready to explode into action at the slightest provocation.

He was so tightly wound she was beginning to get tired just watching him.

"I don't know yet," he said. "Probably the Brotherhood. They haven't been specifically banned from the city, so they're still operating here. And since they're technically not here to kill, only to capture, it'll be harder to root them out with the Guardian spell."

"Because I've got this thing—this Trifero. This medallion." Elise tugged on his arm a little, and he started walking again, carefully matching his stride to hers. "I don't even know why

I bought it."

"It chose *you*, Elise. The Major Talismans are usually at least semiconscious, and this one knew what it wanted. It wanted a fire witch, and they're few and far between. Especially fire witches with plenty of Power that survive past puberty. Most of them get thrown into institutions as arsonists and picked off by the Dark or mindwiped by Thorazine."

That's so cheerful. Thank you ever so much. Elise's stomach roiled. "Gods."

He nodded. "You're lucky, *cherie*. Very lucky. You're alive and free at an age when most Lightbringers have been killed or taken. Or driven into insanity by normals."

"That's pretty grim. How do I know that's really what's going on here?" *In other words, Elise, you're asking him if he's lying to you. Wonderful.*

He *still* didn't take offense, as if he understood why she would ask such a question. "Easy enough to figure out. Have you ever met anyone else like you, or the green witch, or the water witch?" His face was level and serious, his eyes watchful over his sharp nose and straight sculpted mouth. There was a faint blush high up on his cheeks. Was he embarrassed? Ashamed? Angry at her ignorance?

She bit her lip, thinking about it, and felt a cool drop smack against her arm. Rain. It was starting to rain.

"So what would happen if I ordered you to jump up and down on one foot singing Yankee Doodle Dandy?" she finally asked him. They reached Third Street, and she turned left again. He held his arm stiffly, carefully, and she wished now that she had never put her arm through his. He obviously didn't want to be near her.

"I would assume you had a good reason." And, wonder of wonders, a smile quirked up one corner of his mouth. "If only the sheer amusement value."

"You know, you're beginning to develop a sense of humor." She pushed her sunglasses up so that they perched on her head. The light was beginning to fail.

"Anything to please you, Elise."

Damn the man, did he have to say things like that? And not just say it, but say it like he really *meant* it? He sounded sincere. As if she hadn't irritated him in the least.

"I'm not even sure I trust you." Her face flamed with embarrassment again. Hearing him say her name was like being caressed. It just sounded too good to hear his slow accent drawing out the syllables.

"You don't have to." He stopped and looked down at her, which forced her to stop, too. His eyes burned in the gathering pre-storm darkness, golden slashes in his angelic face. "Just give me a chance, huh? That's all I ask."

Elise's teeth worried at her bottom lip. "I suppose you haven't done anything bad so far." In all fairness, she had to admit he seemed serious. And the dream was still bothering her, no matter how much she tried to forget it. Suzanne had never hesitated to tell her when she was being stupid. "I don't think I trust Circle Lightfall," she finished.

He said nothing, his eyes fixed on her face. How could he look like he was paying such attention to her and look so completely alert at the same time?

And he had protected her. In the most visceral, physical way possible. Something like that just made a girl feel mighty charitable.

Elise, listen to yourself. You're dithering. He helps you keep your temper. Who cares about the rest of it? He doesn't seem like an overprotective brainless pile of muscle, like the other two. This guy's something else.

"All right," she said, finally. "You've got your chance, Mr. Remy No-Last-Name. But don't think we're dating or anything. I'm not like Theo and Mari. I'm mean and tough and I'm high maintenance."

"Fair enough." If he would have done anything other than nod seriously, his eyes fixed on her face, she probably would have changed her mind. But he didn't.

She began to feel cautiously optimistic. "Okay. We're going to be doing some research and talking to some people. Can you try not to look so scary?"

"I'll try. I'll do my best to be a wallflower, hmm?"

"Good luck," she muttered, and he did smile at that. It was a small smile, a private smile, and it reached all the way down to Elise's toes. "Come on, big guy. Let me do the talking, okay?"

"Of course, *cherie.* I'll be quiet as a mouse."

Fifteen

She took Remy to a long dim street, curiously deserted, but with evidence of rough living all over it—doorways littered with trash and cigarette butts, and a few stores with heavily barred windows and doors. The storm did not break. Not just yet. Instead, the rain pattered down in random drops and stopped, as if too exhausted by the heat to really get going.

It looked as if Elise came here often, because she walked with an air of familiarity over the cracked pavement. A chill went up Remy's spine as he thought of his witch coming through this part of town alone. Even during the day, something could have happened to her.

Don't think about that. Just do your job, and thank the gods you're here now.

She paused outside the Abracadabra Pawnshop, tucked between a Korean grocery and a Mexican fast-food place. The gilt lettering on the window proclaimed, *We Make Miracles Happen.* More rain flirted down, the storm waiting breathlessly to unleash its fury. *I should have brought a coat for her.* He wanted to touch Elise's bare shoulder, restrained himself.

She had given him a chance. All he had to do now was keep from screwing it up.

The bell over the door tinkled as they stepped into the shop. The smell of dust and human desperation vied with the spicy smell of beef stew with chili peppers. Indifferent hardwood flooring creaked under their feet, and a woman sat behind the counter on a three-legged stool. She had long dark curly hair, liquid dark eyes, and a nondescript face. She wore a blue and silver caftan and large golden hoops in her ears.

She was most definitely not human, and she held a .45 far too big for her slender brown hands, trained on them.

Remy moved between the gun and Elise, who said, "Hey!" and pushed at him. He ignored her, sinking his feet into the floor and meeting the woman's dark eyes, adrenaline spiking his heartbeat before the symbiote took control and forced his pulse back to slow and steady. *She told me not to speak, or I'd ask this woman how she would like that gun fed to her. With a few teeth added.*

"Remy, stop it! Remy—"

"Elise?" the woman asked in an oddly clear, sweet voice.

Remy would have bet his last nickel that voice was the last thing her prey heard. "What the hell are you doing, bringing something like that in here?"

Elise tried to slip around Remy, but he moved again, using his body to shield her. "Dammit, Remy, *quit* it!" She sounded angry.

"She has a gun, *cherie*." He hoped he wasn't breaking the no-talking rule too badly. "Your safety—"

"Abra, please. He won't hurt you, I promise. Can you put the hardware down?" Elise grabbed Remy's arm and tried to peer around him. But she didn't sound angry with him.

The caramel-skinned woman shook her head. The gold hoops swung against her cheeks. "What the hell are you, Gold-Eyes? And what's that thing crouching inside you? Answer me, and I'll think about putting the gun down. I'm sorry, Elise. I trust you, but I don't know this guy."

"Oh, for the love of—" Elise just sounded annoyed, not furious. "You and your paranoia, Abra. Okay. Go ahead, Remy."

His heart eased inside his rib cage. She sounded like she was taking it for granted he would want her permission. Which meant she implicitly agreed that he was her Watcher.

Which made his heart thump again, before the *tanak* tightened its control, bringing autonomic functions back down and chilling the surface of his skin with reaction.

Obedience, Watcher. Do what your witch says.

"I'm a Watcher," he said to the dusky woman behind the counter. If she pulled the trigger, she'd probably fall off the stool she was perched on. Gold glinted under glass throughout the store, guitars were hung on a rack, and there was an accordion in the window. "I mean you no harm, but if you try to hurt Elise, Old One, I will tear out your spine and feed it to you."

"Remy!" Elise began.

"Very cute." The Old One smelled like dust and desperation under the deceptive odor of food. Just one of the many things that lived in—and fed off—cities. She was not quite Dark, but Remy knew enough to guess that her moral system wouldn't precisely be the same as Elise's. "What do you have shadowing you, Remy-the-Watcher? I've only seen its like once before, and that was years ago."

I'll be the last one you see, if you don't put that

goddamn gun down. "Dark symbiote. *Tanak.* Melded to me in the old way."

The woman nodded, measuring him with eyes that glimmered black. A fleeting look of recognition crossed her dark face. "Ah. Elise, are you all right?"

That was surprising. Remy didn't look away from the woman, but he felt Elise relax behind him.

She sighed, letting go of his arm. "Remy, please. Abra won't hurt me."

"Have her put the gun away, Elise. Please." He said it softly, but the glass door rattled in its frame. "I won't risk it." *It's your safety, witch. Come on. Help me be reasonable here.* If this ended up costing him the grudging trust he'd just won from his witch, he was going to think very seriously about getting a little violent on this little bit of not-quite-Dark.

"Abra? Are we gong to do a Mexican standoff all day? I just wanted to ask you a few questions." Elise tried to peek around Remy, and he moved slightly again. She was between him and the waist-high glassed-in counter on the other side of the store, and if he had to he could push her back behind it to provide some cover while he dealt with any problems.

"Well, he hasn't drawn any of his hardware," Abra said, practically. "But just to be safe, Elise, stay over there on that side of the store, okay? I didn't live this long by being stupid or incautious." She laid the gun on the counter. There was a click as she did so. Remy gauged the distance between the gun and her hand, and moved slightly aside so Elise could step out and see the woman.

Elise sighed. "Hi, Abra." She smiled at the woman, who twitched up the corners of her mouth cautiously. "Nice to see you. How did that spell work out for you?"

Now the gypsy woman truly smiled, all the way up to her black eyes. The gold hoops in her ears shivered slightly. "It worked well. I haven't eaten this well in a long time. My thanks. You're going to call in the favor?"

"I might as well," Elise raised her hand and touched Remy's arm.

Even through the coat he felt a prickle of pleasure teasing at his skin. He froze, hoping it would continue.

His witch didn't seem to notice. "Five questions, Abra."

So it was a bargaining game. Remy held himself very still, waiting. Watching.

The Old One shook her head slightly, the gold hoops shivering. "Two. It wasn't *that* big of a spell."

"Oh, come *on*. You've never had it so good. I stopped Robbie from having his guys tear up your part of Klondel too, doesn't that count for anything? Four questions." Elise's fingers dug into Remy's arm. *Stay still and let me talk to her, big guy.* Her voice breathed inside his head.

If he hadn't been frozen in place, that would have turned him into a statue. She had spoken to him. She had actually, positively without a doubt spoken to him privately, used the contact between them that had led him to her in the first place. *If it pleases you,* cherie, he thought. *Still and quiet it is.* His mouth wanted to curl up into a smile. He forced it down and made his face a mask.

Abra shrugged. "You're a nice girl, Elise, and you're powerful. I'll cut you a deal. Three, and you owe me a small favor. I want to ask loverboy there a question too."

"Four questions, and you get to ask him one," Elise said.

Remy felt a faint sense of alarm but quelled it. If Elise wanted him to answer a question, he would. Thunder rumbled outside. When would the storm break? Soon. *Very* soon, there was more rain pattering down onto the cracked pavement outside. A car nosed along the street

"Done," Abra said promptly. She scooped up the gun and put it away under the counter. Elise's fingers tensed on Remy's arm, but he hadn't moved. He was finding it increasingly difficult to stay still and silent. This woman was not human, and she was dangerous. "Ask away, Elise."

"Okay." Elise took a deep breath. "What's the Trifero?"

The Old One blinked. "It's a Talisman, one of the Great Ones. Sitting on a bit of ribbon around your lovely neck, sweets. It's the Stone of Fire and Destruction. The legend is that it was used to sink Atlantis, but I don't think so, *everything* gets blamed for that little debacle. The Trifero's been lost for five thousand years. I think the Catholic Church had it for the last thousand or so. They kept moving it around to keep it away from profiteers. It's worth a lot. Think of a magickal nuclear bomb, Elise, sitting around your neck and just aching to be used." She sounded far more delighted than she should have been.

Remy felt the shiver go through Elise's body. So it *was* the Trifero. He had been almost sure, but it was different hearing someone else say it. Very different. He was not only guarding his witch, but the Trifero as well.

I had better not foul this one up, he thought, without any amusement.

"Number two?" Abra's golden earrings shivered. Remy got the idea that he did *not* want to see what lay beneath the Old One's skin any more than he had ever wanted to see the thing that lay under his own again.

"What do you know about Circle Lightfall?" Elise asked.

Abra's liquid eyes widened. "Ah." Her eyes glimmered as if she'd just put two and two together and hit the jackpot. "A hotshot group going around scooping up psychics. *Real* psychics. Sort of voted themselves the defenders of the psychic population. Lots of predators very unhappy about that. They've got some sort of Hundred-Monkey Theory about what they call Lightbringers, certain types of sensitives. Like you." Abra shrugged, her earrings swinging. "I've heard they don't mess with anyone who doesn't feed on their psychics, if that makes you feel better. They seem to be purely a defensive organization."

Elise didn't respond, and Remy's throat was dry. What was she thinking? He scanned the shop and the street outside again, uneasy. She seemed to be taking it for granted that he would answer the woman's question, whatever it was. Taking it for granted that he would keep her bargain.

Good. Another sign of trust. He was doing well with her, at least.

Or so he hoped.

"That's all I know," Abra said, finally.

"What about me? Anyone looking for me, asking questions where they shouldn't?" Elise sounded thoughtful, but her hand was still tense on Remy's arm. He used his peripheral vision to glance at her and saw she was watching Abra. The Trifero glowed against her pale throat, a reminder of Power. The pawnshop seemed to vibrate a little, tension in the air rattling the glass cabinets and racks of bartered goods.

If the Old One so much as twitches I will have her head, Remy decided. *I don't like this. I don't like this at all.*

"There's a two-hundred-thousand dollar prize for you delivered alive and unharmed to some guy on the East Side," Abra said, as if she was outlining a shopping list. "Which is why it's so surprising to see you waltz into my place like this. I

thought you'd be snapped up by last sunset at the latest." She
shook back her long black hair and looked over Remy again.
"You must be good, loverboy."

Remy's face set. He didn't respond. He was waiting for
Elise to be done with this so he could take her out of this place;
it was enough to strain even a Watcher's patience. Outside,
more rain came down, a hard patter hitting the sidewalk.
Thunder, again. A long rolling peal made the entire place
shudder. Two hundred thousand was chump change for the
Brotherhood. Just an insurance policy, then, in case a
Lightbringer had managed to evade a team of Brotherhood
operatives through luck or good protection spells. It had been
much closer than Remy had thought. Every half-assed
mercenary in the area, human and otherwise, would be pouring
into the city by now to try their luck.

His entire body tightened at the thought of how close Elise
had been to being taken. He had almost been too late. Another
fifteen, twenty minutes and she might have been taken by the
Brotherhood.

I would have had to go get her. He shifted his weight
slightly, very slowly, so he was a coiled spring. *I don't like
this. I don't like this at all.*

"You know, I'm beginning to think that it might be bad luck
to have you in my store," Abra said, once it was apparent that
Elise wasn't going to add anything. "I like you, but I don't want
the entire mercenary population of the city on my ass. Can we
move it along, please?"

Elise shook her head. "You'll have to owe me one. Or you
can give up the question you want to ask him and we'll be
even."

"You're a real bitch, Nicholson," Abra said cheerfully. "I
walked right into that one, didn't I? No, I'll owe the answer,
and I'll ask him this. What made you desperate enough to join
the Black Knife Brigade, boy? Why did you join Circle
Lightfall?" Her eyes were the eyes of a very small, sharp-
toothed creature lying in wait under a leaf in some steaming
jungle, sitting in the center of its steely web.

Remy found himself contemplating what it would be like
to stride across the thinly carpeted floor of the shop and snap
the woman's neck. Control reasserted itself, the bite of the
tanak against his bones familiar and half welcome now, because
the pain reminded him of Elise standing right there, looking up

at him with a faint line between her eyebrows. So she was worried, his red-haired witch.

Obedience, Watcher. Do as you're told.

"I was in jail for murder," he said shortly. "Circle Lightfall offered me a chance to get out, and to stop being a worthless waste of flesh. So I took it." He didn't dare look at Elise's face. "Are you finished here, *cherie?*" He couldn't help himself.

She sounded sad and thoughtful, for the first time. "I guess so. Thanks, Abra."

"Don't bring trouble to my door again, Elise," the Old One said.

"Oh, please." Elise turned to the door. "You wouldn't be the information broker for the entire western half of Saint City if you didn't *like* trouble."

The Old One laughed. "Then let me give you a piece of free advice."

Elise halted. He hadn't moved, still watching the Old One.

"Well?" his witch said, but nothing else.

"Stay close to your Black-Knife loverboy there, Elise." Abra's face was drawn and serious. "There are some serious badasses looking to add you to someone's collection. You might want to stay attached at the hip for a while. I would hate to have to report your disappearance, especially to that green witch friend of yours."

Elise nodded. "Thank you, Abra." As if the news was no big deal.

The gypsy woman laughed, tossing her head. "I give her bad news, and she thanks me. Get out of my store. Don't come back till it calms down."

"You got it. Come on, Remy." Elise glanced up at him, her green eyes wide and worried, and he gave a brief nod to the Old One, who finally looked truly amused and far too satisfied.

He opened the door for Elise and followed her out, careful to scan the street again. Maybe he was being jumpy, but better jumpy than surprised.

Out on the pavement, she looked up at him for a long moment. Rain was flirting down, kissing the pavement in dime-sized, stinging drops. "Breakfast," she said, finally. "I'm hungry. And then we need to find Vann and Trevor. I've got a bad feeling about this."

Relief loosened his hands. He toyed with the thought of telling her he didn't need food, that the symbiote lived on pain and the violence of fighting the Dark. Decided she didn't need to hear it and nodded. His shoulders ached with the strain of keeping himself still. "Should we visit Theo's shop? Safety in numbers."

She still studied his face. He submitted to it, watching the thoughts move in her eyes like silent fish as she worried her lower lip with her pretty teeth. "Maybe." Her beautiful husky voice was a little shaky.

He took a half-step closer to her, wanting to slide his arms around her and provide some shelter from the stinging rain.

"I'm sorry," she said. "Abra wouldn't tell me to stick close to you unless she knew enough about Watchers to be sure of them. I guess maybe I *can* trust you."

That grudging admission made him feel almost charitable toward the Old One. "Let's get out of the rain," he said awkwardly. "Thank you, *cherie*."

She gave him a slightly worried smile that made his heart leap. "I guess I should be thanking you. I'm sorry. I haven't been very nice to you. I'll buy you breakfast."

"No need. I have money."

"Gods," she said, rolling her eyes and taking his arm as they started down the pavement again, "I meet a nice guy and he only wants to go dutch."

"You really think I'm a nice guy?" He sounded hopeful even to himself. *I'm not. But for you, I'd try to be—as long as it didn't interfere with fighting off the Dark.*

"Oh, yeah." As if it didn't matter at all. "Come on, let's hurry, it's starting to rain."

Sixteen

They had a quick breakfast at the Whistle Bar—eggs, pancakes, fruit, orange juice, and more coffee, eaten in a hurry in a red-vinyl back booth. Remy sat with his back to the wall and had a Denver omelet, hash browns, and green Tabasco. Elise approved. Green was the only way to eat Tabasco sauce. Neither of them spoke much. Elise was too hungry and she barely chewed, just bolted her food while glancing occasionally at the rest of the restaurant. It was a relief to feel hungry and to have the food want to stay down for once.

Remy seemed to be content just to make his food vanish, although he had good manners and didn't speak with his mouth full, like Mark used to.

Mark. Elise tried not to think about him. What would he have said about all this?

Assuming she could have told him, that is.

Remy actually paid for the meal while Elise was in the bathroom, and she found she wasn't angry about it. He'd just done it, that was all. She stepped out of the restaurant and stood under the red and white awning providing only a little shelter from the rain starting in earnest now, sheeting down from a bruised sky. *I should have brought a coat. I knew this was coming.*

She stood looking at the rain, Remy a warm bulk beside her. "I've got to get to the Liberty. I'm going to get soaked." Thunder boomed just as she finished speaking.

He slid a cautious arm over her shoulders. After the simmering heat of the past two weeks, the chill in the rain-soaked air was enough to make her shiver. "I'd give you my coat, but it's too long. Should I look for an umbrella, or hail a cab?"

I'm not that much of a wuss. "It's okay. I've walked in the rain before. I won't melt."

He looked down at her, and Elise wondered why she felt so comforted by the heat pouring out from him. The rain might even steam when it hit him, he was so warm. "I want you to be comfortable." He was looking at her that way again—the way Dante looked at Theo. As if she was the only thing in the world that mattered.

"Oh, I'll be all right." Her voice sounded high and breathless. "Really."

"You're shivering." He pulled her closer into his side. "Maybe we should go back to the shop?"

Elise was staring at his mouth. She wondered what it would feel like if she traced it gently with a fingertip, sliding along the bottom curve of his lower lip.

"Elise?" he asked, and she blinked.

I've got to stop mooning over this guy. He's nice, but he's one of them. A Watcher. He's dangerous.

"Um," she said. *You might want to stay attached at the hip for a while,* Abra had said with a wink. She was serious. She had been trying to tell Elise to trust Remy, that he was the safest bet in town right now. And if he had Abra's vote, that was good enough for Elise.

She could take Abra's word, but not Theo and Mari's?

Well, yes, because Abra didn't have a Watcher looming behind her with a gun. She was a free agent, and wouldn't give Elise advice, especially for free, if it wasn't true. It was a huge favor, conveyed in such a way that Elise didn't owe Abra anything...and yet owed her something big. Perfect, and perfectly done. Just like Abra.

"Elise?" he asked again. Lightning sizzled. Thunder boomed.

Gooseflesh rolled up Elise's spine. She shivered, and the medallion around her neck flashed. The rain outside the awning began to steam where it hit the pavement. Elise took a deep breath. *Calm. I've got to stay calm.*

The unmistakable cold shiver of a precognition shook her. Precog was mostly Mari's thing, but every witch had a healthy dose of it—and to Elise, it always felt like cold fingers skating up her back, pressing flabby waxen nails against her skin.

Danger, close at hand, teeth and claws. Something big. She didn't have many premonitions—but when she did, Elise knew something horrible was about to happen.

"Elise?" he asked, for the third time.

She came back to herself, her throat suddenly dry and her breakfast turning to a hard lump in her stomach. "We have to go. Now. There's something wrong."

He nodded and started forward into the rain. Since his arm was around her shoulders, she had to go too, shuddering as the water hit her bare arms. Heavy drops came down in sheets, thunder roiling in the air above. The precognition left almost as soon as it had hit her, and Elise shuddered as water dripped down the back of her neck and started to soak her clothes. *I'm going to look like a drowned rat.*

Remy stiffened slightly and cursed under his breath.

She almost had to shout over the sound of the rain. "What? What is it?"

"Don't know yet." He ducked his head slightly so she could hear him. Water ran through his hair, plastering it to his head. "Will you help me, Elise? Do as I ask, so I can protect you?"

Her heart pounded thinly. She nodded, noticing he had automatically shortened his stride to match hers. He seemed completely calm. "All right. You're calling the shots now."

"Good. All you have to worry about is staying close to me. All right?" His golden eyes were flat and serious. The high-powered radar the Watchers all seemed to have was still going off, making Elise feel as if little crackles of electricity were running over her skin, teasing. She nodded, her wet braid moving against her back. She was going to be soaked. The storm had officially broken, and it was raining as if someone should have been building an ark. There was nobody on the street.

Of course not. Anyone with any sense would have stayed inside, seeing this storm coming. What was I thinking?

The answer was, of course, that she *hadn't* been thinking. She'd been running on nerves and caffeine, too frightened to do anything but try and get away from the Watcher. She'd been hoping she could find a reason to ditch him, she realized.

Why does he scare me so much? It's not because he has guns, or because he's bigger than I am. So why?

She didn't want to think about it. But she had to, because she wasn't a coward.

She wanted to get away because the way he looked at her felt too good to be true. There it was, in all its unvarnished truth.

Elise choked back a half-hysterical laugh. *What a time for introspection, something nasty's on its way, and you have to moan about a guy who seems to like you? Oh, Elise, you take the cake.*

He walked her down the street that was quickly turning into a river, and Elise's braid began to drip water. She began to wish that she had done some weatherworking despite Suzanne's ironclad rule that the weather generally knew what it was doing better than a witch did, and that the best weatherwork was none at all. It would have been nice to have gotten the storm out of the way while she was sleeping last night instead of now, when she hadn't even taken a jacket because she was sure that the storm wouldn't break until she had made it to the Liberty.

Thinking about the Liberty made a sick feeling rise in Elise's stomach, disarranging her mutinous breakfast. The vision was so sudden and immediate she stumbled—the pawnshop empty, a cup of coffee spilled on the glass counter, dripping over the edge and soaking into the thin carpet. That was all. A spilled cup of coffee, an empty shop.

Vann.

No need to worry, he's fine, just upset over the gig last night and weirded out by a big guy in a leather trench coat.

The sick feeling rose again, and Remy stopped, half-turned, and pulled her into an alley that had just opened up to their right.

Normally Elise would have objected. An alley on Klondel Avenue was not a good place for a woman to end up. But then again, with a Watcher at her side, maybe even an alley on Klondel was a Sunday-school cakewalk, especially with this Watcher, with his golden eyes and smooth honeyed voice.

Elise, will you quit it? Something bad is going down.

The two buildings on either side cut the rain's force, but there was still an incredible amount of water coming down, and huge garbage bins hulked on either side. *Thank the gods it's raining so I can't smell it.* The sick feeling rose against her ribs. Their feet splashed through instant puddles, water soaking into her jeans. The vision—spilled coffee, an empty shop, the wet carpet with its rapidly spreading stain—blinked in front of her eyes again. Elise shuddered, and Remy practically lifted her off her feet and over a puddle.

Remy stopped, his hands curling around Elise's wet shoulders. He pushed her against the concrete wall between two gigantic Dumpsters. Then he pressed his body against hers, filling her nose with the smell of leather and rain and a clean male. A knife-hilt jabbed her shoulder, and she tried to move away from it. Remy's eyes closed, sweat stood out on his gold-touched skin. His hands flattened on the concrete on either side of her shoulders. His head dropped forward, his lips burning against her forehead. *Stay still,* his voice whispered in her ear. It was the same voice that had spoken so softly to her yesterday morning. *Very still and very quiet.*

The concrete was cold against her back, and he was scorching. She could almost see the Power spreading out from him, threading through the wall and turning into a reflective shield. Concealment.

I wonder if that's covered in the training. A lunatic giggle rose from some dark panicked place inside her. The danger riding through the storm pressed down on her like a heavy, cold blanket.

It is, he said, calmly. *Just wait a few moments, cherie. Then we'll be on our way.*

"I have to get to the Liberty," she whispered. "Something's wrong."

In a few moments. I promise.

Elise was shaking now. Was he actually talking inside her head? Wonders never ceased. "I have to go to the Liberty," she whispered helplessly. "Now. Please."

He waited just a breath, his skin now wet with sweat under the rain. *Wait until they pass or it will take longer because I'll have to fight. Just a moment,* cherie. *I promise.* His tone was utterly calm, utterly certain.

Elise bit her lower lip, worrying at it. She couldn't see the alley. Remy's body blocked it from sight, and his lips were still against her forehead. Like he needed the contact with her. Something very much like liquid fire seemed to spread through Elise's nerve endings from that soft touch against her skin. If she hadn't been so worried about Vann, and so sick with the premonition of disaster, she might have objected to him touching her like that, not to mention using her head like a radio receptor.

But it was kind of comforting, hearing him like that, she decided before the next wave of nausea hit her.

Thunder boomed, sounding like a gigantic cannon. Elise felt the concrete behind her vibrate slightly. The sense of danger peaked, making her gasp, and she shivered. Remy made a soft sound, part comfort, part effort, under the huge static-laden rumble of thunder.

Something slid over the alley—a shadow, darker than the storm light. Elise's heart fell. She let out a small wounded noise. It *hurt*, scraping against the borders of her consciousness like a knife scraping through paint. Remy was hiding her, she realized, keeping the glow she made from being seen by the thing skimming the rooftops. It was *black*, darker than midnight, and it exhaled cold deadliness untempered by anything human. Under its shadow, the world warped into something malignant and sterile.

Elise came back to herself, shivering while Remy kissed her forehead, stroked her bare shoulders with his thumbs. Just like Dante did with Theo sometimes, comforting, a tender touch. A spark snapped, two, and Elise found her hands were shaking so hard they looked like windblown leaves. "There," he said, quietly. "That wasn't so bad, was it? Let's go. We have to move *now*."

Panic beat with her pulse, a thin reedy rustle like bird's wings. "The Liberty. We have to go to the Liberty."

He nodded and blinked water out of his eyes. Rain slicked his hair to his forehead. "You seem to spend a distressing amount of time in pawnshops."

"I guess I'm just a cheap date," Elise shot back, and then clapped her hand over her mouth, horrified at herself. He had just spent a great deal of Power and effort hiding her from something nasty and huge with leathery wings like a gigantic cartoon bat.

"Me too. Two Coronas and a game of chess, and I'm a happy man. Come on." He pulled her away from the wall, and Elise was suddenly very aware of the cool air brushing her skin where he had been pressed against her. The rain still poured down, slicking his hair down and running off his black coat.

"You know how to play chess?" she asked, as he slid his arm over her shoulders again and hurried her toward the alley's entrance.

"I taught myself in jail. I was in solitary. I don't play well with others, it seems." His tone was cool and sarcastic, but she could tell the sarcasm wasn't directed at her. It just *was*.

"What were you in jail for?" They reached the mouth of the alley and he scanned the street. His mouth turned down at the corners. If she hadn't been watching his face so closely, she wouldn't have seen it.

"Murder. Weren't you listening?" He glanced down at her, his golden eyes suddenly dark.

"Oh." Elise looked at the empty street. Anyone with any sense was inside out of the rain, and here she was, standing in the middle of a thunderstorm with a Watcher. Who had just admitted to being in the slammer for murder. *I might as well ask.* "Who did you kill?"

"The man who was beating my mother." He made no move to leave the alley just yet. "I can understand if that frightens you, Elise. I just—"

"He was hurting your mother?" she interrupted, looking up into his face. A muscle twitched in his jaw. She watched, fascinated. He looked more dangerous than he ever had. There was something dark in his eyes and sliding over his skin, a cloak of venomous red Power.

"She died."

Elise shook her head. *Okay. I asked for that. Gods. No wonder he's so grim.* "We've got to get to the Liberty. I'm glad you run so warm. I think the heat wave's broken."

"Maybe only for today. Elise—"

She knew what he was going to ask, and held her free hand up. "No, it's okay. I shouldn't have asked. If Abra tells me to stick to you, I'm going to stick to you. I don't care what you did before you met me."

That had entirely the wrong sound to it, Elise realized. She sounded possessive. As a matter of fact, she sounded like Theo talking to Dante. Calm and controlled, as if she'd known him all her life. She shook her head, her sodden braid bumping against her back. The feeling of sick urgency returned, making her stomach flip. "We have to get to the Liberty. If you don't mind." *Jeez. What does it say about me that I don't care if he was in prison, I'm just glad he was here five minutes ago when that thing went overhead?*

He stepped out onto the sidewalk, his eyes slipping in controlled arcs over the street. She hurried along beside him. The sick premonition of doom beat in time with her speeding pulse.

It's just a spilled coffee cup. And I think I can handle a spill.

But where was Vann? And why was the entire store empty?

Elise shook her head and sped up. She hitched her purse up on her shoulder and broke into a run, and Remy was right beside her. He had let go of her shoulders so she could run, and he stayed at her side as she pounded down the drenched and swimming sidewalk. The vision meant something awful, she was sure, but try as she might, Elise couldn't figure out *what.*

Seventeen

It was no surprise to Remy, especially after the amount of Dark activity on the streets, and he supposed he should not have allowed her to hope.

"Oh, no," Elise said. Her eyes were huge and dark.

Liberty Loans stood under the drenching rain, thunder rattling in the sky. The glass door had been shattered, and crumbled beads of the safety glass lay across the store's entry. Flickering fluorescent light shone down on thin carpet and racks of leather jackets, electronics, and musical instruments. Remy's eyes covered the entire place in one sweep, taking in the spilled cup of coffee. It hadn't even finished dripping onto the floor from the counter where the register sat. Steam rose in the air. The sharp smell of the Dark grated against his skin. He would have to get her out of here soon. The contamination in the air might make her Darksick. If that happened, he had the idea things would get even more tangled than they already were.

"Is there a back room where he could be hiding?" Remy asked, though he already knew. There was nothing living in this shop or the basement below. Nothing living could hide from Remy's Dark-enhanced senses. There was only deadly silence.

Elise's fingers pressed against her lips, and she was pale. He had cautiously swept the place once, at gunpoint, sheltering her behind his body. He should have tried harder to have her go back to the occult shop with the other Lightbringers. Out here in the open, she was in danger.

Terrible danger. His back prickled and his skin crawled with the thought of it. He should never have allowed her to do this.

Then again, *allowing* Elise to do something was like *allowing* a tsunami to go whichever way it wanted to go.

"Where's Vann?" She looked up at him as if he knew.

Should I lie to her? I can't. "The Brotherhood probably has him, Elise. And if they do, he's as good as dead." Remy slid the gun back into its holster. He didn't like this. She was far too vulnerable here. He could protect her in close quarters, and if there was a safe place for her to stay while he cleared the street he could do even more. But here in this pathetic little shop, he wasn't so sure. She was too used to being alone. He couldn't count on her obeying him in the middle of a fight, despite her promise. And he didn't want her to see the ruthlessness he would have to use, with the amount of Dark loose in the city. The Old One was right. Mercenaries would be pouring into the city and the Guardians were far too new and inexperienced to stem the tide. And there were only three Watchers, one of them on his first witch.

This had all the ingredients of an awful mess in the making. Plus a Talisman and a stubborn, far-too-powerful Lightbringer, and only one Watcher to take care of them both.

"Why would anyone kidnap him—oh." Elise blinked. Water dripped from her braid and jeweled her pale face, making the sodden T-shirt cling to her skin. He had to tear his eyes away from *that*. It was dangerous to his focus. "Because of me." Her tone was flat, not ironic or angry, simply quiet with the utter calm of a disaster victim.

Remy felt his heart twist inside his chest. Guilt, the Lightbringer's worst vulnerability. "I think we should leave here, *cherie*. I don't think it's safe." He deliberately pitched his voice low, soothing, the voice he would use on a feral cat or a fear-crazed horse. If her shock turned to anger, he was the most likely target.

Her eyes were wide, dark, and stunned. "Remy." She licked her lips, looking around the pawnshop. She was numb with shock.

He took her wrist carefully and pulled her out of the brooding little building. Even the spike of barbed-wire pleasure touching her caused didn't make him feel better. He sent a flush of warmth along her skin. If he wasn't careful, she'd go further into shock and hurt herself. "I'll do what I can, Elise," he promised, without knowing quite what he was saying, only that the stunned look on her face ripped at his insides. She should never have to see this, never have to face this.

"But... *Vann*. And Trevor, what about Trevor?" She didn't argue when he put his arm over her shoulders again and ushered her out into the rain. The thunder was loud and almost constant now. He shouldn't have allowed this. He should have cajoled her into staying home, or thought of a good reason to go to the occult shop. At least there, she would have the benefit of defenses—both witch and Watcher shields.

He was about to suggest they find a cab when lightning scorched through the clouds. The resultant blast of light showed him a dark shape, slinking into an alley two blocks ahead on the street. Brotherhood operatives. There was a team up the street—he saw it as clearly as he could remember the first chess set he had ever owned. His brain clicked over to automatic, coldly calculating angles and possible cover, different scenarios. "Elise, is there another way to the occult shop?"

"We could cut up Fourth to the Ave and hike over." Her tone was strangely distant. She stumbled, her wet sneakers catching on uneven pavement. He picked her up by her shoulders and set her on her feet. The water foamed around his toes, splashing up to darken her jeans almost to the knees.

"Calm, *cherie. Tranquille.* You're safe, and I'm gong to make sure you *stay* safe. Come on, not far now."

But it was too far, and he could feel it. Coming here had been a mistake. The Brotherhood was watching the pawnshop, and the field operatives were moving into position. Of course they would have identified her band members. It would have been ridiculously easy. And taking them would be a sure way to catch her if she was alone, without a Watcher. She would have gone blindly into whatever net they prepared, to save her friends. They were almost certainly dead by now, bait in a trap they would never leave alive.

There was a car coming down the street, a green Subaru. Water sheeted up from its tires. Remy's hand closed around a gun. He pushed Elise to his other side and sent a thin tendril of consciousness toward the car, checking—and meeting something very much like a wall of dark crimson fire. Another Watcher.

Remy let out a long sigh of relief.

Dante brought the car to a stop, and the automatic door-locks chucked loose. Remy opened the back passenger door and guided Elise in. Rain drummed on the car's roof, each heavy drop sending up another shower of little drops.

Theo turned around from the front passenger seat. "Hi, guys. Let's go to my house, shall we? Mari's worried sick about you, Elise. Remy, nice to see you again." Her dark-green eyes, lit from within, seemed to go right through Remy's flesh. "What is it? What's wrong? It took some doing, tracking you two here."

"No," Elise said, as Remy slid into the seat right next to her, glad to be out of the stinging rain. Her hand reached for the door release, but the locks thunked down.

Remy reached over and grabbed her wrist. The touch sent

another spike of frustrated pleasure through him, and his jaw set. The Darkness in him turned over, ground against his bones, and subsided. "No, *cherie*. It's best. Truly. Trust me."

She pulled away from him. "No. Vann—*Trevor*—"

"They're already dead. We have to make sure you won't join them." He said it gently, inexorably.

"No." She shook her head. Tears started to well up in her beautiful eyes, and he cursed himself. How could he not have thought that her friends would be targets?

Her friends are not my problem, the cold rational part of him said. *Elise is my problem, and she's whole and mostly well.* The sick rotating feeling in his stomach was pure relief, he realized. The mistake he'd made had not cost her life.

"Honor, brother. Risky to come here." Dante kept his eyes on the road. The shielding laid on the vehicle shimmered at the corner of Remy's vision, and Remy slicked his hair back with stiff fingers. His other hand held Elise's wrist, and he sent another tingle of warmth through her to dispel the shock. The Brotherhood wouldn't strike at a car that held two Watchers. It would only make the Watchers angry and possibly damage the merchandise.

"Duty, brother. She required it of me," Remy said, formally. "All the same, it's good to see you, Dante."

The Watcher's black eyes shifted up and met Remy's in the rearview mirror. "Yeah, they have a way of turning things upside-down. How is she?"

"Elise?" Theo wriggled out of her seat belt and turned around in the seat. She leaned over into the backseat. Elise was still trying, fruitlessly, to twist her wrist free of Remy's gentle, iron-hard grasp. "Elise? Lise, talk to me. Are you all right?"

"I am *not* all right." Elise's small, wounded voice cut right through Remy's chest. "I am very far from all-bloody-right. We have to get them back. Remy, we *have* to get them back."

"Shhh." His fingers gentled, trying to make sure he wouldn't bruise her wrist. "*Tranquille, cherie.* Nothing can be done. I am so very sorry."

"Trevor and Vann," Theo said. "They've been taken by the Brotherhood."

"How do you know?" Elise's tear-filled eyes swung up to meet Theo's.

The green witch drew in a deep breath, as if uncertain.

She gave Remy a sharp look, and obviously decided against questioning him.

"We received a...message this morning," Theo said, as gently as she could. Dante made a low growling sound. "A letter. It was addressed to you, but Mari had one of her flashes and opened it. It said they had Vann and Trevor, and unless you came down to the docks alone, the Brotherhood would kill both of them. Then it burst into flame. Very dramatic."

"And you didn't *call* me, tell me?" Elise gasped. Her pale cheeks began to bloom with color. Fever-spots, high up on each cheekbone.

"I tried your house, but you were already gone. We were waiting for you to come to the shop, and I kept trying to call the Liberty. No answer."

"But they open early on Saturdays." Elise was far too pale, and trembling. "Charlie opens...Oh, my gods..."

"It's probably a good thing we didn't go into the basement," Remy said grimly. "I *hate* the Brotherhood."

"Profit-mongering psychopaths," Dante agreed. "Elise, he's right. Your friends are dead."

"We can't just sit here and do nothing! You have to—I mean, *we* have to—what else are you *good* for?" The windows were steaming up, and a thin trail of vapor came up from Elise's hair.

Dante turned the defroster on maximum and twisted the knob over to "cool." "Theo?" he said, the question clear in his tone.

The green witch tried to calm her down. "Elise, listen to me. Just hang on until we get to my house. Mari will meet us there. Please, just hang on, and we'll talk this out."

"*I don't want to talk!*" Elise screamed. The air inside the car flushed with heat, and Dante rolled his window down. He braked for a stop sign and rolled slowly through the intersection, water spraying up from the tires. The wipers were going as fast as they could, but the windshield was still sheeted with water.

Remy grabbed Elise's other wrist and dragged her across the seat and into his arms. "Shhh." His lips moved against her temple. Her skin was fever-hot, a scarlet haze of pleasure bolting down his body from her touch. The Trifero glittered against her pale throat. "Elise, Elise, *cherie, petite,* trust me. We will find a way. I promise. You might cause a car accident if you keep making the windows steam up, hmmm? We will find something to do, Elise. Just trust me, I promise, but for right now, *tranquille*, shhh, hush..." It was the only thing he could think of.

She made a low, terrible sound, a moan of absolute grief. Remy cursed himself. Why hadn't he thought of this? He *should* have thought of this. After all, if he was the Brotherhood team responsible for capturing her, it was what *he* would do, exert every leverage he could find on her. It was cheaper if she came in by herself, and it didn't require fighting through a Watcher.

Especially a Watcher that the Brotherhood had fought before—and lost to each time. *This is going to wreak havoc on my reputation if it ever gets out. It's not like me to make such a junior mistake.*

She shook against him, and he realized she was shaking as she wept, with a combination of rage and agonizing sadness. The green witch—Theo—reached out to touch her and pulled her hand back, uncertainty printed on her pretty face. Remy shook his head slightly, and Theo's eyes met his.

The green witch measured him for a long moment, then looked down at Elise, who was actually—*miracles do happen,* Remy thought with blind wonder—sobbing with her face buried against his wet, leather-clad shoulder. He kept talking, murmuring soothing sounds, unsure of why it seemed to be working but glad all the same. He stroked her hair gently, rewarded with fresh sobs. She cried as if her heart had broken.

It probably has. It's not every day that you find out your friends have been kidnapped because you're a weapon in the right hands. If I was a Lightbringer, I'd be crying too.

It was much warmer in the car, the air steaming as it billowed out Dante's window. Remy's hair was starting to dry. It was a little uncomfortable. *She has no idea of the kind of Power she possesses.*

That was a frightening prospect. She had the Trifero, and too much Power. One mistake could have horrible consequences; the Brotherhood could catch her and damage her before Remy could reach her, or she could lose control and—

He stopped *that* line of thought in a hurry. He wouldn't screw this up again, he promised himself, continuing to make soothing noises and stroking her back, touching her hair.

What else are you good for? she had asked.

What else indeed. He just made one mistake after another. *She needs a real Watcher, not just a glorified garbage man. I'm trained for this, but I keep making stupid mistakes and it will get us both killed.* The thought of making another mistake made ice roll down his spine. He had sworn not to fail her, and he already had.

"It's not fair!" Elise said against his shoulder. He kept stroking her hair. "It's not fair! It's not fair, it's not fair, it's not *fair!*"

"You're right." His fingers never paused in their even rhythm. "It's not. You're right. The innocents shouldn't suffer. You're right."

She sat up, pushing him violently away. Dante made a left turn, slowing down even more. The volume of water coming from the sky was incredible. Lightning flashed, and Theo watched them both, her mouth pulled tight in a grimace of pain.

"You *bastard.* This is the part where you tell me everything will be all right if I just agree to let Circle Lightfall into the city, right?" Stray strands of Elise's red-gold hair slipped free of her braid, her eyes lit with fury. Fever-spots bloomed bright and unhealthy on her cheeks. Her lips were pale, her hands shaking, and even now, soaked and shivering with rage, she was still the most beautiful thing Remy had ever seen. His very blood recognized her, spoke inside him, swearing to her; his bones sang her name.

"No," he said, because it was true. "This is the part where I say I'm sorry, because I screwed up. I should have thought that the Brotherhood would try this. I should have *guessed.* I'm sorry, Elise. Less than twenty-four hours, and already I've screwed this up. You deserve a better Watcher."

Theo's jaw dropped. So did Elise's.

Remy couldn't quite see the rest of Dante's face in the rearview mirror, but he saw the lines around Dante's black eyes change. Dante was smiling slightly.

The fever-spots on Elise's cheeks faded slowly as she stared at him. "You…" she said, and licked her lips nervously. "Aren't you going to tell me to let Circle Lightfall in?"

It managed to annoy him for only half a second. "Of course not. I'm just saying I should have guessed. I'm guilty, Elise.

I'm sorry. Punish me however you like, as long as you don't send me away." *I can take anything you dish out, just don't send me away.*

Then he shut his mouth with a snap. He'd said enough. Too much, probably. He would be lucky if she didn't order him back to Circle Lightfall in disgrace. He'd spend the rest of his life—what was left of it—shunned by the other Watchers as a failure before he died. Death would be a relief if she sent him away.

Always assuming, of course, that he would have the strength to actually go back instead of breaking his vow of obedience. He strongly suspected he wouldn't. The thought of leaving her, even in a better Watcher's care, was enough to make his head pound with pain and his hands shake.

If you try to send me back, Elise, I swear by every god there is the other Watchers are going to have to hunt me down. Because I won't do it, obedience be damned. If I'm no good as a Watcher I might as well die anyway. As long as I can die between you and the Dark, I don't care.

Elise stared at him, her cheeks now pale as flour. Her braid had come free, and her hair unwound over her shoulders, bright coppery strands drying under the heat of her anger and sadness.

"Remy." It was just a breath of sound, her lips shaping the word, and he was shaken again with that desire to yank her across the space separating them and kiss her. Hard. Until he drowned in her.

This isn't what they told me it would be. This could tear me apart worse than the tanak *ever did.*

He bowed his head, staring at his knees, and waited for whatever came next.

Eighteen

Elise was still staring at Remy, speechless, when Dante pulled into Theo's driveway and Theo pushed the button that opened the garage door. Dante eased the car in out of the rain, and the cessation of noise against the car's roof was shocking. Thunder roiled and muttered.

"This is a bad storm," Theo said. Dante cut the ignition, and the car shut off, its cooling engine ticking.

Theo hit the button again, and the garage door started to close. Dante opened his door and stepped out into Theo's pin-neat garage. Dante's punching bag hung among the bunches of herbs drying on racks for Theo's shop and her patients, and there was a CD player and a pair of sparring gloves set on a new shelf near the bag.

Theo turned again, looking back over the seat. She appeared to want to say something, but she merely shook her head as Dante opened her door. Then she slid out of the car gracefully, taking Dante's hand. The car door slammed shut.

Remy stared down at his knees, his golden eyes burning. He sat there quietly, waiting, with his scarred and callused hands palm-up, resting helplessly. The sight of such a tall, obviously dangerous man waiting quietly to be punished—and that was the word he had used, *punished*—abruptly made Elise feel petty and childish.

It wasn't his fault Vann and Trevor had been kidnapped. It was *hers*. She'd thought she would be safe, that she could have some kind of normal life. She should have taken some precautions with the band, should have known that her freakish Powers would bleed over and destroy any semblance of normality in her life.

Silly Elise, wanting to be a rock star, thinking she could be an *artist*. Theo could heal, and Mari could tell the future, both useful skills. Elise could only set things on fire. Great for birthday parties—useless for the real world.

"It's not your fault." She gulped back tears. Now that she'd started to cry, would she ever stop? They kept sliding down her cheeks, hot and shameful. She never cried. *Never*. At least, not like this, with an awful, wrenching sobbing shaking out from the very core of her body. And he had held her the entire time, talking to her, without trying to use it against her.

He deserved so much better than Elise Nicholson, all-around bitch and nasty girl. She swallowed a fresh round of tears and wanted to scream at the sheer *unfairness* of it. "It's not your fault. It's mine. I'm such a freak that all I can do is destroy things. It's not your fault."

He looked up at her, his hair drying a little, lightening into the familiar gold, springing back up. His eyes were startled now, and dark with something she didn't want to name. Of course—he was going to see that she was only a freak, just a selfish little freak. She'd flamed all over Theo and Mari, and drawn danger to her bandmates, and almost gotten Remy killed, just by being near him.

She had to make him go before her freakish talents killed him too.

Elise took a deep breath, steadying herself. "It's okay." She reached blindly for the door handle. "It's all right. You don't have to go back. You're free. Don't you get it? You're *free!* You can go wherever you want. You don't have to hang around me *or* go back to Circle Lightfall. You're free. Go wherever you want."

Thankfully, her fingers blundered onto the door handle. She yanked on it, wanting to scramble out of the car and run—but where? Where would she go?

There was only one place left to go, one thing left to do. To fix the mess she'd made of things.

His hand closed over her wrist again, but gently. "Elise." His accent stretched the word until it was a brush against her skin. "You are not at fault for the Dark. You didn't make the Dark, did you?"

She shook her head, choking on the helpless tears. He didn't understand, and it was probably just as well.

"I understand enough." He pulled on her arm, and she let him, because the tearing pain was threatening to rip her into pieces. Elise Nicholson, tough and competent girl wonder, was now experiencing major meltdown. "I understand more than you guess, *cherie.*"

"Quit r-r-reading my m-m-mind," she said, then had to stop, because she was sobbing too harshly to speak.

He slid his arms around her again, pulling her against his chest. He threaded his fingers into her hair, his other hand flattening against her back. The thin cotton of her T-shirt didn't stop the heat of his hands from scorching through. He held her, in the backseat of Theo's car, while she sobbed without restraint, and he murmured to her again, little soothing noises, comforting.

It was as if every tear she had ever resisted, ever shoved down into a little black hole inside herself, every sob, every grief, every enraged scream she had ever swallowed and set her jaw against, was coming back to haunt her. She had a brief vision of herself dissolving in a river of tears, washing Theo's car in a tide of salt.

Remy kissed her forehead, her temple, her cheek, tilting her head back with his fingers cupping the back of her neck, sliding under her hair. And then, wonder of wonders, his mouth descended on hers.

Elise tasted salt and gunpowder, and the strange flavor of someone else's breath. He kissed her as if he wanted to drown in her, as if he wanted to pull her in through his skin and carry her around with him, as if he wanted to do more than kiss her but had to settle for her mouth. Just on the edge of pain, skating the precipice before the fall.

She pulled back, and he let her, his forehead resting against hers. She gasped for breath, stunned by the feel of his skin on hers. But he didn't let go of her. In fact, he held her against him so hard she could barely breathe.

"Shhh," he said, his nose inches from hers, and kissed her again, gently, a chaste kiss against closed lips that still managed to feel feverishly intense. *"Tranquille, cherie."*

She drew in a shuddering breath and closed her eyes. *Just for a second. I'll rest for just a second, and then I'll do what I have to do. Just for a second.*

He held her for a long time while thunder played outside Theo's garage. The car began to cool off, water steaming gently off the hood and roof, the thunderous cascade of the rain outside making a muted song that was actually kind of soothing.

Finally, his voice rumbled in the stillness inside Theo's garage. "When I was young, I used to take a boat out into the bayou. There would be storms like this sometimes. I used to think that it was heaven weeping, just what a good little Catholic boy should think. But in the mornings, I used to tie the boat up on an island and climb an old tree. It was my safe spot, and the snakes didn't bother me much. I liked the snakes more than I liked people, to tell the truth."

He took a breath she felt in her own ribs, maybe because she was molded against him in the backseat, her skin blurring against his. "I used to lie there and dream about the girl I was going to marry. I swore to myself I would never do what my mama's boyfriends did to her. I would find a nice, pretty girl, and I would take care of her. Get a good job at the airstrip or the mill, and when I came home at the end of the day, she'd be there waiting."

He paused and took another deep breath. "My mama had awful taste in men. I still don't know which one of her boyfriends was my father. She liked men who loved fast cars and whiskey. The trouble is, men who love fast cars and whiskey are usually mean. She was dating this one man—Jean-Pierre Rocque—and I came back from the bayou with a hopper full of catfish to find him standing over her with blood on his fists and moonshine on his breath...and I saw red. It wasn't the first time, but all I thought was, it would be the *last.*"

Elise half lay against him, his forehead resting on hers. The tears were slowing down, and she could breathe, inhaling great shuddering breaths. She could almost see the hot green of his memories, feel the rage he told her about, so close to her own inarticulate fury it frightened her. Her heart threatened to break for him, and she drew in a deep shaking breath and closed her eyes. The ever-present scorching rise of flame died down under her skin.

He made the fire retreat, made it go away. Made her feel safe.

He continued, his words evenly spaced and calm, though she could feel the horror of his memories sliding under the surface of her own mind. "Unfortunately, our family was poor, and my mama died in the hospital. I caught a handful of bad luck, a prosecutor who needed a slam-dunk and a defense attorney with a serious case of apathy. Happens all the time. So I went to jail, twenty to life. And that nice little Catholic boy turned into a jail cat. I didn't pick a pod to run with, so I had to fight every day to survive. They kept coming, so I kept fighting. I got put in solitary so many times I think I almost forgot how to talk."

His voice was even. Measured, warm. As if he was telling her about someone else. "When the witch came, I was in bad shape. I was an animal. But I was lucky—I had the things Circle Lightfall looks for—some psychic ability, a certain amount of ruthlessness, and a great deal of stubborn endurance. I'm sure there were other things, but that's all I know about. They offered me a chance—*she* offered me a chance. But the funny thing was, the only thing I could think of was that this was my chance to find that girl, the one I dreamed about when I was still a good little Catholic boy. I could do it; make my life into something worthwhile. Redeem myself."

Elise took another deep breath. "How awful." Her voice was husky, and broke on the words. How had she ever thought *she* had it bad? He'd lived through something she could barely imagine, and now here he was, quiet and endlessly patient with her.

I don't deserve him.

"Yeah, it was awful," he murmured. "You're the only chance I've *got*, Elise. I won't go back to being a felon in a dead-end cage if I fail at being a Watcher. I'll die first."

That made her feel like crying again. If she hadn't sobbed herself out she would have probably started to. "I never cry," she said, mournfully. "Gods, how could everything turn into such a mess?"

He didn't answer the question, which was probably just as well. "I should have seen this. I'm sorry, Elise."

You're sorry, I'm sorry, everyone's sorry. The whole world's sorry, goddammit. "I've got to go and get them back. I *have* to. Will you help me?"

It took more courage than she thought she had to ask.

He sighed. "It would be suicide. It's a trap, *cherie*. Make their sacrifice worthwhile, by staying alive. Don't waste their lives by walking straight back into the trap."

"They could still be alive," she said, and he shook his head and then kissed her cheek. His mouth met hers again, as if he couldn't help himself, and Elise had to admit he was pretty good.

Pretty good? Hell, he kissed like a lightning bolt. She wondered where he'd picked *that* up; she was pretty sure it wasn't a Circle Lightfall class.

Why couldn't I have met you before all this? she thought, before she remembered he could hear her. Sometimes.

She broke free, her heart hammering as if it wanted to slam out through her ribs to get to him. *Go figure. I meet the one guy I really like, and he's a Watcher. Suzanne's laughing at me somewhere, I can just tell.*

"They aren't still alive. I know, *cherie*. I've dealt with the Brotherhood before."

Her breath caught, her pulse slowing. "I should...I think we should go inside. It's starting to get cold out here."

I know what I have to do. She wondered if she could keep the thought to herself. If he could hear her through a whole city full of people before she'd even met him, what were the chances he couldn't hear what she was considering now?

"I know what you're thinking," he said, not moving. "No, Elise. I won't let you risk yourself."

Let me? Oh, buddy, was that ever the wrong thing to say. "Isn't it my decision?" She pushed at his chest, ineffectually. "Damn you, let *go* of me."

"The only time a Watcher is allowed to disobey a Lightbringer is when the Lightbringer is determined to risk his or her safety," he quoted, chapter and verse. Just like Dante or Hanson. His voice was still soft and reflective, as if he was thinking out loud. "If I let you go and get yourself taken by the Brotherhood, mindwiped and set up as a weapon, what would that be? *Failure.* I would be failing you if I let that happen."

"They're my *friends*," she said, stubbornly. "And it's *my* fault. And if you go with me, and look out for me, we can rescue them and be back in—"

"No, Elise," he interrupted. "I couldn't protect you there. Are you *crazy?* A Brotherhood trap that they've had God-only-knows how long to set up? What kind of Watcher would I be if I took you there?"

The only kind of Watcher I'd like, cowboy. Goddammit. "I want to go inside and warm up. If you won't help me, I'll do it myself. I took care of myself before you ever came along."

And besides, they'll hurt you, so I can't have you go with me anyway. I don't think I could stand it if you got hurt, Remy. Go figure.

"Elise." Maddeningly patient, as if she were an idiot. "The Dark is out there, and it is waiting for you. You'll be eaten alive. Death would be a mercy compared to some of the things the Dark could do to you. And the Brotherhood is betting on you being silly and stupid enough to go running into the middle of their trap. Do you want to give them the satisfaction?"

She tried to summon the old, familiar rage. Who the hell did he think he was talking to, anyway? It didn't work. The anger was gone. Somehow the crying jag had extinguished it. No more anger, for the first time in her memory.

The Talisman laid against her throat, a lump of warmth. It felt comforting, and she stopped trying to pull away from him. He watched her, cautiously, as the sound of rain filtered down into the car.

Then it happened. A touch, a hot soulless brush against her mind.

help me and I'll help you.

Maybe she just had to be exhausted enough for the Trifero to get a word in edgewise. It was an old, lipless voice, a thread of dark fire in the middle of her mind. Elise jerked in surprise and looked up at Remy, her eyes widening. *What the hell?*

"What is it? Elise?" And that high-powered radar started quivering over her skin. He was scanning for danger, even here.

No place was ever going to be safe. Because she was a freak.

"Nothing," she mumbled, as the Talisman began to speak to her again. A concentrated bullet of information flashed into her head—it had just been waiting, biding its time. It had been hopping from hand to hand, moving through the world blindly in the way of Talismans, working toward her. Because for much longer than Elise had been alive, it had been waiting for her.

Waiting for a fire witch with the Power to use it, waiting for a witch that could truly unlock its potential. It had moved from hand to hand, two thousand miles to end up on the pawnshop counter, waiting for her eyes to fall upon it.

Remy's eyes narrowed. He examined her. "Elise?"

"Get me inside." She straightened, dropping her eyes so he wouldn't be able to read them. She suspected he was better at reading her than he wanted her to know. "I'm tired, and I need coffee if I'm going to deal with this."

He nodded slowly, his golden eyes shuttered and dark.

i know how to help you, the Talisman whispered. **i am the Trifero, the stone of Destruction. i can help you, if you give me what i want.**

What is it you want? Her fingers stole up to touch the Talisman's hard, pulsing warmth at her throat. It felt alive against her fingers, warm and pulsing like a quick alien heartbeat.

just your love, witch. to be used, used as I was made to be used. It was a ribbon of fire, the fire that had lived under her skin all her life, just waiting to be called out.

Just waiting to be *used*.

All this time, she thought, wonderingly, as Remy examined what he could see of her face. Which couldn't be much, she was looking down, thankful that her hair was free so she could hide her expression. *All this time I thought it was Theo who was the most powerful.*

But I have this thing now, don't I? This chance to make it all right.

If she had the Trifero, she could protect them all. Theo, Mari, Vann, Trevor—she could fry anyone who hurt her friends. The Talisman itself could teach her how to use it, and she could untangle this whole awful mess.

She could even protect Remy. Relief made her boneless, and she slumped against the door, hoping he couldn't read her mind. His hand was warm on her wrist, gentle. It felt too good.

Finally, Remy let go of her, one finger at a time. She squirmed away from him, away from the heat of his body and the burning memory of his mouth on hers. He let her, but his eyes followed every move she made. "I'm sorry, Elise. I should have thought of this. I should have known."

Elise dredged up a smile. It was a bright, sunny smile, her lips peeling back from her teeth, and he actually flinched as he met her eyes. "It's okay, Remy. It's not your fault. It really isn't. It's mine. I'm a freak. I've always been a freak. I should have known better."

"Elise—" he began.

She fumbled for the door handle again. "Coffee. Get me some coffee. And keep Theo and Mari off me, okay?"

He nodded, his fair hair falling forward over his golden eyes. "Why? They're worried about you."

"Didn't you just tell me you're supposed to *obey* me?" Elise flinched away from his hand as he reached for her again.

His hand stopped in midair. The flash of hurt on his face before he schooled his expression twisted Elise's heart. The doors behind his eyes slammed shut. He nodded. "All right, then, *m'selle.*" His hand dropped. "I'll be a good little boy and obey. Thank you."

What the hell is he thanking me for? Elise opened the car door. The windows were opaque with condensation. How long had she been in the car playing tonsil-hockey with him?

Way to save the world, Elise. Can't you do anything right?

"Elise?" he said. "I mean it. Thank you."

"For what?" She heard the irritation in her voice, hating it. *How can you be so cruel, Elise?*

I have to be cruel. They'll try to stop me, or come with me. I can't let them do that. I have to fix this on my own. It's my mess. Clean up your own mess for once, Elise.

"For not sending me away," he said.

"I haven't made up my mind yet." She wriggled out of the car. Her entire body ached from the adrenaline, running in the rain, being closed in a car with him—for how long? How long had she let him kiss her? "Don't get too comfortable."

I could really make him hate me. Her heart threatened to tear itself out of her chest. It hurt to think that a sharp word from her would cause him pain. He was rapidly turning into one of the few people she didn't want to hurt.

He exited the car on his side and looked over the roof at her. "I won't get comfortable at all, then."

"Good." Elise stalked past the car and up the single concrete step into Theo's house. The Trifero whispered inside her head, cajoling, tempting. How had she never heard it before? She knew what to do now, and how to do it. If she had the courage, she could do it.

I have the courage, for a little while at least. Now let's see if I have the brains.

Nineteen

The green witch and the water witch both came running for Elise, but Remy stepped around her, holding up his hands as their bright auras made the pain start in his bones, the *tanak* flinching away from the light. "Please. She doesn't want to be touched."

Theo stopped, her skirt swirling around her knees. The blond witch stopped too, and the look of baffled pain that crossed her face would have worried Remy if he hadn't been following orders.

Don't get too comfortable, Elise's voice whispered. Where had he gone wrong? One moment she had been in his arms, soft and willing, and the next she had pulled away, her eyes blazing, her mouth setting itself in a grim line. What had he done?

Story of my life, I'm not even sure where I screwed everything up. Wonderful.

The green witch's home was full of books and plants, clean and pretty and smelling of cedarwood incense. The kitchen was spotless, decorated in green and yellow, and something that smelled like chicken soup was simmering on the stove. Coffee was brewing, of course. They would know Elise, and know what she wanted. The green witch wore a long dress of deep-green silk, but she looked less calm than Remy remembered.

"She doesn't want to be touched?" Dante's eyebrows rose. Remy made a slight movement, hands spreading, expressing resignation. *I'm just the Watcher, don't ask me.*

The blond witch—Mari—peered around him. "Elise, what's going on?"

A slight sound of motion told him Elise had folded her arms. Her tone was cool and even, and terribly sad. "Theo, can I use your guest room? I'm tired, and I've had a *really* bad day. Now he's telling me I just have to leave Vann and Trevor to be eaten alive or something by a bunch of two-legged elephants. I've had it. And *this* joker—" She poked Remy between his shoulder blades, not hard enough to hurt, but hard enough that he felt it like a knife to the heart. "—won't even go with me to get them. Says it's crazy. Says he's supposed to obey me—but not this time. Well, that's enough. I want to go to bed for a week and forget about all this. And when I get up, I don't want to do this anymore."

"What are you talking about?" Mari's big blue eyes were fastened on Remy instead of Elise, and he shrugged helplessly.

"I want out," Elise answered, low and furious. But the air in the room didn't stir. "I don't want to be a Guardian anymore, and I don't want to be involved with Circle Lightfall any more than I already am. I don't want a Watcher. But I'm stuck with all this. The least you guys could do is give me a little time to rest."

What did I do wrong? Remy wondered. She was blocking him, closing him away from her with a surprising new strength and efficiency. And the Trifero...Did it feel more alive now? Had it moved against her throat? He couldn't be sure, replaying the scene in the car in his head. He'd been too damn distracted.

"Elise," Theo said quietly, with a patently *I-am-so-patient* tone, "you don't mean this. I'm sorry. I would send Dante to rescue your friends, but these are ruthless people we are dealing with. Dante wouldn't lie to me about this."

"I'd go myself," Mari said softly, "but it would just get someone else killed—me, or Hanson, or both of us. Elise, I'm sorry, I'm so sorry."

Remy's witch was unimpressed. "Save it for the funny papers. I asked to go lie down, not for a goddamn sermon."

There was a long hurt silence. The water witch brushed back her blond curls and looked at Theo. Dante straightened from leaning over a low table full of scattered papers. "You should be more careful with your tongue, Elise." His tone was excessively mild.

Remy looked at him. "We should stay out of this." His eyes held the other Watcher's black gaze. The air creaked with tension.

Hanson appeared from what Remy guessed was a living room, dusting off his hands. "I've got the fire going. Took a bit of doing. Hi, Elise."

She made a short derisive sound. "Don't even talk to me." She swung past Remy. The smell of her anger—burned paper and candle wax—was missing. Why? What was she planning? "I'm gonna use your spare room, Theo. You just figure out how to kick me out of the Guardians, and I'll be all set."

"Elise," Theo began, but Elise brushed past Hanson, her coppery hair floating on the breeze she made as she moved, and disappeared into the living room.

"Let her go, Theo," Mari said. "You know how she is. Anyone who goes after her now is going to get a face full of porcupine quills. She'll calm down and see reason soon enough." She looked up at Remy, blinking. Her eyes were red from crying, and there were damp spots on her blue T-shirt and ragged jeans. "Thank you, Remy. I was worried about her, but I knew you were with her, so I was a little *less* worried. If that makes sense."

She's calm enough. Remy realized why he felt so unsettled. Elise in a fury he was fairly sure he could handle, if only by patiently bearing her sharp tongue until the storm was over. After all, her anger was a shield over a heart that felt too deeply.

But a calm, rational, determined Elise with her mind set on doing something foolish—*that* was a prospect he had shivers thinking about. "My thanks, Lightbringer," he said, formally. "And my apologies, brother." This he directed at Dante, who still watched him, black eyes depthless.

"I missed something," Hanson said pleasantly enough, but he hadn't missed the tension between the other two Watchers.

"No hard feelings." Dante sounded grimly amused, and his face was still and set. "The gods know it's hard enough to deal with one Lightbringer taking suicidal chances. Three of them is a damn Chinese puzzle."

"Worse than a Bishop with a Seeker." Hanson looked relieved. "And I should know."

Remy listened for Elise's footsteps. She was going up the stairs, but not stamping and muttering imprecations. He waited until the footsteps stopped and took a deep breath. "I don't trust this. She's too calm."

"You call that calm?" Theo arched an eyebrow, her pretty face momentarily very much like Elise's sardonic look.

Remy shrugged. He didn't want to argue with a Lightbringer. His personal stock seemed to be a bit low with this group at the moment. "It doesn't smell like a fire in here. When she gets upset, it smells like burning, and the air gets warmer. I don't sense that now."

There was a low, intense silence when he finished speaking. He looked from the Lightbringers, who were exchanging worried glances, to the black-eyed Watcher, who looked suddenly thoughtful.

"You know," Hanson said thoughtfully, "you have a point."

Mari smoothed her tank top nervously. "What now? What do you think she's planning?"

"With Elise, it's safer not to guess." Theo sighed. "Come on, have some soup. We'll give her an hour or so to take a nap and calm down, and then I'll take up a tray for her and try to make her see reason." There were dark circles under her beautiful eyes.

"I hate this," she continued, swinging around to look at Dante. "I *hate* this. I've met Vann and Trevor. They're good people. I..." She shook her head, tucking her long dark hair behind one ear. "We didn't even think to do protection-work for them. I thought that just being the Guardians of the City would be enough. I wish Suzanne..." She cut the words short, and set her slim shoulders.

"I wish so too." Mari touched the other woman's arm. "Guess we got more than we bargained for. Like usual. I wish there was something we could *do*."

"When Elise calms down, we'll brainstorm a spell." Theo nodded smartly. "All this Power should be good for something. I think it's time we asked the guys, too. They're bound to have some ideas." The smile she flashed at Dante was weary but hopeful. "I'm talking about you as if you're not here again. Sorry."

Dante's lips quirked fractionally, giving the impression of a smile. "It's not so bad, Theo. All my life I've dreamed of listening in on women."

Hanson gave a short snort of laughter, sliding his arm over Mari's shoulders. "If they only knew." His face changed when he touched her, relaxing.

Remy felt his shoulders slump with relief. Surely here in a Guardian's house, with two other Watchers, was the safest place for Elise. The house was well-shielded, and he could ask the other Watchers what he should do now. *I'm just a glorified garbage man. How could finding one artifact and one Lightbringer turn into such a tangle? She'll hate me now, and I don't blame her. I don't blame her at all.*

He cocked his head, listening. There was no sound from above. Maybe she was crying again, her face in a pillow. He could feel her aura, fiery reds and golds, stationary over their heads. It seemed a bit flat, two-dimensional, but she was probably concentrating fiercely, trying to keep him out of her mind. It wouldn't work for long—he was far better tuned to her than she thought—but for now, he was willing to give her some privacy. She deserved it.

Remy sighed. Theo was getting down bowls, and Mari poured coffee. Hanson helped, getting the milk out, catching a spoon when Mari dropped it, and making easy little jokes to make his witch smile.

Dante was still watching Remy. "You're a good Watcher," he said, when Remy's eyes met his. "Don't worry so much. You did what you should have."

Remy nodded, setting his jaw. "I've only hunted down artifacts. I don't think I'm prepared for this."

"We never are," Dante said sagely. "Come on, have something to eat while you can. My instincts tell me this is going to get far worse before it gets better."

I agree with you. I really wish I didn't, though. I'd love to be wrong.

Twenty

Elise quietly shut the door and spent a few moments swearing softly and viciously, using every obscenity she'd ever heard. Then she sank down on the bed, her hands in her lap, and waited.

It took a few moments for her breathing to even out. Her head felt ringingly clear but heavy in the aftermath of her crying fit. She had never cried like that before in her life, even when her real parents had died. Of course, she had only been six years old and hadn't fully understood everything happening around her. If her Power—her control over fire—had been active then, she might have been able to save both of them. But as it was, she was lucky to have survived their house burning down around them. All her early memories seemed tinged with smoke.

Elise shut her eyes. Theo's spare bedroom was pleasant and comfortable, even with the rain beating on windows. It seemed to be easing up a bit now, the thunder retreating. An awful storm. Some of the lower parts of town might be flooded.

There were bookcases in here, and spider plants and ferns hanging from pretty brass hooks. Theo had hung one of Elise's paintings over the bed—the painting of a rose garden under summer sunshine, a single monarch butterfly pausing on one of the white roses. Elise was proud of that piece. The butterfly almost seemed to tremble, ready to flutter away. There was a comfortable chair sitting in front of the window, across from a dresser Theo used to hold spare clothes, and a full-length antique oval mirror in a dark wooden frame. A cherub's face grinned from the frame over the mirror, wings delicately carved on either side of its chubby smiling cheeks. The mirror itself was clear and flawless.

Perfect.

The Trifero pulsed against Elise's throat. She'd read about magical objects that seemed to have a life of their own, but she hadn't really believed it. There was a whole lot she'd read about that she hadn't believed until she'd met Suzanne, and a whole lot more that she'd never dreamed possible until Circle Lightfall had ruined their lives.

Oh, to be absolutely fair, they didn't ruin our lives, she thought, wincing. *They're trying to help. It's my freakish ability to set stuff on fire that's ruined my life.*

Vann didn't deserve to be kidnapped for her sake. Neither did Trevor. The drummer had only answered an ad in the local rag about the Tragic Diamonds needing a new drummer. She barely even knew him beyond practice sessions and a few obligatory brewski-pounding matches.

Theo and Mari had to be protected. They'd be safe enough with three Watchers in the house. Remy...

Her chest hurt to think of it, but she had to leave him here. Unless she was right about the Trifero, it just might be suicide for him to come with her. She didn't want that—she wanted him safe. No matter how lethal he was, the thought of him facing down whoever or whatever had taken Vann and Trevor made her feel unsteady and breathless with worry. If the Trifero was the equivalent of a magickal bomb, and she was the only one who could use it, she owed it to everyone to fix the mess she'd made.

Elise took in a deep breath, shaking away worry and fear. She needed to concentrate for this.

Another deep breath, and the familiar floating feeling began in her stomach. Thanks to her practice with Suzanne and the others, she could fall into a light trance with no effort at all, even under these awful conditions.

The Trifero sent a warm, tingling rush of Power through her. **the mirror,** it whispered. Heat rose under Elise's skin. **the mirror, fire witch. easier with the mirror.**

She rose slowly to her feet, taking another deep breath. Then she ghosted over the floorboards, her wet sneakers making slight squeaking sounds against the wood. Her feet were soaked. If she ever got dry again, she would probably smell like mold.

Her reflection greeted her. A triangular face, wide eyes, a sharp nose, her thin silver nose-ring lying dark against her damp skin.

I look like hell.

Pale cheeks, glowing green eyes, her hair had escaped her braid and now tumbled around her face. Her mouth was pulled tight, as if she tasted something bitter. The T-shirt was sodden and clung to her chest and belly, rode up to expose her belly button. Her jeans were dark with water and were beginning to chafe.

He had kissed her as if he loved her.

Elise shoved that thought away and faced the mirror. *What*

do I do now?

As soon as she thought it, the answer appeared.

Theo could heal, and Mari's visions told the future. Suzanne had always told Elise that her gift would become apparent, and Elise had always privately thought that setting stuff on fire whenever she got angry was enough of a curse. She didn't need any more.

The Trifero knew differently.

power. you have the power to use me.

She put her hands up, palms out, facing the mirror. "To see, to feel, to shape, to be," she whispered. "Shape and form for all to see. Shape and form for all to see. Shape and form for all to see, in a form that matches me. Come out, come out, come out to me. Come out, come out, come out to me."

The chant never became more than a whisper, but it didn't need to be louder. The Trifero glowed at the throat of the woman in the mirror, and its carved scales shifted. A red spark began in the depths of the central jewel, pulsing in time with Elise's heartbeat. Her skin flushed with heat.

The ecstasy of the Power building was juice swelling against the skin of a fruit, a sweet bursting pain. She was heavy with Power, her skin stretching to contain the heat, her eyes glittering under half-closed lids, taking on a mad gleam. "Come to me. Come to me. Come to me. Come to me."

Glamour is the oldest of witch skills. Suzanne's voice sounded distant, whispery. *It can be a great blessing, when one has need of it. But take care. The lesson of glamour is that seeming becomes truth.*

Elise's palms met the mirror. Or met something cool and smooth that felt like the mirror's surface, and at the same time felt like warm skin. Human skin.

The Power crested, spilled over her in a wave of tingling sparkles. A spark snapped. Elise would have been worried—that much Power in Theo's house would have brought all of them up the stairs at a run—but the Trifero absorbed the extra Power, making sure not a ripple of it escaped. It was the closest thing to a surgically neat spell Elise had ever experienced.

A part of her was vaguely troubled by this. To be able to work a spell like this was impressive enough, but the kind of Power that could keep the spell silent was even more impressive. And that much Power, at her command, was downright scary.

Scary, and exhilarating too. Like a fast ride or a hot jam, like a roller coaster or a thunderstorm.

The *doppelganger* stepped out of the mirror. Elise's fingers slipped free and the Power drained from her, leaving only a shaky sense of satisfaction. Fire was the element of illusion and the burning away of illusions. Why hadn't she thought of this before? It felt so natural, so *right* she could have started to cry again if she'd had any tears left.

The *doppelganger* glided to the opposite side of the bed and sat down, the springs of the mattress creaking. Its mussed hair was an exact copy of hers, and it burned with her shifting red and gold aura. Elise was now the closest to invisible she could get. The copy of her wouldn't last more than an hour or two, especially if one of the Watchers came close to it. The venomous red Power the Watchers carried would tear the illusion to pieces.

She had to hurry.

Elise crossed to the window and looked down over the street at the front of the house. Theo, Mari and the Watchers were in the kitchen. She could hear them talking back and forth in worried tones.

Don't worry, guys. I'm going to take care of it all.

She swung the window open. The rain came down steadily, but not in waves as it had earlier. She slid out onto the narrow ledge that ran over the living room windows. The bedroom window slid down behind her, closing most of the way, and Elise looked down onto Theo's juniper bushes.

If I break a leg, I'm going to look very silly.

Then, gathering herself, she jumped.

It was an awful impact, but the bush took most of it. Elise muttered a quick apology as she rolled off, hitting the ground on her hands and knees. Her teeth clicked together painfully, and her hair fell forward. Theo's garden was spongy with rain, mud squelching between her fingers and soaking into the knees of her jeans. *Great.* She ignored the flare of pain in her left wrist. *I'm going to be the Mud Avenger. Jeez.*

She made it to Theo's garden gate and bolted out onto the wet sidewalk, running for the high yew trees that separated Theo's house from the low red ranch-style place next door. Once she passed that hedge, she was safer.

Okay. She skidded to a stop to catch her breath in the shelter of a huge cedar tree three doors down from Theo's.

Now what?

Go back, Suzanne's voice replied over the sound of the rain. *For the love of the goddess, Elise, go back. You're being stupid. What will you do, march in there and sing them to death?*

Clapping a lid on that voice, Elise pushed her damp hair back and set her jaw. *Now, I find myself a cab.*

Twenty-One

"Well." Theo set a bowl of steaming chicken soup on the green Japanese tray. "I'll take this up to Elise. She'll be a little calmer now, I think."

Remy automatically rose from his place at the round table. Hanson moved his chair over slightly, so he could ease out from behind the table. The Watchers had all taken off their leather coats, and they lay draped against the chairs like sets of black wings.

Mari had her elbows on the table, sipping cherry soda through a straw. "I don't think she'll be calmer, Theo." Her face was pale under her bright golden curls. "Maybe I should go up."

Remy stretched, his weapons-harness moving with him. "Maybe I shouldn't have left her alone."

"No, trust me, it's best." Theo picked up the tray. "Elise can be very…well, harsh. But it's like a candle, quickly lit and quickly gone. Once she gets over the first step, she's all right."

"Yeah." A fading rumble of thunder underlined Mari's voice. "But that first one's a lulu."

Theo made a small face at Mari, who laughed. But her laughter didn't have quite the same easy, ringing tone it usually had.

Remy glanced around the bright, cozy kitchen. It was warm enough that his clothes were mostly dry, and the other Watchers were dry as well. Hanson shuffled Mari's deck of tarot cards, his pale blue eyes thoughtful, and Dante buttered a slice of Theo's wheat bread. It was a calm, peaceful scene…but somehow Remy didn't feel peaceful. As a matter of fact, he felt less peaceful than ever.

Elise hadn't made a sound, but the red-gold glow of her aura had remained bright and stable. *A half-hour should be enough time to cool her temper, just a little.* He felt a prickling of unease run up his spine again. She hadn't been furious. No, she had been curiously calm.

Almost too calm.

"Well, let's go, then." Theo smiled at him. He nodded, the bright clear green of her aura dragging across his nerves like broken glass. Being in a room with these two witches was a torturous experience, especially with Elise—and that damnable spill of pleasure each time he touched her skin—right upstairs.

"Yes, ma'am," he said automatically. Mari seemed to find this very amusing and laughed again.

Theo led him through the living room and a front hall, both welcoming and full of green growing things. A black cat curled into a round shape on a battered green linen couch, one golden eye half opening to examine them as they passed through. Books were scattered everywhere. This was more of what he had imagined a Lightbringer's home would look like, but he found himself missing the clean clarity of Elise's house. Missing especially her bedroom, watching her sleep against the black sheets while he rested in the red-velour chair, occasionally glancing out the window. He'd memorized her face during those long hours, and wondered what it would be like to touch her.

Now he knew, and all he wanted to do was touch her again, as many times as she let him near her.

"You're very quiet." Theo started up the stairs. "Then again, so is Dante."

That brought him up out of memory. "Really?" He had no idea of what to say, but that seemed fairly safe.

"Yeah. Elise calls him Stoneface, when what she really means is *uncommunicative*. She was very upset when he showed up, and they have no idea of how to talk to each other." The witch climbed the stairs slowly and gracefully, balancing the soup bowl and the cup of coffee faultlessly on the tray. "She's been very lonely, for a very long time. I'm glad you're here. I think she is too."

Remy found his mouth was dry. "She doesn't seem too glad." *Don't get too comfortable,* Elise's voice echoed in his memory.

"Oh, that." Theo sounded cheerful and dismissive. "She likes to act tough. Did you know she feeds all the stray cats out behind the store? I caught her using her own money to buy cat food. I told her to just take what she needed from the register, and she looked as horrified as if I'd suggested she rob a little old lady." They reached the top of the stairs, and Theo glided down a dark hall with an Ansel Adams print hung on one wall. "She's all prickly on the outside, but she's just a big marshmallow inside."

"I'll remember that." The unease returned, even stronger than before. What was *wrong* with him? Danger? From where? The other Watchers would be here if they sensed anything.

In lieu of knocking, Theo kicked gently at the door to the spare bedroom, making a small polite noise. The door swayed, closed but not latched shut. "Elise!" she called, softly. "I have some dinner here for you, and some coffee. I'll bet you need some caffeine."

No answer.

Theo pushed the door open with her foot. Elise sat motionless on the bed, her hands clasped loosely in her lap. Remy could see her coppery hair, messy and mussed, stray strands of red-gold curling free. Her head bowed forward, almost as if she was praying. "Elise," Theo said, firmly, "don't be childish. We'll brainstorm a spell to help Vann and Trevor, I promise. But we need you strong if we're going to..."

Theo's voice trailed off uncertainly.

Remy slipped past her and approached the bed cautiously. His skin wasn't ringing with Elise's nearness, and the green witch's aura scraped painfully at his nerves.

Something was very wrong.

He was almost around the bed when Elise began to waver, as if she were underwater.

Remy cursed. Theo let out a gasp.

The *doppelganger* winked out with a puff of cinnamon-scented air. The Power holding it in place fled, and the temperature in the room dropped at least ten degrees.

Theo shivered. "Dante." Before the word finished, Remy heard boots on the stairs.

He kept staring at the bed in stupefied wonder. The sheer Power she would need to do something like this astounded him.

How did she do it? How did she create a double that strong under our noses, without even a stray breath to warn us? How? "Why didn't anyone tell me she had the Power of glamour?" he asked the thin air. It hadn't been in the file.

"We didn't know," Theo answered with the utter calm of the utterly stunned. Remy looked at the window. It was open only a quarter of an inch, and cool rainy air came in through the crack.

He crossed the room to the window and wrenched it open. The juniper bush below was flattened, and even from here he could see deep imprints in the soft muddy earth. Mystery solved. She was gone.

How did she do that? The amount of Power she'd need,

and not even a whisper to warn three Watchers downstairs.
Gods. Gods above.

The Trifero. Of course.

How could she use the Trifero? Or was it using her?

Dante skidded into the room, a curse that would have made a dockworker proud escaping his lips.

"Glamoured a double and slipped out," Remy said grimly. "Three guesses where she's going, *mon ami.*" He was vaguely aware that his voice made the window rattle in its frame. The rain still came down in a silver curtain, and a far-off afterthought of thunder resounded in the sky.

"Oh, for the love of—" Dante tipped his head back, his jaw working.

Theo had set the tray on the bed and now stood with her fingers pressed to her mouth. "Dante. You have to…You *have* to go after her. You *have* to."

"I know." His black eyes met Remy's. "Let's go."

"Stay here with your witch," Remy said. "I should have known. I should have—the fault is mine. I should have—"

"Don't tell me what to do, brother," Dante snapped, sounding more like Elise than he probably would ever know. "Theo's asked me to fetch her, and you'll need all the help you can get."

"I'll get the car started," Theo said, and Dante put out one broad hand.

"Don't even think about it, Theo. You'll stay here."

"She's *my* friend," Theo began hotly.

"We have no time for this." Remy pushed past Dante. "I need my coat. Get out of my way."

As soon as he was in the hallway, sick dread beating behind his heart, he began to run.

Twenty-Two

The storm lay over the city like a pair of folded wings.

By the time Elise paid the cabdriver, it was late afternoon. It looked much later because of the clouds massed in the sky. The sea heaved under the pilings, a moaning noise in the wind coming ashore hard and fast enough to make her shiver and wish again that she'd brought a coat.

The message had been simple. *Come down to the docks.* There were miles of docks, really, but Elise was a witch. If she couldn't tell where Vann and Trevor were being held by a bunch of two-legged elephants, what kind of a witch was she?

Elise slid out of the cab and shut the door behind her. The rain kissed her already wet hair and cheeks, not to mention soaking her T-shirt again. As soon as the cab disappeared down the empty, waterlogged street, she dropped the pretense with a sigh, and heat popped out in shimmering waves.

The rain turned to steam around her, and Elise blinked, looking around. Now that she wasn't trying to hide, this part of town blurred and ran with Darkness.

I'm seeing auras. Just like Theo. It would have been wonderful if she hadn't been seeing such awful, twisted dark shapes hiding in every warehouse, leering in every corner.

Elise walked down the sidewalk. Vann and Trevor. She had to concentrate, to think of them, and find them.

She stopped in the shadow of a giant warehouse perched on one side of the railroad tracks, and closed her eyes. *Vann.*

She began to hum. Her fingers twitched, remembering chords, following the song. *Lowdown Jimmy Jingo, that no-good dirty beast...didn't even know 'nough to treat a woman right at least...Lowdown Jimmy Jingo, that no-good dirty dog...walking around like Elvis and smelling just like a hog—*

She'd written that for Theo, after the last boyfriend debacle. Suzanne had helped. Vann had suggested a new bass line for it, and Mark had done some inspired drumming. It was kind of a hit among the hip in the city, and there were requests for it all the time. Especially when someone had just broken up.

Elise hummed quietly and began to feel a tugging on her hand. It felt just like someone leading her.

What else could she do but follow?

She edged down the cracked pavement, the rain turning to steam before it touched her, so that she looked like she was being trailed by a white cloud. Her T-shirt was drying, and that was a good thing. Parts of the street had turned into a river, and thunder still breathed in the sky. The worst of the storm had probably passed.

Unless we're just in the eye of the hurricane. What a comforting thought that is, Elise.

She walked past a giant open pier, glancing out to sea. The waves on the bay roiled. It was probably really bad out past the protected waters, and Elise shivered. She knew a few dockworkers, and they always wanted a night of heavy drinking after storms like this. It was hard to work near the sea and not want a good stiff drink once in a while, seeing that much casual power.

It was kind of the same way Elise felt about Theo. If Theo wasn't so gentle, Elise would have been frightened of her. If Theo could heal a cut, she could probably create one. *A witch who can't hex, can't heal,* Suzanne's voice drifted up from Elise's memory.

Come to think of it, that's how she felt about the Watchers too. So much Power, so thinly controlled; so much lethal intention and grace and such a small margin for error. The only thing that kept the Watcher from running riot was the training, Elise supposed. But what did they have to do to turn men into fighting machines like that?

But they're so gentle. Hanson treats Mari like she's breakable, and Dante would never even raise his voice to Theo. And Remy...

She shut that thought off in a hurry. It hurt too much.

Elise found herself going down the slippery ramshackle wooden stairs to the beach under the pier. Down here was a good place for transients and junkies, and she felt a momentary shiver as she reached the bottom and peered around. She shouldn't be here. It was like an alley on Klondel Avenue, not a good place for a woman to end up.

Nobody was here, though. The weather and the persistent smell of doom probably had driven anyone who lived here up into town to find a warm dry spot if they could.

Elise smelled salt, and darkness. There was a long strip of beach down here, sandy, rocky, and littered with trash. Several hunched buildings were built on piers, climbing out over the sea on sticklike legs, and Elise's throat scorched with bile as she thought of rats. Dock rats were huge, and they probably had very bad tempers.

Well, they would burn just like anything else, if they attacked her.

That thought surprised her. The Trifero glowed against her throat, a quiet warmth. *So much Power.*

She picked her way carefully down the trash-littered beach. One of the buildings attracted her eye, hulking over the water and exhaling cold darkness in every direction.

there. The Trifero whispered inside her head, as familiar as her own thoughts.

Okay. Elise started out, balancing on rocks, and at one point having to splash through knee-high shallows since the tide was coming in. Tide plus storm would mean high waves and a lot of stuff washed up in the parks. Mari would want to go beachcombing.

Thinking of Mari and Theo made a spike of pain go through her heart. She'd ditched them both. They were going to feel so betrayed and angry.

That led her thoughts right to where they didn't want to be. To a pair of golden eyes and the feel of his mouth on hers, his body hard and warm and—

Oh, stop it. You're acting like a teenager. He's just a Watcher, just another one of Circle Lightfall's goons.

Only he wasn't. He was smart and quiet and funny in a morbid way, just like Mark had been. And he had protected her, put his body between her and danger, held her while she cried. It was hard not to feel like a hormonal teenager. It was hard not to wish he'd come with her. He would probably have a better idea than scrabbling on some trash-laden beach. He seemed so competent.

But she couldn't stand the thought of him here, getting hurt because of her.

She reached the building that was breathing out darkness into the air. There were two spindly ladders coming up from the beach, both leading to trapdoors. *Now that's weird. Is it an old cannery or something? Probably not. Those are probably trash chutes—don't ask about garbage, they won't tell you.*

She had to wade though waves up to her mid-thighs to get to the closest staircase. It was festooned with seaweed and rust. The water bubbled around her feet, steam still trailing her.

She hauled herself up out of the waves and began to climb, hoping it would carry her weight.

It took a long while to reach the top, and she began to feel sick even before she got there. The Trifero sparked, sending another flush of heat along her skin. *I could burn this entire building down.* She shivered, fever flushing through her skin. *I'm not sure I'm ready for this.*

The trapdoor wasn't even locked. Elise balanced on one ladderlike step, pushed up on the trapdoor's splintered wood with one hand and peered through.

There seemed to be a pile of something in front of the trapdoor. Elise shoved the heavy wood up slowly, trying to look in every direction at once. It stopped halfway up, and Elise wriggled through onto a splintery wooden floor. After her feet slipped through, it closed with a muffled thud. Elise rolled up into a crouch, looking around.

There was a huge pile of what looked like discarded clothing blocking the rest of the cavernous open space from view. Elise edged to one side of it, peering. The only light filtered in through holes in the walls and the gaps between the boards on the windows.

What she saw was strange. There were lumps and piles of what looked like clothes everywhere except for along the west wall, where boarded-up windows let in the whistling wind from the sea. There was a thick, clotted smell Elise recognized. *Darkness.*

She peeked around the lump of stuff, looking for any sign of life.

On the western wall, there was a large, wet stain. She didn't want to know what it was. But down to the side, chained to the wall with huge iron cuffs and a chain that looked like it could hold back Cerberus, was a thin young man with dark hair that she recognized.

"Trevor!" Elise whispered, and bolted for him.

She threaded her way through the piles of clothing, and finally reached him. "Trevor," she said, going down on her knees next to him. "Hey, Trev. Trevor!"

His eyes were almost swollen shut and his lips were cracked. He rolled his head to the side, and his dark eyes glittered feverishly under the sweep of his charcoal lashes. "Lise," he croaked. "Elise."

He wore his Green Lantern T-shirt and a torn and tattered pair of jeans now crusted with dried blood.

Thank the gods. Maybe I can actually pull this off. "Where's Vann? I've come to get you out of here."

He shook his head. "Lise...*no*..."

She examined the chains, blinking furiously against tears and the dimness. There was a simple spring lock, and she popped her purse open. It was soaked with sea and rainwater, steaming as the heat around Elise blurred through it, but everything inside was still okay. She dug until she found the thin, flexible piece of hairpin she kept more for old times' sake than for any real breaking and entering. "Just relax. I've come to get you out of here. Where's Vann?"

Trevor's head rolled on his neck. He tipped his chin up, indicating the large dark stain on the wall between two boarded windows. "Goddamn...Something. *Ate.* Him." He coughed, a tubercular sound she wasn't sure she liked.

"Oh, no." Tears rose behind her eyes, hot and prickling. She pushed them down. "I'm so sorry, Trevor. I'm *so* sorry. I'm a freak. I should never have even tried to be normal."

"Get out," Trevor said, husky. "Trap."

"Anything comes along and I'll fry it. I'm a witch, Trev." The lock popped open, and the cuff around his neck clashed, falling to the floor. "Sheesh. I should try to be quieter, shouldn't I."

"Lise, it's a...trap." He coughed weakly, and a ribbon of red appeared at the corner of his mouth.

"I've got a friend who's a healer." Elise fiddled desperately with the cuff around his right wrist. *Hell of a time to wish I'd kept up on my lockpicking.* It popped open obligingly, and she began to work on the last one. "If we can get you to her, you'll be okay."

"Elise...*Elise.*" He pushed fretfully at her hands.

She shook her head. Strands of her hair were lifting on a hot draft that seemed to come from nowhere. "I'll get you out of this, Trevor. I *swear* I will. And I'll get you to Theo. She'll help you and Vann...Gods, Vann..." She angrily wiped tears away with the back of one hand. *Stop your crying, Elise. Just get it done. Quit being a coward and do something right for a change!*

There was a low, thick, burping chuckle behind her.

Elise froze. Then the worst happened.

"Quiet, Rork." It was a low, soft, evil male voice, quiet and full of something chill that made Elise's entire body turn to a block of ice.

The Trifero flared, shattering the ice, and her heart pounded thin and high in her temples. The last cuff fell open under her fingers. She stood, her knees creaking, and turned around.

It was the elephant things. At least ten of them. Elise swallowed. The wind coming in off the bay keened and whistled against her back. They were each at least seven feet tall, their bald heads shining with an oily gleam in the uncertain light coming in through the gaps in the walls and the boarded-up windows. Razor-sharp tusks jetted out from their thick faces. They all wore long gray trench coats, and Elise saw the gleam of metal under the coats. *They're copying the Watchers.* The lunacy of the thought made a traitorous giggle rise up under her breastbone. It died away, tearing a hole in her chest, and Elise's numb hands curled into fists.

There was a slim dark man, not much taller than Theo, with a thatch of short black hair dyed Kool-Aid red on one side and a pleasant, bland face that was nevertheless mostly nose. *Vann?* Elise blinked, looking under the glamour, and her knees started to turn to water.

She collapsed on the floor next to Trevor. "Oh," she said, a hurt little sound. "No."

Whatever it was, it looked like the shadow of cold, sterile batwings. But that wasn't the worst.

The worst was that it was wearing Vann's body like an ill-fitting suit. She could see it crouching inside his flesh, inside his nervous system, the Darkness it radiated warping Vann's flesh. His familiar face had already been twisted, changed into something different.

I did that. I put them in harm's way. I did that. It's because of me. All because of me. "Vann," she whispered hopelessly.

"A nice little morsel." Its voice was lipless and dark as the mouth of a poisoned well. "Oh, he struggled, but I was quick. I was *merciful.* Now, you're here. Let's talk business."

Elise felt all the strength run out of her. Remy had been right. This thing...There was no way she could fight it. Not while it wore Vann's face, not while it leered at her with his familiar mouth.

fire, the Trifero whispered. **do not despair. despair is its weapon. see the truth.**

"Lise," Trevor said. "Circle...Lightfall—"

She stared at him. *What? How does he know about them?*

"He's a spy," the thing wearing Vann's body said, thickly. "A spy from Circle Lightfall, sent to gather information about the Guardians. To decide the best approach to use to worm their sanctimonious asses into this city under your very nose. They lie, Miss Nicholson. They *deceive.* And you are a pretty prize to add to their collection." The thing's voice was low and evil, worming into her head.

Elise's heartbeat slowed. She stared at the thing, seeing Vann's nose collapsing slowly into its face. It was eating his body from the inside. Was Vann still in there, feeling this?

"No," Trevor whispered, with a lung-racking effort. "Lightbringer. I'm a Lightbringer. I came here for sanctuary."

She looked down at him, jerking her eyes away from the bat-thing eating Vann's body from the inside. Wearing it and eating it at the same time. Elise's stomach declared mutiny. *I'm going to throw up,* she thought, oddly amazed. *I really honestly think I'm going to puke.*

It was looking down at Trevor that saved her from the thing's mesmerism. Its hold on her snapped, and she saw Trev's eyes drifting closed. He looked too exhausted to breathe, and as she watched, some essential spark in him dimmed.

Fury rose up inside Elise. Not for herself, but for Trevor, and for Vann, and for Theo and Mari and every other person in the world who had suffered because of Elise and the Dark. A wave of liquid crimson flame filled her veins, and the space inside her skull ignited as if she'd been drinking rum again, matching Mark shot for shot.

"No." she said, reaching down and blindly feeling for Trevor's shoulder. Her palm met blood-soaked cotton, and fire roared through her.

It was a different kind of fire than the one she was used to. Pure Power. It whipped down her arm and forced itself into Trevor, who screamed and convulsed.

The thing wearing Vann's body chuckled again. "See? She'll make a good one, won't she, boys? I'm afraid she won't come quietly. Take her. Kill the other. He's a nice snack."

"With pleasure," a low rumbling voice like earth moving under wet rocks said. Had to be one of the kobolds.

Strength returned to Elise's legs. She slid her arm under Trevor's shoulders and struggled to her feet. Wonder of wonders, he came with her. Under the crust of blood, color flushed back into his face, and his eyes were no longer puffed shut. *I healed him.* Blank wonder colored the thought. *I thought that was Theo's trick.*

What else can I do?

The Trifero sparked again. **they are coming, witch.** Its anger began to burn under her skin too. It was a slow, white-hot fire, like a charcoal seam burning underground. **they are coming to slay or capture you.**

Trevor leaned against Elise, coughing weakly. "Elise," he whispered. "Don't."

But it was too late. The kobolds lumbered forward in a loose semicircle, and one of them licked its lips. They stared at Trevor, shivering against Elise. He was thinner than her and usually full of nervous energy, but now he slumped with his head on her shoulder, too exhausted to stand upright.

The thing wearing Vann's body chuckled again. "Don't fight. It will only make it worse. The Brotherhood will be your new home, fire witch. When we're finished with you, you won't even remember your own name, let alone *his.*"

That's it. I. Have. Had. Enough. The rage crystallized inside her chest. Pure protective fury, like the fire of Sekhmet.

"No," Elise said, and flung out her hand.

The Trifero's force melded with hers, ran down her arm like a whip of flame, and shot through the dark, wet air. Cooked air expanded with a thundercrack that blew Elise's hair back and made the wood groan.

One kobold stopped, stiffened, howled, and burst into flame.

"Elise," Trevor choked. "No, you can't. Don't."

"The hell I can't." Elise's teeth ground together. The kobolds stopped, staring at the one she'd ignited. It burned like a huge waxy candle, and a gout of black smoke billowed up. "The hell I *won't.*"

The fire roared up inside her. It wasn't her usual sharp irritation with a world that moved too slow and ran too cold. This was absolute *fury.* This was the rage a volcano must feel, forcing liquid stone up through cracks and vents.

This was true destruction.

She opened herself to the Trifero completely, and the Talisman hissed with delight. It had been centuries since it had been allowed such complete freedom, the freedom to *burn*. The stone ran and shifted against Elise's collarbone, the central jewel flashing white-hot.

Thunder boomed.

Trevor clutched at Elise's shoulders, jerking in surprise. Living flame blossomed, radiating out from Elise in lines of force eating into the sodden wood of the building's floor.

Five of the elephant-things immediately went up like torches. Black smoke gouted, and high whistling screams filled the air. Elise coughed, smoke stinging eyes and throat, and the smoke suddenly *shifted,* streaming away from her on a hot wave of air.

One of the kobolds had a gun. He raised it.

Elise's eyes narrowed. The firebolt smashed into the elephant-thing, and the bullet detonated inside the gun's chamber, shrapnel flying. A thin slice of metal kissed Elise's right arm and she let out a thin little cry like a hawk's scream.

She stopped, looking at the remaining kobolds as the Trifero flashed again, humming. They stared at her as if she'd grown another head.

"Elise—" Trevor started to say, but she shook her head. Her hair streamed up on a hot breath of air. Stray strands whipped across his face.

"You want me?" Her eyes felt hot, as if streams of fire were pushing out from them. Her voice held the rush and crackle of an inferno, the hungry heart of the sun. "Come and get me." And her lips peeled back from her teeth.

"*It's just one witch!*" the thing wearing Vann's body howled. "*Get her, you brainless—*"

Elise's fingers flicked. Another whip of fire sizzled. The thing that had hijacked Vann's body vanished in a sheet of flame that boomed up from the floor and caressed the ceiling.

Every window still left intact blew out in silvery tinkles. The roof ignited with a sudden *wump!* that shook the entire building.

"Oh," It was all Elise was capable of saying, a small breath of air lost in the huge noise. She hadn't expected it to be this powerful.

The Trifero howled, a long note of rage and satisfied Power. Elise's own voice rose with it, breathless, screaming. The

Power rode through her nervous system, jacked into her just like an amplifier jacks into a guitar and turns even the lightest breath against the strings into a crashing chord.

The remaining kobolds vanished into a wall of living flame, Trevor yelled something shapeless, clutching at her. Elise screamed again, a short cry of satisfaction underlaid with rushing flame. How dare they? How *dare* they? She was Destruction. She was Fire. She was the way the world ended, in flames.

Not with a whimper. Make them burn.

Make them pay.

The building groaned. Tilted. Fire exploded out, caressing Elise's skin like a lover.

Trevor clung to her, screaming with hoarse surprise. The flames played over them both harmlessly, like water. *"Elise!"* Trevor yelled.

It was meaningless. Nothing mattered but the fire. Nothing mattered but the *burning*, the cleansing of the world in flames. To burn away all the darkness and the sickness and the suffering, to revenge herself and her friends on everything that had ever chased or attacked them. To purify.

To *cleanse*.

The wall of flames made a rushing waterfall sound. There was a curtain of flame, a mirror made of it, and Elise stared at the fire she'd let loose on the world.

It was beautiful.

And then, something dark hurled itself out of the flames and wrapped its scaly claws around Elise's throat. She went over backward, not even having enough time to scream, and Trevor fell heavily against the smoking floorboards.

Twenty-Three

"Keep them in the car," Dante said. "You hear me? Don't let them out in this. If it comes down to it, leave. We'll find our own way back."

"Now just a minute—" Mari began.

"Don't." Hanson turned around from the driver's seat. "You're here, and if Elise is still alive, they'll find her and bring her out. We need you two to work some protection. Can't you feel the Dark here?"

Mari's blue eyes were dark and haunted. She shivered, looking out the Subaru's windows at the deserted, leering warehouses. Shadows flitted between them, and the rain had taken on a flashing, needlelike appearance. "I've felt those before, those flying things."

Remy, who sat behind the passenger's seat, had his hand on the door-latch. "She's there." He pointed down International Street to a low, hulking warehouse building that had been built out over the water. The faded sign on the front announced that it had once belonged to the Salvation Army. It teetered on its pilings, glittering with Power. Something was happening inside it.

"No doubt." Dante checked one of his guns. "Can you two do that? Stay here and weave protections? We'll need all the help we can get."

"Go," Theo said, her large dark eyes worried. "Just go. Bring Elise out safely. That's all that matters."

Amen to that, Remy thought grimly. The sick feeling in the pit of his stomach—his witch alone and unprotected in the middle of a Brotherhood trap—intensified. He pulled on the door latch and climbed out of the car. "I'm going. Thank you."

"Wait a moment." Dante opened his door too. Theo reached out from the backseat and touched his shoulder. He paused.

"Be careful. Come back to me." The green witch looked serious, her teeth worrying at her lower lip.

Will Elise ever look at me that way? Remy had to clap a lid on that thought and shove it away. It hurt too much.

"Of course," Dante told her. She let go of him and he surged out of the green Subaru.

Remy closed his car door and examined the street. Kobolds and Grays, standard Brotherhood teams of eight. At least four teams he could spot.

"This is not good." He slid his left-hand gun out.

"You can say that again." Dante slammed his own door, and the locks inside flicked down. "I can't believe I let Theo talk me into this."

"I can't believe you did either," Remy said. "But I'm hardly one to talk. My own witch seems to hate me."

"She doesn't hate you." Dante moved forward. Remy followed him, gun held low and ready. "You'd be a pile of ashes if she hated you."

"Comforting." It was combat zone banter, and it failed to ease his nerves. His training clamped iron control down on the part of him that wanted to run pell-mell down the street, screaming Elise's name. To find her, shake her, and demand she never do anything like this *ever* again.

The Dark won't have to get me if this keeps up. My heart will fail from worry. The thought, sardonic and morbid, helped him focus. If he was going to rescue Elise, he needed to be cold and clear.

And ruthless.

I can do that.

"Should be comforting. How many teams you mark?"

"At least four. Standard formations."

"Predictable." Dante's lip curled in his severe face. The glow of a Watcher—venomous red Power—spread out from him in a haze.

It was at that moment that the first Brotherhood team came boiling out of the alleyway to their right, and the building they had been heading for exploded in a breathless rush of flame. The explosion knocked down two kobolds and shrapnel began to rain down onto the wet street. Thunder boomed.

Time was up.

Twenty-Four

"Pretty," the bat-thing said, its hairy, razor-toothed snout inches from Elise's face. Its breath smelled like rotting meat in a blind hot corner, squirming with things best left undiscovered. Its hands tightened on her throat. "That *hurt*. But don't worry, I'll take it out in trade when we break you."

It was the thing that had taken Vann's body, now naked of any human form, and strangling her.

The fire looped away from her, uncontrollable. The building leaned crazily to the side because the fire was eating at the support pilings. Despite the rain, the wood burned merrily. Steam hissed and wreathed. The kobolds were only indistinct melting shapes in the twisting flames. The screaming from the elephant-things had stopped.

"You'll join us," the bat-thing said, "or you'll die choking on your own blood." Its snout pulled back in a genuinely cheerful smile. Elise couldn't even get the breath to scream. Her lungs started to burn. "By the time we're done, you'll beg to kill your pretty little friends yourself. I like that, it's poetic."

The horrible choking sensation broke Elise's concentration. The Dark scraped against her, turning her stomach and poisoning her aura with a spreading stain. Fire roared, escaping her control, spreading, but she couldn't strike at the Dark thing crouching over her. It was too strong. Its foul breath washed over her, draining her, draining the Talisman. Its fingers tightened on her throat, malignant and twisted and too horribly strong. Her fingers plucked uselessly at its scaly claws.

She tasted blood, and a dark cloud began at the corners of her vision. Over the rush and pop of the flames, she heard Trevor screaming. A surviving kobold was stalking him, its skin shiny with the heat. Trevor tripped and fell, the fire miraculously curling around him, keeping him safe. But the kobold just kept coming, with scary fluid speed.

No. Elise struggled to think, to do something, anything to save him. *No, please—*

And then the thing was torn off her and flung back. Elise sucked in a gasping, retching breath. Trevor grabbed her arm weakly and tried to pull her to her feet. His blood-encrusted T-shirt smoked. "*Elise!*" he yelled. "*Control it! You've got to control it!*"

Remy was there.

He stood in front of the black bat-thing, his sword reflecting the firelight in a sharp bolt of gold and orange. His golden hair was dry, stripped back from his face by the fire's backdraft. Elise, coughing and choking, clung to Trevor. Tears squirted out of her burning eyes, her throat swelling closed.

"Not on my watch," Remy said softly, but the icy rage in his tone cut through the insane roaring of flames and the rushing pop and crackle that was the entire building being consumed. "Not on *my* witch."

He looked furious. He looked *lethal*.

He was the most comforting thing Elise had ever seen.

Dante was there too. He pulled Elise to her feet with a single movement, bringing Trevor with her too. Trevor's face was gray, and he coughed weakly. The Watcher's black eyes were alight with something hard and cold Elise had never seen before, a kind of fierce joy she recognized. The thrill of combat, the glory of destruction.

In that one moment Elise understood something about the Watchers. She might be pushed to destruction to protect her friends and her own life, but she didn't like it. It frightened her. It went against the very core of what she was.

A Lightbringer. A light in darkness, a candle flame against the Dark.

Remy's voice echoed in her head. *It takes the Dark to fight the Dark.*

Now Elise understood. Protect Remy? She might as well try to protect a tornado.

"Got them!" Dante called over his shoulder.

"Get her out," Remy said, still in that same calm, inexorable voice. "I'll deal with this."

The bat-thing laughed. "A Watcher. How *cute*. A nice little pre-dinner snack." Its voice hissed, poisonous and sliding. It was gathering itself to leap for Remy, and Elise's entire mind narrowed to a single point of concentration. She couldn't let it hurt him.

Elise cried out weakly, and the flame erupted around the bat-thing. It roared, its fur smoking, beating at the flames with its hairy, clawed hands.

Elise coughed, but Dante picked Trevor up, slung him over one broad shoulder, and grabbed Elise's arm. "Hold onto me," he yelled. "The whole damn place is burning down."

"Remy—" Her throat exploded with raw burning acid. It had shrunk to the size of a straw, her breath whistling through the suddenly narrow passage.

The bat-thing leapt for Remy, who fended it off, steel clashing and slithering against its wicked claws. "*Go!*" Remy yelled. "*Get her out of here!*"

There was a shuddering, crashing sound, and the entire building tilted like a mad carnival ride.

"Elise!" Dante yelled, and yanked her with him.

"*Remy!*" Elise screamed, trying to tear herself free of Dante's grip. He swore, his fingers clamping down like steel bands, and the bat-thing moved for Remy again.

His sword flashed. Red, pulsing flame coated his left hand. **firefirefire,** the Trifero whispered. **burn. burn them all, burn them all, BURN THEM ALL!**

Elise screamed. The Talisman fought her, struggling to rip free. The bat-thing closed its hands around Remy's throat, and both of them tipped over, vanishing into the flames, Remy's sword slicing down in one last, convulsive movement.

Dante snarled something, and the floor tilted and jerked again.

The fire rose in Elise's veins.

burn them all.

The Trifero pushed. It pressed. It muttered, and it cajoled.

It could burn the city, if she let it. Melt the concrete of the skyscrapers and turn the entire town into a molten slag pit with a new volcano pulsing in the middle, sending streams of lava into the suburbs, the earth itself ripping free and steaming, shrieking, moaning in pain. It could, and it wanted to.

Elise! It was a faint, faraway cry. Mari, her fingers locked with Theo's, in the backseat of a car. *Elise, no! Fight it! Fight it!* They were both chanting, adding their strength to hers, a thin layer of protection between Elise and the hungry Talisman.

The floor disintegrated, flaming little bits of wood plunging like stars into the hungry sea. Dante leapt, caught his balance, and leapt again, Elise hanging from his arm like a doll, Trevor flopping limply over his shoulder. Elise's nerves burned, sparking with pain. She screamed again, a long despairing howl of abused breath. It hurt. Agony rubbed against her very core as she fought against the Trifero's hunger for flame and death.

It's not easy to put the genie back in the bottle, is it, Elise? Suzanne's dry, academic voice sounded inside Elise's

head, in the maelstrom of chaos and pain and fury that had
swallowed her whole. Elise coughed, choked.

Dante swore. The entire building tilted again, crazily,
waltzing on its burning supports. The floor fell out from under
them.

Weightlessness. The rain hissed before it touched the
flames, and the sound of the sea below was as hungry as the
flames.

"Now fight it," Suzanne whispered in Elise's ear as they
fell. Elise took one last gasping breath of smoky air before
they hit the waves with a terrible shock that drove all the breath
from her abused lungs. Her throat and eyes burned fiercely.
"Fight it, Elise. Rule the Power, or it will rule you. Use your
will. *Fight.*"

Elise floated. No, not floated. *Sank.* Dante had lost his
grip on her, and now she was drifting toward the bottom of the
sea.

burn...The Trifero sank into quiescence. She'd won. She
hadn't let the Talisman loose to turn the entire city into ash.
Dante had saved Trevor.

But Vann, poor Vann...

The last bit of air left her, squeezed out of her lungs. The
bubbles were silvery, and Elise's hands weakly scrabbled.
Blackness, then, closing over her.

Mari. Remy. Vann. I'm so sorry.

"Don't give up." Suzanne's voice, almost physical. Then
there was a sudden jolting wrench as an iron-hard hand closed
around her wrist and yanked so hard it nearly dislocated her
arm.

Too late.

Elise fell down into endless night and the sound of waves.
Her last thought echoed in blackness.

If I have to die, I'm glad I protected them.

Twenty-Five

The pain was incredible. It was agony. It was the worst Remy had ever been injured.

He didn't care.

"Elise!" Remy screamed, splashing through the shallows. Water streamed from his coat and hair. Burning wreckage fell into the water, steam billowing up to make a plume into the bruised sky. The entire left side of his face burned as well, and his broken arm grated, sending a fresh spike of agony up his shoulder into his head. "*Elise!*"

There was a roaring popping hiss, and a beam fell, water splashing up. Remy dived to the side. Dante had already surfaced, and he was having enough trouble keeping the other Lightbringer's head above water, as he made for the shore.

Remy was in deep, over his head and diving into the next roiling wave. The downside of greater strength was greater density of muscle and bone, and he was wearing his boots and several pounds of metal and equipment. He could alter the rules of the physical world slightly, but it was savagely tiring to do it.

I don't care, Elise is down there. He dove.

The water was black, the shallows stirred up by all the debris falling from above. He saw something and lunged for it, fighting the resistance of the water and his own exhausted body, his broken arm and cracked ribs, salt stinging against the burned mess on the left side of his face.

His hand closed around Elise's wrist.

He pulled, shoving himself for the surface now, kicking furiously, his lungs burning, a spike of pleasure from his witch's skin blazing through his overloaded nerves.

His head broke the surface and he had to flounder aside to avoid a burning pile of debris. He dragged her up, her hair swirling in a cloud around her head. The Trifero, dark and dead instead of flaming with golden light, bumped against her collarbone.

Remy pulled her face up to his. The Dark coiled inside his bones. It reached, blurring through her skin, ignoring the agony in his own body. He clamped his lips over hers, puffed a breath into her lungs, and then *squeezed*, physically and mentally.

Water jetted out of her mouth and nose. She retched,

coughing, an awful hacking sound.

It was the sweetest thing Remy had ever heard. She was alive.

There were livid bruises around her throat. He struggled for the shore, avoiding burning wreckage while she coughed and choked weakly, her head lolling forward whenever she almost passed out. He had no breath to spare, or he would have tried to say something comforting.

His boots touched rocky sand and he staggered. Now he had to drag her out of the helping arms of the water, and he did it. Dante was on the beach with the other Lightbringer, the male. The drummer. Remy had let *that* one slip through his fingers, he'd been so focused on Elise. Next to her, the drummer was only a faint glow. Another mistake Remy would have to atone for. The kobolds hadn't killed the boy because he was a Lightbringer and had the potential to be profitable. Maybe the *kalak* hadn't been so sure Elise would come, and it had kept one hostage alive as potential insurance. Or because they had already been sated with another death.

His heart pounded thickly, rage boiling under his skin. A red haze clouded his vision, only slightly diluted by the fact that she was in his arms. He hoped she would live, that she was miraculously unharmed.

If she wasn't, nothing and nobody on earth would be safe from him.

Have I finally gone over the edge? I'm going to need a psych eval and some nitroglycerin for the heart attacks this woman's going to cause me.

He dragged Elise out of the waves. Her hair streamed, spilling black water onto the sand.

"Dante—" Remy started. He meant to warn the other Watcher. *Be careful. I'm two inches away from snapping.*

"Can you fight?" The black-eyed Watcher looked like hell. His coat was torn and singed, and his black hair was crisped on one side. He was favoring his right leg a little.

Remy bent over, retched, and produced an amazing quantity of seawater. It stung his mouth and nose, and he spat to clear his mouth when it was finished. "I can fight," he rasped. "If I have to."

I'd love to. Point me at them. Let me kill them.

Let me kill them slow.

"The Brotherhood," Dante said grimly. "We've got to get

out of here."

"I can't wait." Remy's arm burned, the ends of the bone fusing together. It was a messy, incomplete fix and would hurt more later, as the Dark went through and repaired it properly. But for right now he needed the use of the arm, quickly. "Lead the way."

Elise shuddered and coughed again. "Remy?"

He was surprised to find that his racing heart leapt to his throat at the sound of her voice, even cracked and husky as it was. Relief slammed into his chest, breaking the shell of killing calm wrapped around him.

Thank you. Whatever god looks after suicidal Lightbringers, thank you. "Are you hurt? Elise?"

She seemed only half-conscious, her eyes burning green under partly closed lids. "Remy," she said again, and sighed. It was a tired sound. Her head rolled on her neck, and she laid her forehead against his shoulder. "Trevor…is he…"

I could care less, cherie, *as long as you're safe.* Remy glanced over. The drummer was standing up and talking rapidly in a low, husky voice between deep lung-clenching coughs. "He's fine. We've got to get you under cover, Elise." He printed a kiss on her wet hair and tasted salt. "Gods above and below, woman. What were you *thinking?*"

"Protect you…" she whispered, and passed out.

I'll have to carry her. He dragged her over to Dante and the drummer. "She's out, Dante. We have to move."

Dante nodded. "Look, there's a staircase up to the pier. Let's go. The drummer's a Lightbringer, came here for Sanctuary. He's Caroline Robbins's brother."

Remy's jaw threatened to drop. He bent stiffly and picked Elise up. His arm grated, but the bone held. *It's only pain,* he told himself. *Ignore it. It's only pain.* "*The* Caroline? The Mindhealer?" He forced the anger down, leashing it with an effort that almost made him sweat through the cold glaze of seawater weighing down his clothes.

Dante nodded. "*The* Caroline." He steadied the skinny young man, whose knees didn't look too stable. "Quickly, now."

The two Watchers limped up the stairs, and the drummer had to pause halfway up to retch and spit seawater. The rain wasn't bad, because they were under shelter, but the thunder rolled closer. The Trifero pulling on all the available Power inside the city limits had skewed the already unstable weather systems. It was going to be a mess in the lower areas of town. *Ask me if I care.*

Elise made a low thready noise and started to cough, hacking. It didn't sound good. Remy murmured to her, soothing little noises, comforting words. What he really wanted to do was shout. *Why? Why did you do that? Was getting killed by the Dark preferable to being in my company? Didn't you believe me when I told you it was a trap?*

Protect him, she'd said. Protect *him*. As if she didn't trust him to protect *her*.

The thought made rage rise again, and he shoved it down. He had to *think*, he had to stay calm.

They finally reached the top of the stairs, and Dante scanned the broad open expanse of the pier. "Nothing. Wonder if Hanson's still on the street."

"Who knows?" Remy said. "Would the Brotherhood pull back once the building went down?"

"They're just stupid enough to do that. You look awful."

"You're a fine one to talk." Remy hacked and spit to one side. It glittered wet and red in the failing light, the *tanak* burning in his bones as it fought to repair internal bleeding. The clouds had thickened. One last dying glitter of gold showed the sun, sinking into the western sea. Night was coming.

And with night, the Dark.

Gods help me, but I'll kill them all if they come near Elise. I swear I will.

Dante helped the drummer out onto the street. "I've never seen anything like it," the boy rasped. "She made the fire come." He coughed, and the light coming from him, never very strong in the first place, dimmed even further. He needed the healer, and quickly.

"The Trifero," Dante said. "Did she lose control of it?"

"Seems likely." Remy hacked and spat again. *I hate smoke poisoning. Hurts worse than a bullet, that's for sure.* Elise was a dead weight in his arms, her hair still dripping over his arm. Her face was chalky and almost blue, her pulse rapid and thready. "It's old and tricky."

"She blew that entire building like a missile," Dante said. "Remind me not to piss her off anytime soon."

"I'll do that." Remy scanned the street. The Subaru stood there, its lights on, the engine running. It began to creep forward, and Remy gave a sigh of relief.

"Oh, damn," Dante growled, and Remy's head snapped up.

One last team of Brotherhood operatives, coming from the right across the street, where they would have been out of the fallout zone of Elise's destructive Power. "Damn." Remy made a short sharp sound of frustration. It was too far. They couldn't hope to reach the safety of the car.

Elise's eyes blinked and opened. "Suzanne?' she breathed, and Remy's wet skin chilled at the floaty disconnected tone. She looked like a sleepwalker, her pupils shrinking to pinpoints, as if staring into a bright light.

"Get as close to the car as you can," Dante said. "I'll draw them off, and you get them to safety."

"But it hurts, Suzanne." Elise's voice was the slow, stunned tone of a child in a fever. "It *hurts.*"

"All right," Remy said, whether to her or Dante he didn't care. *This is going to get ugly really quick-like out here.* He was tempted to stay, to unleash some vengeance on the Dark. Training bit harsh across the red roil of bloodlust. His first priority was to get her to safety.

The Subaru accelerated. Hanson must have seen the hulking shapes of the kobolds.

"Remy." Elise stiffened in his arms. "Where are they?"

"Where are who, *cherie?*" He kissed her fevered forehead. *If I'm going to die I might as well. I'll go down fighting, Elise. Let's hope it buys you some time to live. Even if it's just a few more breaths.*

Heat rose from her skin. His cracked, bleeding lips printed a dark crimson mark on her wet forehead.

She made another short sound of exasperation. "The bad guys, Remy! Where are they?" Her pupils dilated. She looked like she had some sort of concussion. Two spots of high color burned high up on her aristocratic cheeks, and her mouth hung slightly open.

"At my two o'clock, *cherie*, coming in fast. Just keep breathing." He didn't know why he was answering her. Dante pushed the drummer ahead. The thin young man was walking under his own power now. Jerky, disconnected, and slow, like a marionette, but still walking.

"Protect you," Elise whispered. "I'll protect you all."

"Elise, no." He didn't know what to say to call her back from whatever dream she was in. At least she was talking, alive.

The Subaru spun forward, and both passenger-side doors opened. *"Come on!"* Hanson yelled, and Remy began to run.

No time. No time, not going to make it, they're coming in too fast. Gods help us all.

Elise's eyes rolled back into her head, and the Trifero sparked with life.

A flash of gold so hot it was white burned through the air. Hanson yelled something Remy couldn't hear.

A thunderclap rattled down the street, the Subaru rocking on its springs, and he shoved Elise into the car, pushing the drummer in after her. Mari scrambled over the backseat into the cargo area, and then she leaned over the seat, pulling the drummer in. Dante was laying down covering fire. Remy glanced up to gauge the distance, his hand dropping to his own gun.

The kobolds were burning. They blazed like huge candles, and the thin, high keening screams made Remy's lips pull back from his teeth with satisfaction.

Didn't expect that, did you? Neither did I. I hope it hurts.

A Gray leapt for the hood of the car, and Dante shot it. He ducked into the car. "Go! For God's sake, go!"

Remy dove in and dragged the door closed as Hanson stamped on the accelerator.

"Be careful with my car!" Theo yelled.

"I'll buy you a new one," Dante rasped over his shoulder. "What *was* that?"

"Did I get them?" Elise's voice was small and childish. The Trifero settled, its gleam quiescent now. Damped.

"Yes, *cherie,*" Remy said. Iron blood and rage turned bitter on his tongue. He struggled for control. "You got them." *How did she do that? Was it the Trifero or just her? Something got them, at least.*

Mari pulled the drummer back into the cargo hold, and Theo said something low and fast. The smell of the healer's Power—green things, rich dirt, growing plants, a warm summer scent—filled the car, and Remy took a deep breath. His arm gave one last agonized twist of pain.

Theo pushed Elise into his arms. "Keep her here for a few moments. Talk to her. He's more badly injured." Her hands glowed green, a beautiful deep color like the sun behind a forest canopy. She wriggled up, half-lying over the back of the seat, and clamped her glowing hands onto the drummer's head.

"Elise," Remy whispered into her hair. "Don't leave. Don't leave. Stay with me. Just a few moments, and Theo will help you. Stay with me, please, *cherie,* stay with me."

He kept talking to her, into her hair, his lips moving against her forehead. She was crusted with salt and burning with an unhealthy heat he could feel even through his scorched and tattered coat. She made a small whimpering sound, and her breathing took on a rasping sound he didn't like. Her face was turning an awful chalky blue, and if her heart paused or her breathing halted Remy wasn't sure he could keep his rage leashed.

Don't you dare leave me here. Don't you dare. The words were colored crimson, and he shut his eyes, struggling to contain the Dark under his skin.

"Hold on, Elise," he whispered. "Just hold on."

Twenty-Six

Warmth. Softness.

Familiar smells. Paint. Dragon's blood incense. Her own house. Her own bed. She'd somehow been put in her own bed. There was no smell of smoke, thank the gods.

Elise opened her eyes. It took three tries. Her eyelids were leaden and burning with exhaustion. She had been dreaming of the sea, of drowning, of fire boiling out of cracks in the sea floor, vents full of superheated water and strange volcanic gases.

Light lay across her bed in a thick golden bar. Blessed sunlight.

She reached up—her arm was so heavy, too heavy, it took effort to raise it—and touched her throat.

It was there. The hard, warm stone resounded under her fingertips, purring like a cat. **fire?** it asked, sleepily.

No, she told it, and it obeyed her, falling back into a sleepy, quiet watchfulness. Her will was law, now. She'd stopped the Trifero from destroying the city, and it wouldn't test her again.

Or so she hoped. But if it tested her again, she'd fight it. And she'd win, if she had to.

It purred under her touch, stretching sleepily, and she sighed. Was she dead? She vaguely remembered...What? Asking Remy if she'd gotten them. Focusing the Trifero's Power, funneling it. The Talisman pushing savagely against the confines she placed on it, wanting to leap free and burn the city and keep burning until the whole world was a scorched wasteland.

It hurts, she had moaned to Suzanne, who had stroked her cheek and hummed, as she always did.

It hurts, Suzanne had agreed. *Everything hurts, Elise. That is the lesson of your gift. Everything worth having is worth fighting for, and your pain is the pain of birthing. Control the Talisman, Elise. Save us. You're the only one who can.*

And the Power, flooding her. She was strong enough. She had controlled it, forced the Talisman to her will, and saved them.

Remy's voice in the chaos of fever her mind had become. *Hold on, Elise. Just hold on.*

Cool fingers touched her forehead. They felt good against her hot skin. A great cool wash of Power filtered through her, calming the fire, carrying the fever away.

I know that touch. "Theo," Elise croaked.

Theo's face swam into focus above her. "Just rest. We're all okay. Trevor will live. He's got a cracked rib, but it's healing nicely. All four of you had smoke inhalation, and the guys had some burns, but they're much better now."

Theo's long dark hair fell down, brushing Elise's face. She smelled, as always, of sandalwood and green growing things. Elise sighed. Her throat burned like a desert.

"Thirsty," she croaked.

"I don't doubt it. I'll bring you some water." Theo's face disappeared.

But Elise fell back asleep before Theo came returned.

There was a long time of darkness, and when she woke up again, at first she thought she was dreaming. The room was dark except for something glittering by the window, and there was the sound of rain on the roof.

The glitter near the window was a pair of eyes.

Golden eyes.

Elise lay against the pillows, dreamily considering that glitter.

Then he moved and gained his feet in one fluid motion. She could only see him when he moved because he wore a dark T-shirt and jeans, and the twilight from outside showed in his light hair.

He reached the side of the bed. "Do you need a drink of water?"

Elise discovered her voice had failed her. She nodded. Even that was a struggle. Her entire body felt heavy, leaden.

He slid an arm under her shoulders and propped her up. Then he held the glass to her lips, gauging it perfectly. She could only take small sips, and she drank half the glass before he took it away.

"More later, but let's see if you can keep that down." The skin of his arm burned against her bare skin, and she felt silk against her shoulders. One of the short slips that she often wore to bed, which was why her back was bare.

The T-shirt must have been ruined. She surprised herself by giggling wearily.

His tone was as calm as ever, but sharp as a knife. "I'm glad to see you're in better spirits. You've been out for twenty-four hours. You'll probably be in bed for a week."

She cleared her throat. It hurt. "Remy," she began, but he shook his head.

"Don't worry. I took this shift because everyone else was exhausted, and I didn't think you'd wake up." Not quite as calm as she'd thought, his voice shaded into raggedness at the end of the sentence.

What? She blinked up at him. The silence of night enfolded both of them, his face hidden in the darkness. She could see nothing but his glowing eyes.

"You were right. I should have thought of your friends, and I should have gone to retrieve them from the Brotherhood. The boy—Trevor—is safe. Circle Lightfall's asked to send him a Watcher, since he wants to stay in the city. But the decision is, of course, up to you. We're still trying to find some way to explain Vann's disappearance to the police, and Circle Lightfall has offered to help there, too. But like I said, the decision is yours." It sounded like a rehearsed speech. Like he'd been saying it to himself over and over again.

He took a deep breath and gently laid her back down against her pillows. "I'll be going invisible in the morning," he said, softly. "You won't have to see my face again."

"You...leaving?" Her voice was a harsh ruin.

Well, what do you expect, Elise? You treated him horribly, you told him not to get too comfortable. Of course he doesn't want to be around you.

It hurt far more than she thought it would, more than the Trifero's savage mind-shattering fire. It hurt down deep in her chest, as if her heart was breaking.

He said nothing, retreating to stand away from the bed, his hands loose at his sides. She could see his outline, faint details of him in the uncertain light.

Finally, he said, "If you can't stand to be around me so much you go running for the Brotherhood that should tell me something. I won't trouble you, but if you think you're going to wander around without a Watcher you've got another think coming."

"Remy—"

"I'm only going to say this once." Now he didn't sound calm at all. The window rattled under the fury in his voice, the bits of chandelier she'd hung on the bedstead stirring as if touched with a brisk breeze. "I am *your* Watcher. They turned

me into an animal in prison, and I thought Circle Lightfall had
changed me back into a man. But they *didn't.* They just made
me a better killer than I already was. If it scares you, or disgusts
you, I understand. But the Dark is after you, *cherie petite*, and
I will *not* let it get to you. I may be a fucking failure as a
Watcher, but I'm yours and I'll do what I have to. Is that clear
enough even for you?"

Elise took a deep breath. "Don't." The blackness was
closing in again, her body rebelling against the demands she'd
made on it. "Please."

The air had turned hot and hard, pressing against her skin.
She should have been furious. She should have been scared
out of her mind.

Instead, she felt vaguely comforted.

Before she could make her mouth work, he spoke again,
softly. "There's going to be chaos. The Brotherhood's massing
for another try, and I don't know if you'll be well enough to
invoke your Guardianship with the other three and ban them
from the city. Dante's promised that he and Hanson will take
shifts, and I'll hang around and do what I can. But you don't
have to see me, Elise."

Oh, for the sake of every god there ever was, shut up.
"Stay," she whispered. "Stay, please. I'd...miss...you."

She was rewarded with thunderstruck silence. He paused
for a long second, standing by the side of her bed. The rattling
in the air went down, anger submerging. "You're my witch,
and Circle Lightfall can't order me away from you. I won't go
even if they—"

"Oh, shut up," she said, taking a deep breath. "Stay. Please."

Slowly, he lowered himself onto the bed. It creaked its
familiar creak, and Elise closed her eyes. His warm fingers
threaded through hers. "Do you want me to, Elise? Do you
really want to look at something like me every day?"

She tried to lift her hand. He helped her. She slid her arm
around his nape, feeling short golden curls tickle her fingers.
Then she let her arm go mostly limp, dragging his head down.

Their mouths met. Elise didn't care if she had a dry mouth.
She wanted to kiss him, and the way he made a small sound in
the back of his throat and leaned into her made her think he
didn't mind anyway.

She melted into him, trying to tell him how much she wanted
him to stay. When he broke free, kissing her cheek and her

forehead, she sighed. "Don't leave."

"I'm not a nice guy," he whispered back.

Well, we're pretty evenly matched, wouldn't you say?
"I'm not a nice girl." Her unreliable voice cracked, a lump in
her throat. "I want you to stay." It took all her fading bravery
to say it. "Please?"

He went completely still. His skin was warm, and he rested
his chin against the top of her head, the blankets crushed
between them. Somehow, his arm was suddenly under her.
She breathed him in, grateful he was still alive.

"You don't get it. I'm telling you I'm breaking my vow of
obedience as a Watcher. I am *not* going to let you waltz around
unprotected, Elise. If I have to tie you up and sit on you, I will."

You idiot of a man. We'll just see about that. Irritation
rasped faintly under her breastbone. "Shut up." Her throat
tickled with the urge to cough. "I want you to stay. Promise
me."

"I promise."

"Good." She wriggled slightly, getting comfortable. He
inhaled sharply, going still. "You came for me."

"Of course. Why did you do it, Elise? What the hell were
you thinking?"

Don't you know? "Wanted to protect...you. All of you."

"Elise—" He was about to argue with her, but she shook
her head. Time enough later. She was so tired.

She made an exasperated noise and fell back into sleep.

Twenty-Seven

Remy was tranced out in the chair and only half aware of Elise getting up and stumbling to the bathroom. She didn't ask for help, though, and she didn't fall, so he let her be.

However, when she came out and started down the hall toward the stairs, he swung himself out of the chair and strode down the hall, catching her arm as she almost overbalanced. She was pale and there were fever-spots in her cheeks again.

"Careful," he said. The feel of her skin made his entire body clench, and sweat sprang up on his back. She wore only a thin red silk nightgown, the shape of her slimness under the silk just begging for his hands. He invoked control again, and was actually surprised when he didn't grab her by the shoulders and shake her. *Protect me. She said she did it to protect me. Gods above.*

The thought of her protecting *him* made something warm uncurl in his chest, the only soft thing left in him. He was struck with two opposing desires—to either shake her until her teeth rattled or kiss her until he lost the sick fear of losing her. He wondered which one would win out.

Her eyes were dark with something he didn't want to identify as pain. She nodded wearily, her red-gold hair spilling forward over her shoulders, tangled from sleeping. "Coffee." Her voice was much better, a little husky but not croaking.

And as always, it threatened to stop his heart when her green eyes met his.

"I'll bring you some." He kept his tone neutral.

"Okay," she said. "And some cereal. I'm hungry."

"Good." He stood there, just watching her. Waiting for whatever would happen next.

I'm not even half the Watcher she should have. She's going to come to her senses and tell me to get the hell out of here any moment now. And then I'm going to have to disobey, and we're going to have trouble. Lots of trouble. This woman excels at trouble.

She leaned against the wall, rubbing her forehead with two fingers, as if her head hurt. It probably did. The Trifero had fired the entire warehouse and blown out every window in two city blocks still left intact from the economic downturn. There was nothing left, just a few charred stumps of the building's supports sticking out of the hungry water. The fire marshal was calling it "spontaneous combustion" and attributing it to a lightning strike. After using that much Power, it was a wonder she wasn't blind with backlash.

She reached up and touched his face. The burns had healed painfully, leaving only a faint shadow of scarring—a benefit to being a Watcher. The healing had been awful, and Theo had tried to help, but her being a Lightbringer only made it worse. So, he had sat there and waited and healed, watching Elise sleep. She examined him, her fingertips on his cheek, and the burn of pleasure her touch caused slid down his skin. But her hand dropped, and she almost flinched.

That small flinch tore at his heart. She was afraid of him. She'd seen what he was, and she was going to turn her back on him, order him away.

All hell's going to break loose. He struggled to stay contained, to shove down the tide of red anger sweeping through him.

What she said next stunned him. "Are you staying?" The corners of her mouth turned down. "Or are you going back to Circle Lightfall? I know I'm a disappointment, but—"

The rage retreated, back down into its hole. *What the hell?* "No," he said, and she stopped speaking and stared at him. The look on her face—hope warring with caution and pain— was uncertain enough that he felt the urge to smile. Theo was right. Under the spiky exterior, Elise was as soft as silk, using her anger to keep herself from being hurt.

No more. I won't let anything hurt you, Elise. I swear it.

"You'll never be a disappointment, Elise." *You're the only thing that makes me feel human.* He was searching for more to say when she smiled. It was a fleeting grin, but it made her eyes light up, and he felt the spike of pleasure again. His chest unloosed, and his hands relaxed. "A complete bloody frustration and a suicidally foolhardy witch, but never a disappointment."

She rolled her eyes and yawned, swaying. He caught her other arm and set her back on her feet. "I feel like the entire world is rocking," she said, softly, and leaned forward into his arms, almost overbalancing him. He caught her, and she rested her coppery head on his shoulder, pushing a knife-hilt out of the way and leaning her entire weight against him.

Remy froze. She sighed. It was a sigh of weary contentment, and his heart started to pound. The pleasure burned through him, and he risked dropping a kiss on the top of her sleep-mussed head. He took a deep breath. He had to say it.

He had to *make* her understand.

"Don't *ever* do that to me again, Elise. Do you know what it was like for me to find that thing upstairs in Theo's bedroom and know you were walking into a trap alone?"

She shrugged. "I'm sorry. Well, I'm not sorry I did it, but I *do* apologize."

Stubborn to the last. He had to strangle the desire to laugh at that. Instead, he just held her, feeling incredibly lucky.

Blessed, even. Elise was in his arms, and all was right with the world.

She wants me to stay. As miracles went, it was a good one.

"Come on, let's get you back to bed. I'll bring you breakfast, and coffee." But he didn't move, standing there and holding her in the hallway, feeling her body against his, her heartbeat against his skin. Even the honey-spiked pleasure of holding her was secondary to the relief of having her alive; secondary also to the relief that she was resting against him, apparently content to be in his arms because she had asked him to stay.

"Not unless you're going to stay. Are you?"

I'm going to stay. The only question is, can you stand to look at me? "Do you want me to?" he asked again.

She made another one of those short, exasperated sounds, not quite a sigh, almost a groan. "Remy," she said slowly and clearly, as if she was talking to an idiot, "of *course* I want you to stay. I've asked you to stay *how* many times now? You're dense, even for a Watcher."

"Hmm." The last of the fury drained away, leaving him grateful and just the slightest bit shaken. "Of course I'll stay, if you want me."

"Oh, for the love of—" *Now* she was truly irritated, and he smiled into her hair. She sounded much more like herself. His shoulders relaxed, he stroked her back with his fingertips, marveling at the heat of her through the silk.

He couldn't think about what he'd like to do to her now. She was still sick and weak. But when she got better, maybe…

Yeah, hope. That great human drug. But it seemed as if he might have a chance after all. If she could stand to look at him, maybe he was redeemable after all.

"I'm staying. You need *someone* to clean up after you. There's a hell of a mess down at the docks." He gently stroked her bare shoulders and slipped his fingers under her glorious hair, cupping the back of her neck and inhaling, smelling her, cinnamon and heat. The urge to kiss her was overwhelming. He settled for kissing her hair again.

"Mmh," she said. "I never did play well with others. Theo and Mari. Are they okay?"

I couldn't care less, witch. You're safe. That's all that matters. "They're fine. All right, back to bed. I'll bring coffee and breakfast. All right?"

"I guess," she said, dreamily. "In just a minute."

He held her, barely daring to move, until he realized that she had fallen asleep standing in his arms.

Where she belonged.

He carried her back into the bedroom and laid her down on the bed, drawing the sheet and the velvet comforter over her. The heat wave had broken, and now it was raining. There was flooding in some of the lower areas of the city. They hadn't been able to determine if it had been a natural storm, or if the Talisman had been playing merry hell with the weather. The Trifero was nothing to fool with.

He stroked her hair back from her forehead. Her skin against his caused a pleasurable burn, more intense each time. *I don't want to stop touching you.* He touched her cracked, beautiful lips. *I don't think I can stop. It's a good thing you didn't want me to leave. You have no idea how close to the edge I can get, firehair.* "Coffee, and breakfast. You need something to eat."

But then he leaned down and gently kissed her forehead. *I swear I won't fail you. Thank the gods you don't want me to leave.*

She made a small, sleepy sound, and his heart twisted inside his chest. *The Brotherhood won't rest until they have you. And I won't stop until you're safe.*

"Remy?" she said, sleepily.

"I should make you breakfast," he said, to remind himself.

She yawned and reached up blindly, her fingers closing around his wrist. Then she pulled on him. "Idiot. Come here."

He found himself pulled onto the bed, grateful he wasn't wearing his boots or his weapons except for the knife in its sheath at the back of his belt. She turned over, presenting him with her narrow back, and pulled his arm over her so that he had to turn onto his side. She spent a few moments moving around, getting comfortable, and the sharp spill of velvet blurring through his body made him take in a sharp breath.

He froze as soon as she stopped moving, holding her, and she made a low inquiring sound. Then she sighed again. "You guys." Her voice held the slurred slowness of a dreamer. "Those big black coats. Not exactly kind and cuddly."

You have absolutely no idea. "Guess not." Remy propped his head on his arm, barely even daring to breathe. How the hell had he ever gotten this lucky? She *trusted* him...and she wanted him to stay.

She wanted *him* to stay with her. Somehow, he had done something right, and she wanted him to stay.

"Still," she yawned, "you've got some sense. Stoneface and Prince Charming are idiots. You can help keep them in line. Keep them from messing with us."

She was talking about the other Watchers. Remy found he was smiling. He buried his face in her hair and drew in a deep long breath. "I suppose so," he murmured. "Under your close supervision, of course."

"Stay with me." She blew out a long, sleepy breath.

"Of course." He closed his eyes. "As long as you'll have me." *Just try getting rid of me. It won't work.*

"Good. For keeps, then."

He should get up, make her breakfast, and start planning a defense of the city...and he would.

But not just yet.

"For keeps," he whispered into her hair.

"Of course. You're my Watcher."

Absolutely. Remy nodded, his chin moving against her hair. "I am. Elise?"

But she was asleep. Remy lay there, quiet and still, his entire body sparking with the pleasure of holding his witch, and listened to her breathe.

Printed in the United States
50262LVS00002B/162